HIDDEN LOVE

HIDDEN LOVE

Eskay Kabba

4 Horsemen
Publications, Inc.

Hidden Love
Hidden Love Series Book 1
Copyright © 2021 Eskay Kabba. All rights reserved.

4 Horsemen
Publications, Inc.

4 Horsemen Publications, Inc.
1497 Main St. Suite 169
Dunedin, FL 34698
4horsemenpublications.com
info@4horsemenpublications.com

Cover by by 4 Horsemen Publications, Inc.
Typesetting by Autumn Skye
Edited by Muñeca Fossette

All rights to the work within are reserved to the author and publisher. No part of this publication may be reproduced, stored in a retrieval system, or transmitted in any form or by any means, electronic, mechanical, photocopying, recording, scanning, or otherwise, except as permitted under Section 107 or 108 of the 1976 International Copyright Act, without prior written permission except in brief quotations embodied in critical articles and reviews. Please contact either the Publisher or Author to gain permission.

This book is meant as a reference guide. All characters, organizations, and events portrayed in this novel are either products of the author's imagination or are used fictitiously. All brands, quotes, and cited work respectfully belong to the original rights holders and bear no affiliation to the authors or publisher.

Library of Congress Control Number: 2021951161

Paperback ISBN-13: 978-1-64450-447-5
Audiobook ISBN-13: 978-1-64450-445-1
Ebook ISBN-13: 978-1-64450-446-8

DEDICATION/ ACKNOWLEDGMENTS:

Dedicated to Binty "Queen B." My first fan. And my sister TJ: You can read it now.

CONTENTS

Chapter 1 Who the fuck is
   flirting with my girl? 1
Chapter 2 Your cover story? 15
Chapter 3 You're like my perfect match......... 39
Chapter 4 We're just ... dating? 64
Chapter 5 Jesus Christ,
   who is this person I'm becoming?........... 82
Chapter 6 We'll just be
   scared shitless together. 101
Chapter 7 And suddenly
   I was good with that.................. 121
Chapter 8 Look who's attached now? 144
Chapter 9 I get you better now.............. 164
Chapter 10 Me. I needed him.................. 194
Chapter 11 What the
   fuck am I missing here?................ 215
Chapter 12 It was the perfect day........... 236

Author Bio................................ 258

CONTENT WARNING

Racism, homophobia, and incidents of violence

CHAPTER 1

WHO THE FUCK IS FLIRTING WITH MY GIRL?

~~~September 2009~~~

Who the fuck is flirting with my girl? I thought angrily. Okay, Afia was not *exactly* my girl. But she kinda was, so I got to say and feel things like that when someone was actively trying to get in her pants. And she was eating it up which was like *uuuugh!*

The moment I walked into her family pharmacy, I saw him leaning on the counter, talking all sultry to her. I didn't know what he was saying, but based on her shit-eating grin and whispered replies, I knew he was saying all the things she wanted to hear. Always the professional, she kept her hands flat on the counter and stood straight up as if she were serving a customer. But I knew that look on her face.

I casually walked over and passed another waiting customer who was also witnessing this display of lust. She looked up at me, wide-eyed, and said, "Hey, Connor. Connor this is Tyrell; Tyrell, Connor."

We shook hands, then he leaned back down on the counter and turned to Afia, clearly not threatened by me at all. *I know…It's because I'm white.* If I wasn't actually at her side, holding her hand people dismiss the idea of me as her partner. I mean, what would a blond-haired, blue-eyed white guy be doing with a brown-skinned, beautiful black woman like her?

He asked, "So, have I earned the right to take you out yet, Ms. Afia?" *Um... what?*

I had to mark my territory, so I smiled and said, "Ms. Afia has a date with me right now, so…"

He looked up at me in disbelief while she gave me the coldest glare ever. *Uh-oh, she likes this one.* So, I backed down. Suddenly, the customer that was waiting came over and stood on the other side of Tyrell. He looked at me first, then looked at Tyrell and asked in a calm, deep voice, "Is everything okay, Ty?"

Afia answered in her sweet voice, "Everything is fine, but Connor's right. I do have plans with my *friend* right now."

She emphasized "friend" and touched his hand. I resisted the urge to roll my eyes and stepped back slightly, leaning my forearm against the wall near the counter. I waited for her. She grabbed a pen and a piece of paper from the counter and started writing her number. It was her real number too; I saw it. I averted my eyes; *She can have that one.* My eyes landed on the person I thought was a customer, who also stepped back slightly. He was obviously Tyrell's friend.

♥♥♥ Chapter 1 ♥♥♥

No, not a friend. Relative. Brother. He had to be. They looked alike, but he looked older than Tyrell, who was about my age. They had the same features: Strong jawline, high cheekbones, full lips, small ears—I notice ears. And eyes. They both had gray eyes. Their similarities stopped there. Tyrell was thinner, a couple of shades lighter, curly-haired, and he had a laid-back way about him. The brother had dark brown skin, a muscular build, and a dark Caesar haircut with circular waves going around. He was gorgeous. And he was definitely military. I could tell because I'm a Marine. And we military persons have a way about us.

From a few yards away, I kept giving subtle looks to this attractive man who wasn't leaving much to the imagination. He was wearing black bicycle pants that showed off his muscular calves and thighs, his strong, tight ass, and nice, big bulge. A white t-shirt, that barely covered his bottom, showed off his muscles, especially since his arms were folded across his broad chest. I would have given anything to be in between those thighs at that moment. I literally found myself growing at the thought.

In one of my subtle glances, he caught me, and I quickly averted my eyes to look over his head. He turned back to Afia and Tyrell, who continued their low talking and flirting. I waited a bit and took another chance, casually letting my peripheral vision lead me into staring at his profile again. I accidentally turned my head slightly. He turned his head and looked right into my eyes. I couldn't turn away even if I wanted to. He wasn't smiling, but he wasn't upset that I was looking either. We watched each other for a moment, then his eyes slowly traveled downward. I realized while I was trying to be subtle, he was now overtly checking me out.

I was wearing work clothes, a black Comcast short-sleeved shirt and khakis, so there was nothing special about it. But his eyes took their time anyway. He took in my blond hair that I had been growing out since I left the Marines. He looked at my arms which, while not as big as his, had some definition. I used to run and lift weights but not as often anymore. My pants weren't tight, but I've been told I got a pretty nice ass. His eyes reached back up to mine, and he was staring into my bright blue ones as I was drowning in all the silver he was giving me. His eyes traveled down to my midsection, and I was hard as fuck. Fuck it. There was point in hiding it. So, I didn't. I let him see how hard he had made me. He pulled in his bottom lip to bite it a little, looked up at me again, and smirked. I didn't smile back.

We broke eye contact when Tyrell pulled on his arm. "C'mon, Mel. Afia, I'll call you later, sweetheart."

"Bye, Ty!" she called after them. Mel allowed his brother to take him away without a glance back at me. But I didn't give a shit because I got to see that tight ass all the way, and it did everything to keep my dick hard.

Afia clapped her hand in front of me. "Hey! Don't do that again."

"Huh?" I looked at her.

"Don't cock block me, asshole. I don't do that to you. Don't do that to me," she said angrily.

❤❤❤ Chapter 1 ❤❤❤

I laughed her off. "Listen, if I scared him off, then he wasn't for you."

She rolled her eyes. "Dad," she called toward the back, "I'm gone for the day."

"Okay Fifi, see you at home," he called back. She hated when he called her Fifi. But he was the only one who still did, so she let him.

Afia took off her pharmacy tech jacket and hung it, grabbed her bag, and met me on the other side of the counter. As she came toward me, I thought, *she looks so pretty.* She was wearing a bright blue, spaghetti-strapped sundress with yellow shapes and such on it, showing off her smooth, unblemished, almond-colored brown skin. Her dark brown hair fell naturally to her shoulders, but she recently put a couple of weave tracks in it to make it travel down her back. Afia had been my best friend since she was 14 years old and I was 15, and I had helped her about 100 times with her hairstyles, so I knew a thing or two about black hair.

She linked her arm through mine, and we left Williamson Pharmacy together in College Hill. She loved to talk, so naturally she started talking, and I listened as we walked over to Manhattan Bagel. It was our Wednesday ritual. I would meet her at the end of her shift at 3pm, and we would go to Manhattan Bagel to hang out with our friends until I took her home. Today, she was talking about Tyrell, which was the first time she had mentioned him to me, and I found that very interesting.

"So, he's been coming in monthly for like six months to get his father's blood pressure medication, and he just says hi to me. But for the last couple of weeks, he's been coming in almost every other day, buying stupid shit. I know it's just to talk to me. He bought Advil and hemorrhoid cream on Monday. Like, dude, really? So, finally I was like, do you really have a headache and boils on your butt or are you just coming to see me? He was shocked I was so bold, but he said, 'You're right, I just came here to see you.' So, we just got to talking, and he is really sweet. He came yesterday, too, just to talk. Today's the first day he asked me out. He works with his dad. They own a contracting company, but he's getting his plumber license soon so he can do contract work like his brother."

My ears perked up at 'brother.' "Oh, the one that was with him?" I asked casually.

"Yeah, his brother Jamel is a certified electrician, and he is contracted by mortgage companies, realtors, other contractors and private customers to inspect houses and repair electrical issues, but he also works for their dad. Ty wants to be able to do the same for himself."

I nodded. "Cool." *Jamel. Got it.*

She continued talking excitedly about Tyrell. As I was listening, I thought about Jamel. *What a sexy-ass man. I had no idea if he was straight or gay or bi. If we ever meet again, and he gives me the signs he was giving me today, I will have no choice but to fuck his brains out. Or even better, let him fuck my brains out.* I smiled to myself.

She noticed. "What are you smiling about?" she asked curiously.

"You." I played it off. "You seem really interested in this one, Lovie." I used the name that only I called her. I opened the door to the cafe and held it for her to

Chapter 1

walk in first. We liked that nobody really came in here in the middle of the day. Our table by the window was open so she made a beeline for it.

"Yeah, I think I am. Did you see his eyes? Man, I could swim in those silvers all day," she said dreamily. I nodded and smiled. As different as we were from each other physically, we were so much alike mentally and emotionally.

I went up to the counter and ordered our usuals: Thintastic Avocado BLT for her, a fruit cup for Winter, ham and swiss for me, and chai tea lattes for all of us. Because it was still a little warm for September, I ordered our chais iced. I ordered four because Mina was on her way too. I ordered her a Thinstastic Turkey with apple slices.

I pulled out my phone and looked up Grindr profiles as I waited for our food. It had only been three days since the last one, but my encounter with Jamel gave me an itch that I needed to scratch— probably tonight. I welcomed all races, ethnicity and nationalities, but as a blond-haired, blue-eyed white guy, it was mostly other white guys checking for me. My profile was simple and not sexy; I wore a nice smile and a tight shirt to show off my muscles. That might have been part of my problem. Maybe I needed a picture to show how kinky I really was.

I ignored the guys who left dick pics in my messages and started scrolling for sexy African-American guys. After a couple of pages, I came across "Xavier, 23, lives in Rhode Island, looking for relationships and a good time." He had his shirt off and was wearing sweatpants. He obviously wanted people to see what he was working with. He had milk chocolate brown skin and locs that were golden with shells at the tips. His smile was genuine, and he had a look that said, "Okay, here I am if you want me." He was online. So, I messaged him:

[Connor: Hi, I'm Connor.]

He messaged me back immediately: [Hi Connor. I'm Xavier but people just call me Lex. How you doing?]

[Connor: I'm good Lex. You?]

[Lex: Good good. Sooo what's up?]

[Connor: Nothing much. Just looking for something to get into later.]

[Lex: Something or someone?]

I smiled. [Connor: Yeah. That.]

[Lex: Well, I don't have any plans. I live in Elmwood, so I don't know if you want to come out this way or if you want me to come your way.]

[Connor: No, Elmwood is good. There is a Spanish restaurant I like out there, but I always forget the name.]

[Lex: La Gran Parada. I live walking distance from there. Do you want to meet there?]

Chapter 1

[Connor: That works perfectly. Yeah, let's meet there.]

[Lex: OK cool. What time should I meet you?]

[Connor: Let's do 8pm.]

[Lex: OK cool. I'm looking forward to getting to know you better, Connor. You're beautiful. And sexy.]

[Connor: Funny, I was thinking the exact same thing about you, Lex.]

I grabbed our food tray and headed back to the table. I put Afia's stuff in front of her, put the fruit cup and a drink next to me and put Mina's stuff on the table before the empty chair. She looked over at Mina's empty seat and said, "I wonder if she will tell us where she was?"

I shrugged. "I don't know. Jack's not talking either. He just said, 'We needed to get away, and now we're back.' I'm not going to press him about it, I'm just glad he's back. Glad they are all back."

"I know, me too," Lovie said. "I saw Brayden last week and he looked like shit. Like he hadn't slept the whole time they were gone. And I barely saw Liam."

"I did. He wasn't looking too good either. And nobody had seen Ethan at all except at Mass. He just held himself hostage at the inn the whole time."

"So, what do you think happened?" she asked.

We had been talking all day about our friends' disappearance a few weeks ago. Jack, his sister June, and his cousins, Mina and Henrietta, just up and left one day with barely a note to anyone, not even their significant others. The whole town of Rockville gossiped about it. No one knew if they were hurt, dead, or kidnapped. The consensus was that they were on the run from something. But they all came back on Monday and resumed their normal lives: Henrietta with Brayden, June with Liam, and Jack with Ethan. And Mina said she would meet us here on Wednesday like she always did.

"I don't know. I'm kinda hoping Mina tells us something," I said.

As the words left my mouth Mina came through the door. Mina Frazier was stunningly beautiful. Even gay guys noticed when she walked in a room. She had long blonde hair, dark blue eyes, and an apple round bottom. Guy or girl, I loved to see a nice ass. She was wearing a very short, black and cream romper to show off her bottom. She breezed in like always and smiled when she saw us. We both got up and hugged her tight.

"I missed you," I breathed in her hair.

She reached down and held my butt with one hand and said, "And I missed you." She also liked a nice bottom, which was how we became lovers in high school. I laughed and pulled away first.

Winter Sutton, who came in right after her, was wearing tight jeans that showed off the shape of her hips and derriere. She had a pink cutoff top to show off her flat belly and belly button ring, as well as the curve of her melon-shaped breasts. When she walked, you could hear drums. That's how sexy she was. Her mother is Brazilian and her father is white, so her skin bronzed instead of turning red in the sun. Her curly brown hair was not in place, so we could all tell she

♥♥♥ CHAPTER 1 ♥♥♥

had fought with it that morning. She was wearing big shades but took them off, revealing large hazel eyes that drew people in. She saw Mina, and they ran and hugged each other.

When they finally let go, Winter plopped in the chair next to me, kissed my cheek, and sighed. No one touched anything, and we all looked at Mina, who was smiling hard at us. "What?"

Winter spoke first. "Bitch, out with it. What the fuck happened?"

Afia, always the diplomatic one, touched Winter's hand and said, "What Winter means to say is, we have all been so worried about you. Are you okay? Is everything okay? Can you tell us why you left?"

Mina's smile faded a bit. She looked thoughtfully out the window, drumming her fingernails on the table. Then she said, "Yes. I am okay. We are all okay. But no, I can't tell you anything. Because it's not my story to tell."

"Then whose story is it?" Winter asked. "Jack, right? He was always starting shit when he was younger. It probably finally caught up with him."

Mina did not answer. She just took a sip of her chai tea and opened the wrapping of her sandwich. We knew she wouldn't say more, so I let it go for all of us.

"I'm just glad you all are okay. We all are." I meant that, as Jack and Mina are two of my best friends. I opened my sandwich as well. "Are you back at school too?"

She looked at me grateful. "Yes. I was able to resume my clinicals and keep the majority of my classes so I will graduate on time."

"That's awesome," Afia said.

♥ ♥ ♥ Hidden Love ♥ ♥ ♥

Mina was the only one of us that actually went to a four year college. We all graduated from Rockville High, but I went into the Marines for four plus years. Afia, who was a year behind us, did two years of community college and got her Pharmacy Tech degree so she could work in the family business. And Winter did two years of Cosmetology school and worked in a hair salon. But Mina said she was going to college. For the first three years, she bounced around a couple of majors and then settled on becoming a nurse. She was almost there and we were so proud of her. I told her that just then.

"Thanks, guys. Okay, enough about me, out with it. Whose dicks have we been sucking since I was away?" Her eyes sparked with amusement.

Winter started with her previous night's sexcapade that left her looking disheveled this morning. Mina talked about fucking Sam in the back room of his bar yesterday and on the day she got back. She planned on fucking him tonight too. Whatever happened to her had her looking for comfort because it was Sam she turned to whenever she needed to feel loved and safe. They had been fucking around since forever, but Mina didn't want to commit to anyone. I told them how I drove over an hour to meet a guy last week and possibly another one tonight. His big dick and long tongue were worth the drive. And Afia, the only one of us that is not a whore, talked about Tyrell.

This was my crew, my tribe, my family. I love them all, but I love Afia the most; that's why I call her Lovie. I slept with all three of these women at one point in my life—Mina and Winter in high school and Lovie

♥♥♥ CHAPTER 1 ♥♥♥

twice: Once when I was 18 and she asked me to take her virginity from her on her prom night; and then again accidentally when I came home for good almost three years ago. I shouldn't say "accidentally." That's not fair. We both wanted to. It was nice and sweet and felt like home.

We never did it again, but we had no regrets either. Not one bit. Lovie knows who I am, and she would never try to change me. At 16, after I had sex with Jack for the first time and then let him fuck me, Lovie was the first person I came out to. And in the middle of my existential crisis of sexuality, she said happily, "Great. Now we have something else to talk about—Boys!" She is my rock and my everything.

Lovie's also been my beard since my last few months of high school and when I left the military three years ago. I never asked her to. She just kinda fell into that role as we fell in step of always being together. Everyone assumed we were a couple, and she never corrected them. Her habit of kissing me on the lips didn't help. Mina and Winter rolled their eyes every time she did it in front of them. It was Lovie's way of protecting me.

My tribe and I sat, talked, and laughed for about two hours, then kissed, hugged, and promised to do it all over again next Wednesday. Afia took my arm again, and we walked the couple of blocks back to my car. We drove the thirty or so minutes home to Rockville. She was still talking about Mina and what she didn't say, and about Tyrell and whether he would call her, and how she wished she had big boobs like Winter. I just loved the sound of Lovie's voice.

When I dropped her off, she kissed me on the lips and said, "Be safe tonight."

"Always," I told her. I drove slowly to my parents' house, thinking of ways to avoid them as I made my way to my apartment over their garage.

CHAPTER 2

YOUR COVER STORY?

I got to the restaurant and immediately saw him. Lex was even more gorgeous in person, and I hoped he found me attractive too. His wide smile told me that I was. He was wearing a regular black and yellow polo shirt with black jeans. His eyes are almond-shaped, wide, and brown, and his face was smooth looking, younger than his 23 years of age. His locs were pulled back in a French braid and hung a couple of inches below his shoulders. He stood up when he saw me, and I automatically went to him.

"Hey, Connor." He held his hand out for me to shake.

"Hi, Lex," I greeted him. He had nice, strong hands. We shook once then he pulled in his four fingers to meet mine tightly before letting go. I sat across from him.

He looked at me, then chuckled. "I didn't know if you actually wanted to eat or..." He trailed off. I could tell he was a little nervous, and I liked that this wasn't something he regularly does. It made me want to fuck him more.

I gave him a reassuring smile. "Yeah, I could eat." He looked relieved.

He called the waitress and spoke Spanish, which was a pleasant surprise. He asked me, "What are you in the mood for?"

"The last time I was here, I had half a chicken with Spanish rice, black beans, and fried bananas. I could eat that again."

"*Plátanos*," he said with a smile. "Not bananas." He ordered for the both of us in Spanish. When the waitress left, Lex turned to me. "So what's a nice white boy like you doing on Grindr, Connor?"

I laughed. I liked Lex's humor already. "I'm just looking for someone to hang out with. Someone more my speed."

"What? Dick pics aren't your speed?" He laughed, and I laughed with him.

"No, but I'm just saying you wore sweatpants in your pic for a reason." I held his gaze.

He licked his lips, looked away shyly, and chuckled. "Yeah, you are right about that." Then he asked, "Just someone to hang out with? Nothing more, nothing less?"

"Nothing more, nothing less," I told him candidly. "I'm not really in the space to be in a relationship right now." Most people in my life don't know I'm gay, but I left that part out of the conversation. "So I'm just meeting people and having fun."

"Okay. I'm cool with that," Lex said. We held eye contact until the waitress arrived with our water, chips, and salsa.

♥♥♥ Chapter 2 ♥♥♥

"So, what kinda work do you do?" I asked. We talked for the next hour about our work, our lives, and other random things while we had dinner. We each had a beer. I like to be completely lucid for the first time. At the end of the night, the waitress brought the check and placed it on the center of the table. Lex and I both reached for it at the same time, our fingertips touching.

He smiled, and I chuckled. "Let me pay," he said first.

"No, I hit you up, so let me." I tugged a bit, but he didn't budge.

"I plan on seeing more of you, Connor. If you plan on seeing me again, then let me pay today, and you can pay next time."

That was his way of saying he liked me, even though we hadn't bumped our cocks together yet. And I liked him too, but committing to seeing him again wasn't something I wanted to do. I'd have to fuck him first to see if it was worth it. Running the risk of hurting his feelings, I said, "How about we split it right down the middle for now, and after tonight we can decide if we want to see each other again?"

He nodded slowly, slid the paper from my fingers, and gave me the total. I had cash and he had a card. I gave him cash, and he paid the check with his card, leaving a couple of dollars from what I had given him as a tip.

After the waitress picked up the receipt, Lex said, "I live about two blocks from here, Connor."

"That's what you said."

"I have a roommate, but she isn't there right now."

I nodded and waited. *He's adorable.* He was really new to this. He had no idea that this conversation was unnecessary. From our first initial contact, we both knew where and how we would end up. But I let him take the lead anyway.

"Do you want to come over for a little while, Connor?"

I think he likes to say my name. Almost all of his sentences end in him addressing me by my name. I think I'm gonna make him say my name.

"Yes," I said.

He smiled and looked relieved as if I would have turned him down. *He has no idea how sexy he is, but I am ready to show him,* I thought in my head with a smile.

We walked down to the apartment complex making small talk. By the time we got into the elevator to go to the fourth floor, Lex was quiet and I could feel his nervousness. As the elevator began to move, I reached over and pressed the stop button. The elevator jolted.

He looked up stunned, almost scared. "What—why did you—"

I didn't let him finish. I pressed my lips against his and pushed him back against the wall of the elevator and rested one hand near his head. I reached in between us to feel his groin with my other hand and kissed him on his closed mouth a few times. I kissed his jaw, his smooth face, and went to find his ear. I sucked his earlobe as he wrapped both hands around me and reached up my shirt to rub my back. *That's it. Let go a little.*

♥ ♥ ♥ CHAPTER 2 ♥ ♥ ♥

And he did. He got tired of my closed-mouth kisses and pushed his tongue through my lips. I immediately sucked his tongue. He was getting hard, and I was already hard. I moved my hand off the wall and placed it behind him. He reached down to grab both my ass cheeks and pulled me closer. Here we stayed, hands on each other's bottoms, cocks pressed tightly together, tonguing each other down. I slowed down first, and he opened his eyes to look at me. I'm about 6 feet, and he was about 5'11, but for some reason I was towering over him.

I asked him softly, "Are you okay?"

He nodded and said, "You have the prettiest blue eyes." They are icy blue, and I knew how enticing they can be.

I smiled a little. "You have the prettiest ... everything. Everything about you is sexy." He blushed, a bit of red showing up on his brown cheeks. I asked him, "You ready?"

"Yes!" he said excitedly.

I reached one hand back and pressed the button. The elevator moved again, I resumed holding onto Lex. We didn't kiss for the rest of the ride; we just embraced and stared into each other's eyes. When the elevator door opened, quickly spun me around and reached for my hand, but I gave him my arm instead. We turned down several halls until we faced two doors. He got out his key with one hand and opened the door, pulling me inside.

As soon as the door closed, he pounced on me. All his nervousness was gone. He grabbed me by my neck roughly and attacked me with his tongue while his hands pulled at my belt buckle. I let him kiss me as rough as he wanted while I mimicked his movements. He was faster and managed to get my cock out before I could pull his zipper down. He got on his knees and put me in his mouth, and holy shit, he could suck dick. It was like a warm, wet, tight suction surrounding me. I felt his tongue moving all around like he was rolling his r's on my cock. He pursed his lips on the underside of my head before making his way back down. With every bob, he moved me deeper and deeper in his throat. He hummed, twisted his head, and moved his tongue, and I had to make him stop before I busted a load right in his mouth.

I called his full name to get his attention, "Xavier."

He looked up at me with my dick in his mouth, and I could have came right then. Nothing in the world was sexier to me than having my dick in a man's mouth. Instead, I moved him off me and lifted him for a kiss. We kissed a lot gentler but still with passion. Then I asked him, "What do you want?"

He knew what I was asking, and he answered as candidly as we had been all night. "I want to fuck you. Then I want you to fuck me." *Good plan.* Although I am typically the one taking charge, I liked to get fucked too, which was why I only reached out to versatile guys like me.

I kissed him again. "Where is your room?"

He led me into the apartment. The apartment had a spacious, open floor plan and a balcony. There were two doorways in the living room area, and Lex led me to the furthest one. His room was basic and clean. I had pulled up my pants but didn't buckle them. I sat

Chapter 2

on the bed and took off my pants as Lex closed and locked the door. He came over and helped me take off my shirt. Then he took off his. We kissed and touched like old lovers.

He dropped his pants and boxers, then moved closer to me until I was at eye level with his dick. Just like the rest of Lex, it was beautiful. I happily put his brown cock between my pink lips and sucked. He let out an intense moan as I deep-throated the fuck out of him, cupped his balls, and massaged his perineum with one finger. Then accidentally-on-purpose, I put my finger in his hole. He let out another loud moan as I continued to deep-throat and finger-fuck him.

He said breathlessly, "If you don't stop, I'm going to cum."

I chuckled as much as anyone could with a thick, long penis in their mouth and pulled off him slowly, watching him watch me since he liked my eyes so much. I moved back on the bed, and he slowly followed, not breaking eye contact. When he got between my legs, he reached over and opened the top drawer of his nightstand as I stroked him. He placed two condoms and lube on the bed. He put a condom on himself first, then lubed up his hands and started moisturizing my pucker with his whole hand first. He inserted two, then three fingers. I moaned wildly. He liked watching me squirm while he fingered me.

When he felt I was ready, he guided himself between my open legs noticing my flexibility. He eased in with no trouble, and I squirmed to adjust to his size. Once I adjusted, we were good to go. At first, it seemed he wanted to take it slow. But he soon started pounding into my hole, groaning the whole time. I allowed myself to be used up because it felt so fucking good. He was also a shit talker. Usually, I'm the one talking shit, but he was topping, so I gave him what he needed.

"Fuck, Connor fuck, this fucking ass of yours is so fucking tight! You like this, Connor? You like this dick all in your ass, Connor? I know you like this big Dominican dick in your ass, Connor. Fucking tight ass."

Dominican, not African-American? Okay, sure. "Fuck Lex, ugh, fuck me harder. Ugh. Love this thick Dominican dick. Ugh, fuck me in Spanish, ugh, fuck me harder, ugh, dick is amazing, ugh!" I meant it too. His big dick was amazing; it hit my sweet spot, sending electric waves all through my body. And he complied, speaking in Spanish as he was slamming into me.

"Ay dios mío, este culo apretado se siente tan jodidamente bien. Podría follarte toda la noche. Dios mío, me voy a volver loco con este culo apretado. Coño, me voy a correr—"

One day, I'll figure out what he said, but it didn't matter because he sounded sexy. Then he switched to English and gasped. "Fuck Connor, I'm gonna cum, fuck Connor, I'm gonna cum, fuck fuck this tight ass I'm gonna—" He gasped again, came, then collapsed on top of me. "I'm sorry," he said. "I thought I was going to last longer, but you're fucking tight as shit." He slid out and sat up, took the condom off, tied it, and put it in the trash near the nightstand.

I chuckled a bit, annoyed that he came before me, but I had a feeling he was gonna make it up to me. As soon as I thought this, he leaned down and started

Chapter 2

sucking me off again. His dick-sucking skills were top-notch. He could have done that all night, and I would no longer be annoyed. Instead, he blew me until I was erect, then put a condom on me. Without another word, he stood above me and fingered himself, lubing his asshole. It was the sexiest thing he could have ever done, but then he knelt and eased himself on my cock. I already could tell he did not have sex this way often. He was fucking tight. Literal tears were making their way out of his eyes, so I held onto his waist and guided him until he was all the way down.

"You okay, Lex?" I asked.

"Yeah, it always hurts the first time, but I'll be fine in a few. Just give me a second."

He took a couple of breaths, and then he began to move, circling his waist against me like we were dancing to reggae music. I let out a special occasion moan that only comes out when I am getting fucked. Because even though he was the one bottoming, he was still doing the fucking. All I could do was hold on and let him take me for a ride. He moved like the waves of the ocean, pulling me forward and backward. He saw what he was doing to me and went a step further. He pinched my nipples hard and twisted them until I moaned like an animal in heat. My nipples are extremely sensitive.

"Fuck, give it to me, Connor. Give it to me," he repeated as he pinched my nipples. I didn't know what "it" meant, but I hoped I was giving "it" to him.

He started moving faster, and I started moaning louder. Because I was already so close to jizzing, I quickly forgave Lex for how fast he came. I was not doing much better. I held on as long as I could. But when he started pounding back, and I involuntarily started thrusting up to meet him, it was over for the both of us. He froze again into his climax as I kept pounding into his hole. He exploded cum on my chest, clenching his rectum making me burst inside the condom.

We laughed and caught our breath together. He rolled off and took the condom off me, tied it, and put it in the trash. We laid side by side. Neither of us were snugglers, but we wanted to be close.

I asked, "Xavier, why do they call you Lex?"

"My last name is Lemos. In school in the DR, I was Lemos, X. So the name just stuck."

"So you're from the Dominican Republic. Cool."

He turned to face me. "You don't seem the type to fuck with a lot of Dominican guys."

I smiled. "If I'm honest, you're the first. I mostly fuck different variations of white guys."

He chuckled, then asked, "So is this like a fetish for you now? You're going to start knocking off ethnicities one by one?"

I laughed. "No. I don't usually pick someone off Grindr based off of skin color." Although I totally did that time, thinking of Jamel's sexy ass again. "I'm not usually the one messaging people. People message me all the time."

"That's because you're the American Dream, Connor. White, masculine, blond hair, blue eyes, perfect body, big dick, tight ass. If they don't want to be you, they surely want to fuck you."

Chapter 2

I laughed, but his comment made me uncomfortable. Mostly because I knew he was right, and I didn't want to be seen that way. My life was far from perfect, and I got a lot of fucked up issues, so no one should ever want to be me.

I told him, "Yeah, I guess I am. But there is so much more to me than what I appear to be."

"I can see that," he said softly. I turned to look at him as he was already looking at me. "But if you haven't shown people the real you, so how could we?"

I turned my head to avoid his eyes. *Nobody sees the real me. Except Lovie.* I changed the subject, and he allowed me to do that. I asked about his apartment and roommate, and he told me about her—a home health aide that works nights. It was her apartment, and he was paying rent to her.

After some time, he asked me the question that I knew was coming, "Do you want to stay the night?"

I replied casually, hoping not to hurt his feelings too much, "I can't. I have to work early in the morning."

"Okay."

"But ... can I see you this weekend?"

His face lit up, and he tried to hide it. "Yeah, sure."

I told him I was working Saturday morning, but I would be free Saturday night. He said, "Okay." We were silent for a moment, then he asked, "Are you leaving now?"

I looked at his hunger for me. "Not yet."

I leaned in and kissed him. Since we had both came, we felt a lot less pressure and enjoyed touching each other. I bit his neck and left him a souvenir hickey. I changed positions first and knelt on the bed. He knelt with me and stroked both of us. I was close, but Lex came first, cumming all over my cock and his hands. He looked like he wanted to say sorry again, and I kissed him so I wouldn't hear it.

I used his jizz as lube and told him, "Kneel against the headboard."

He moved the pillows out of the way, faced the headboard, and held on. He knew what was coming. I entered him bareback, remembering but not caring about my promise to Afia, and I pushed all the way in. He moaned in pain, and I knew his eyes were stinging. I didn't care about that either. I didn't take it slow at all. I reached one hand around his chest to hold onto the front part of his shoulder, wrapped the other around his midsection, and I fucked him hard and mercilessly. I held him in that position for a long time. The headboard hit the wall as he moaned in Spanish.

As I reached my climax, I bit his earlobe a little hard and said, "Say my name."

He repeatedly moaned, "Connor, Connor, Connor," until he came again, and I came right after.

I kissed him on his neck, told him I'd see him Saturday, put on my clothes, and went home.

♥

~~~October 2009~~~

A month later, my phone rang on a Sunday morning. I looked at it groggily. It was Afia. *Why the hell is she calling me at 6:03 am on a Sunday?*

♥♥♥ Chapter 2 ♥♥♥

I answered, "Somebody better be dying."

"Connor!" she shrieked in my ear. "I have so much to tell you, so get the fuck up!!"

She must have gotten laid, I thought. That's the only time she got that excited, when she finally had something to gush about at our Wednesday tribe meetup. I knew she had a date with Ty over the weekend, and they hadn't had sex yet. That must have been it.

Sure enough, she told me about her ninth date with Tyrell, which started on Friday and ended that morning. The good best friend in me sat up, lit a cigarette, and listened. Ty had wined and dined her and took her back to his place on Friday where they talked all night and didn't make love until Saturday morning. Then they spent the whole day talking and fucking like good lovers do.

Of course, like the good best friend that I am, I asked Afia all the important questions: How big is his dick? Did he go down on you properly? Approximately how many times did you cum? Did he worship your tits? Afia was a B cup and very sensitive about her appearance, but her body was perfect to me. She detailed how Ty was an excellent lover, worshiped every inch of her body, including the boobs, and kept her cumming.

I had an average level of interest in the conversation until she said, "And I have to tell you about his brother Jamel who asked about you!"

This just got ten times more interesting. I finished my cigarette and asked, "Why would he ask about me?" I tried to keep a conversational tone, but who was I kidding? Not my girl, that's for sure.

"Shut up, Connor. You don't think Ty and I noticed you and Jamel eye fucking each other when you met?"

I laughed and lied, "I was not eye fucking him."

"Okay, whatever, but listen. Tyrell said that after we went out last week, Jamel had asked if you had been around, giving Ty any problems about being with me. Ty told him that we were just friends, and we've been friends since we were kids, so there was nothing to worry about. But then he said that Mel started fishing for details about you, asking if you were military, how old you were, things like that. So I asked why he was so interested in you? And Ty says, just like that, he says, 'Mel probably wants to fuck him. My brother is gay.' Did you hear me, Connor!? He's gay!" She shrieked again.

She sounded so happy about finding out someone else was gay I laughed with her. But then I got serious. "You didn't tell him about me, right?"

"Oh, Connor. No, of course not. I just said, 'Oh wow, I didn't realize he was gay.' I have seen him again after that one time at the Pharmacy, and he's pretty cool. I think you would like hiiiiiiimmmmm." She sang that last word and made me laugh again.

"Calm down, Lovie. Stop trying to play matchmaker. I'm good," I lied again. I was interested and she knew it.

"Stop lying. You want this. And I'm going to need you to actually date people, man."

"I'm dating Lex, remember?"

"No, you're *fucking* Lex. Since your first date, y'all haven't done much outside of his apartment."

"And what's wrong with that?"

"Ugh, Connor, you cannot spend your life on Grindr going from one fuck to the next. Date people! Meet

Chapter 2

someone! Fall in love for a little while like the rest of us out there."

"That doesn't sound appealing at all."

"Connor!" she whined.

I cut her off and asked, "Are you coming to Sunday dinner tonight?" She was quiet for a moment.

Afia hates being around my family. But if I was not working on a Sunday, then my family expected me to be there at dinner. I only asked Afia to join when I didn't feel like going on my own. And I didn't feel like it that day.

Afia said, "I will go to Sunday dinner if you agree to talk to Jamel." I rolled my eyes as Afia continued. "I'm going to their church today in Providence, and Jamel will be there. I am going to plainly ask him if he wants to get to know you. I want your permission to tell him about you, and I want to give him your number. Those are my terms."

I could picture her cute and defiant face as she waited for my answer. A gay guy in Providence knowing I'm gay was not a big deal. If my parents traveled outside of Rockville just a bit more, they would probably know about me, but they were small-town people with small-town minds. So really, there is little risk for me and all the angst for her. She must have realized that, and it must have been a huge deal for me to meet this Jamel-called-Mel so I happily gave in.

"Sure, Lovie. Tell him I'm gay. Tell him I was eye-fucking him too. And give him my number. I'm good with all of that. Just please come over tonight."

She sighed. "I'll be there, Connor. Love you."

"Not as much as I love you."

Afia showed up like clockwork. She looked beautiful and respectable as always in her Sunday best. She kissed me on the lips, and I pulled her into a hug.

"Thank you," I whispered.

"Um-hmm," she mumbled.

My mom, Katherine, walked past the door and said, "Afia, nice that you came today."

"Hello, Mrs. Katherine." They gave each other respectable hugs, and she handed my mom the shoe-fly pie she made for the occasion. My mother is always Katherine, not Kate or Katie or Kat. I think she named my sister Mary Kate to have a Kate in the family. But we call her MK.

Mary Kate curtly greeted Afia and walked to the back of the house without waiting for a response. Afia didn't bother acknowledging her at all. After knowing Afia for ten years, you would think they would be less icier to each other, but my sister can be an icy bitch when she wants to be. She's 21-years-old, 5'6 in height with heels, cute, blonde-haired, blue-eyed, and popular, so things tend to come pretty easy for her. MK has a talent for burying her head in the sand.

I took Lovie's hand and walked her into the living room, where we sat on the love seat and waited for dinner. She wore a long burgundy dress, draped her legs over one of my legs, and held my hand. We watched TV and talked in low voices as she told me about her day with Ty, Jamel, and their family.

Chapter 2

"I told Jamel, and he had this look on his face like he wanted to smile but not in front of me. I think he's excited to talk to you. Yay!" She was so gleeful.

I rubbed her thigh and said, "Calm down, Lovie. He hasn't called me yet." But I have to admit I was a little excited too.

My baby sister Angela came into the room. She is seventeen and the only family member I can stand. Maybe it's because her generation doesn't give a shit about what older generations say about social media consumption, interracial marriages, gender fluidity, or non-religiosity. Or maybe it was the way she goes head-to-head with my father on such issues until he curses her out or threatens physical harm if she doesn't shut up. She was unlike the rest of us who either agree with him, like Matty, my 28-year-old brother, or cave to him out of fear, like Mary Kate and myself. I wish I had her strength.

Angie is 5'8, and like MK, she is cute, blonde-haired, blue-eyed, and popular. Or more like, infamous. She's always doing the craziest shit, like setting up an auction for the white cheerleaders at Rockville High for Black History Month so they can know their "worth in humanity." She then got a bunch of other students she considered marginalized—Blacks, Hispanics, immigrants, disabled, gays, nerds—to forcefully throw pennies at the cheerleaders. Angie was proud of her suspension.

Angie and Afia exchanged genuine smiles. Afia got off me to hug Angie, and Angie sat at our feet to talk about the latest social media craze. I listened to them thinking, *Teenagers are awesome.* Afia must have been thinking the same. I looked at how she took in every word Angie said and gave her advice on bad relationships. Afia is the youngest of three girls, so she has always treated Angie like the baby sister she's never had. I loved that they were so close.

Mom poked her head in. "Dinner is ready."

We sat at the table, and it was just the six of us—my mom, dad, me, Afia, Mary Kate, and Angie. I thanked God my brother wasn't here. We took our places: Dad at the head of the table, my mother to his right, Mary Kate to his left, and Angie next to my mother. I sat next to Mary Kate. Afia always sat to my left, except when Matty would take the other end of the table if he was around, then Afia and I would switch seats. My father would never let me sit at the other end of the table.

Dad said grace, and my mom, sisters, and I conversed easily. My father, Owen McIntyre, is a military guy. He served as a Staff Sergeant in Vietnam and retired after ten years of service. My father doesn't say much and focused his life on being the family breadwinner and disciplinarian. But when he has something to say, it was usually something highly offensive or disrespectful, and that's when the problem begins. He is a white Christian man who is sexist, racist, xenophobic, and homophobic.

Toward the end of dinner, the doorbell rang, and I could feel Afia tense up next to me. Matty walked in, upset. She reached over, squeezed my leg, and laced her fingers with mine—our sign to keep calm and keep our mouths shut.

Chapter 2

"Dad, you're not going to believe what just happened," Matty said. I knew he was about to say some dumb, racist, sexist, or homophobic shit. *Let's spin the wheel.*

He sat in his spot at the table and started talking, but my dad stopped him. "Say hello, Matty. I didn't raise you in a barn."

"I'm sorry, sir," he said respectfully. He looked around. "Hey, Mom." He got up to give her a kiss. "Hey Connor, MK, Angie ... Afeeeeeya." He said her name stupidly, as always, and smirked. She never acknowledges him when he did it, but his narcissistic ass never notices.

He turned back to my dad. "Dad, this spic bitch—"

"Language," my mom warned, and I thought, *Oh, a twofer today—racist and sexist.* I squeezed Afia's hand, and she squeezed back.

"Sorry, Mom. This spic female dog just swiped my car! This is why women shouldn't be on the road. None of them can drive, especially illegals." My mom said nothing, and Afia and I exchanged eye rolls that Mom was okay with "spic" but not "bitch."

"Shut up. I can drive," Mary Kate said lazily.

"Well, you're not a spic bitch," he said.

"Well, you know how those people are," MK said. I felt Afia tense up again.

"I'm not kidding. Stop cursing at the table," my mother repeated.

Matty ignored her and said to our father, "Can I bring it to the shop? See what they can do about it? My insurance will go through the roof if I have to submit a claim." My dad owns a car dealership and service center, the only one in our small town of Rockville, Rhode Island. American cars only, of course.

My dad said, "Sure, bring it by."

Matty continued to go on a rant about the Spanish woman who swiped his car. It didn't matter that it was most likely an accident because she was probably an illegal who should be rounded up and blah blah blah. We all had to sit there and listen until Angie spoke up.

"Matty, how do you know she was Spanish?" She cocked her head to the side, a sign that she was about to lay into someone. I sat up straighter.

"What? Because I know an illegal spic when I see one," he said dismissively.

"Really? Because Hispanics can be anywhere from my complexion to Afia's skin tone, and some darker, like South Americans, Dominicans, and Puerto Ricans." My heart kinda jumped as I thought about my Dominican lover, who was just a few shades darker than Afia. I nodded.

Matty looked at Angie like she was stupid. "Why is that important? She kinda had an accent. That's how I know."

"There are a lot of people in this world with accents. How do you know it was a Spanish one?" She was pushing him. Afia and I were here for the show.

Matt had the nerve to look at her like she was the one who didn't get it. He yelled, "You think I don't know a spic accent from a Russian one? And why does it matter? She swiped my car!"

Angie yelled back, "It doesn't matter, but you brought up her supposed race or ethnicity like it does."

"When did I bring up her race?" he said incredulously.

Chapter 2

"You did just now, you dummy! You used a racist term to describe Hispanics, and you don't even know if she is actually Spanish-speaking or not."

He snapped at her, "Were you there, Angie? No, you weren't so what the fuck do you know? And anyway, no one was talking to you. You just wanted a reason to spit your liberal PC bullshit around. Take that fucking shit somewhere else!"

Katherine yelled, "Okay that's it! Out Matty. Out, Out, Out!" She shooed him from the dining room. He got mad and stormed out of the house. Angie sat back, looking satisfied, and I winked at her. *That's my girl.*

♥

I walked Afia to her car, holding her hand. "Thanks for coming over, Lovie."

She hugged me and said, "Let me know when Jamel calls, okay?"

I pulled my phone out of my pocket and started to say, "If he calls. We don't know if—"

But the little light was blinking, letting me know I had a missed call. My ringtone was off for dinner. My eyes widened, and so did hers. I opened my phone. It was a number I didn't recognize that came in thirty minutes before, but the person left a voicemail.

I was about to hold the phone to my ear when Lovie grabbed my hand forcefully and said, "You better put that on speakerphone so I can hear, or I will break your fucking fingers."

I smiled and pressed the voicemail icon and speakerphone. A baritone voice came through. "Hey,

Connor. It's Jamel. I got your number from Afia. Hit me back up at this number if you want to talk. Bye."

I'm not going to lie, my dick twitched at the sound of his voice. Then Afia said, "Damn, his voice just made me wet. Is it bad that I'm wet from thinking of my boyfriend's brother that way?"

I nudged her a little. "Boyfriend? After one month?"

"Yes, boyfriend," she said. "I like him, he likes me, we're exclusive, and we want to see where this goes. If that's not a boyfriend, I don't know what is."

I pulled her in for a tight hug. I let go and held out the car door for her. Right before she got in, she kissed me on the lips. "I love you, Con."

"Love you more. Drive safe. Text when you get home."

She nodded and drove off. Instead of going back into the house, I walked to my garage apartment and pressed the missed call number.

Jamel answered in the same deep voice I heard in the voicemail, "Hello?"

"Hey, Jamel. It's Connor."

"Coooooonooooor." He dragged out my name in his deep voice. It was incredibly sexy. "I'm glad you called me back. I've heard a lot about you. You're an interesting guy."

"Yeah? You got all that in the three minutes you saw me a month ago?" He chuckled, and that was sexy too. "What's so interesting about me?"

"The way you were all protective of your friend Afia. Like you were more than friends. But Afia and I talked a little about you, and she assures me you are

Chapter 2

not more than friends. She assures me it's quite the opposite. I find all of that very interesting."

"I love her. I'd physically protect her with my life if she ever wanted or needed me to. But I'm not physically interested in her. She's my best friend."

"Your best friend and your beard? Your cover story?"

Cover story? Okay, this conversation just got uncomfortable. I opened the side door and went up the stairs to the main entrance of my apartment. "She's so much more to me than that. She's thoughtful, kind, authentic, and beautiful inside and out. She protects me and keeps me grounded. She's the best part of me, so she's more than just a cover story for me."

"Damn. I was just teasing you, but I see you're a little sensitive about it. It's cool."

"You don't know me like that to tease me." Maybe I said it with a bit more edge, but I didn't like him belittling her role in my life.

I plopped on my bed as he said, "Then let me get to know you. Let me take you out. I'm not really a phone person, so I'd rather talk in person."

Wow, he's forward like me. "Okay," I said casually. "When do you want to go out?"

"There's a restaurant in South Providence; a hole in the wall you probably never heard of, but they have the best pasta in all of Rhode Island. And I would know, I travel up and down this state for work. Thursday night okay?"

"Okay, yeah. Thursday." I had a "date" with Lex, but I could cancel it. "Give me the address, and I'll meet you there. Eight o'clock okay?"

"That's perfect. I'm looking forward to this." I could tell he meant it.

"Me too." And I meant it too. "Good night, Jamel." I'm not a phone person either, so I rushed off the phone to make that clear.

"Good night, Connor." He hung up first.

I thought about my only encounter with Jamel as I zipped down my jeans, grabbed my cock through the slit of my boxer briefs, and slowly started stroking myself. I closed my eyes and tried to remember every detail. I'm six feet even, and he seemed a bit taller than me, maybe 6'1 or 6'2. Brown skin, the color of hot chocolate made with water and not milk, small curvy ears, full lips with a thin mustache, and an even thinner goatee. I lubed with my pre-cum as I thought about those lips, thick biceps and triceps, and broad chest with his nipples poking through his fitted, white exercise shirt.

Those thoughts brought me closer to climax. I traveled to Jamel's muscular ass, and a moan escaped my lips. I couldn't wait to bury my nine-inch dick in that ass. My thoughts moved to his equally thick thighs, and I could almost feel them wrapped around my waist, his heels digging in my lower back. I heard him draw out my name, "Coooooonooor," and I lost it, cumming all over myself and my shirt. I licked my fingers out of habit, then took off my shirt and cleaned myself up. I laid back down, still wearing my jeans and shoes, and fell into a dreamless sleep.

CHAPTER 3

YOU'RE LIKE MY PERFECT MATCH.

I saw him at a booth near the back of the Italian bistro. He stood up as I came closer. I was in blue jeans and a plaid button-down shirt; he was in black jeans and a gray sweater that brought out his eyes. *He is fucking gorgeous* I thought, and my heart pumped a little faster. He held his hand out for a shake, and he folded his four fingers in the same way Lex did.

"Connor," he greeted.

"Hey, Jamel. Or Mel?" I asked.

"Either is fine." He motioned for me to sit. As I sat across from him I casually put my flip phone on the table. I was on call this week and if it rang I would explain it to him.

The waiter came over with warm bread and olive oil, rattled off the specials, and took our appetizer order. Jamel ordered a bottle of Riesling for the table. I like my beer bitter and my wine sweet, so I was happy about that.

He started, "So, you're military?"

I answered him, "Corporal McIntyre, U.S. Marine Corp, based in New River, North Carolina. Three tours in Fallujah, Iraq, four and a half years of service."

He nodded. "Sergeant Jones, U.S. Army, based at Fort Riley. Four tours in Afghanistan, seven years. I just got back three years ago."

"Me too. So we were over there at the same time." I took a sip of my water and relaxed.

"Seems like we were. What made you enlist?"

I shrugged and gave the standard answer. "I wanted to serve my country. And I wanted to make my dad proud of me. He served in Vietnam."

"Same," Jamel said. "My dad did twenty-five years of service before he retired. I'm an Army brat, so we moved around a lot. It was natural for me to want to enlist. But I'm the only one in my family that served, other than my dad."

"Same," I told him. "My older brother, with all his talk of God and country, is chicken shit. He would never serve. I have two younger sisters, and they never had an interest in enlisting."

"Well, none of my brothers are chicken shit, but after my first tour, I implored them not to enlist. This war is never-ending. I have two younger brothers behind Ty, one at Morehouse College starting his last year, and the other is a senior in high school."

"Wow, we have a shitload in common," I said, surprised. "My middle sister just graduated with her bachelor's degree in May, and my youngest sister is a senior in high school like your brother. We should hook them up."

♥♥♥ Chapter 3 ♥♥♥

Jamel chuckled. He had a pleasantly deep and soft laugh. "I don't know about all that. Lavell is a real nerd. He's into anime, comic books, chess club, and he's on the debate team. He wants to be the next Obama. Not so much because of politics, but because he wants to be a really important, smart black guy."

I laughed. "Well, Angie is pretty smart and a real activist for social issues. And she loves Obama but wasn't old enough to vote for him the first time around. She can't wait to vote for his second term. She is going to go to law school and become a civil rights lawyer."

"Does she know you're gay?" he asked me.

I shook my head slowly. "No one in my family knows I'm gay."

"Why?" he asked with genuine curiosity.

"My family is," I paused, "extremely conservative."

He raised his eyebrows. "So, homophobic."

I cringed a little and smiled. "And racist."

He let out a big laugh and said, "Holy shit, Connor. What the fuck are you doing here with me, a gay black man?"

"I'm a rebel, I guess." I laughed and gulped some wine. "They've gotten used to seeing me with Afia, so they know to keep their mouths shut, at least around me."

He nodded and said seriously, "That must have been really hard for you, growing up in a family like that."

"It's still hard. They have no idea who I am."

"What do you think will happen if you told them?" he asked.

I answered him honestly and with a straight face. "Well, my father would probably try to kill me."

He looked at me for a moment, then said, "You're not kidding."

"No. I'm an abomination. A sexually immoral cretin that should be eradicated from this earth."

"He doesn't talk like that for real, right?" Mel asked in disbelief.

I nodded. "Among other things. Homos, liberals, and baby killers deserve to die the Old Testament way, death by stoning, an eye for an eye kinda thing. My older brother, Matty, believes what he believes. My sister Mary Kate and my mother play their role in keeping quiet when the men talk about these issues and don't express an opinion. Only Angie challenges them."

"And what do you do? What role do you play on this stage?"

I blinked a few times as he awaited my response. "I… I disappear. I shrink in my chair while they say all the horrible things they could say about gay people and hope they don't notice that I am one of the people they are talking about. It's better when Afia is around. She holds my hand and gets me through it, helping me stay present. She protects me." *Why did I tell him that?*

"Shit, Connor," he said, shocked by my predicament.

I nodded again. "So telling my family wouldn't be them accepting me. At best, it would be me accepting that I no longer have a family. At worst, having to watch my back. But as terrible as they are, they're still my flesh and blood. I'm not ready to let go of them just yet." *Or maybe they aren't ready to let me go.* I took another gulp of wine.

❤ ❤ ❤ Chapter 3 ❤ ❤ ❤

"So you've been through actual war, only to come back to a personal war on the home front."

"Yes, it feels like mental warfare. Everyday. At least on base or in Iraq I could be myself, but here…"

Jamel watched me for a moment, and I stared back. He didn't look at me with pity. It was something else. Almost like he was in awe of me, which was weird because I sounded like a coward to myself. But he said, "That's heavy. But you're strong; I can see that. Everyone deserves to live their truth, though. I hope you find some peace about it, and soon."

I felt a little warm spot in my chest. I didn't think of myself as strong, but it was nice that he thought so.

"Me too. But in the meantime, I'm keeping them in the dark and living my life." *Enough about me. I need to turn the tables.* "How about you? You've always known you're gay? Lived your truth?" I took a sip, or maybe another gulp, of wine.

"Yeah, I've always known, but I didn't say anything to anyone until right before I deployed, literally days before. I told my mama and told her to tell my pop. I was chicken shit too." I laughed a little. He continued, "My dad came down to the base and took me out that following Saturday. We went for a long drive. He shared things about his childhood that he had never told me before, namely about his not-so-great relationship with his father. His parents were functioning alcoholics, and he joined the Army to get away from them. I never knew that. We played hoops, had dinner, and then he told me he loved me. It was the first time he's ever said it and he will probably never say it again. He also never brought up me being gay. But by telling me he loved me, he was saying he accepted me, no matter what. He said nothing and everything in the nine hours we spent together that day. Then I went to war."

"That's awesome. You're one of the lucky ones, fully accepted."

"I know. I will never take it for granted. My brothers were equally cool with it, and that really meant a lot to me." He paused. "You should tell Angie. Something tells me you won't lose her."

Nope, we're done talking about me. "Maybe. But back to you. You didn't test the waters as a teen at all? No crushes?"

Jamel said, "I had crushes, but no. I didn't start dating until I joined the Army, and then I really experimented."

"The military is arguably the best place to experiment," I threw in, and we both laughed. The waiter brought our appetizers and took our orders, chicken and shrimp Alfredo for me, sausage and gnocchi for him. "So, are you still experimenting? With white guys now?"

He smiled. "I've only ever been with one white guy. So yes, I guess this is an experiment for me."

"What made you want this experience with me?"

"I don't really know. There is something about you. I've known it since I first saw you."

"When was your last experiment, in general?" I just wanted to know if he was willing to fuck me tonight. *If it's been a while, he just might.*

Jamel paused, then said, "A few weeks ago. But I don't really like causal sex. I'd rather date and get to

Chapter 3

know someone." *Uh-oh.* Jamel threw the same question my way. "When was the last time for you?"

I wanted to be forthright and said, "Two days ago."

I looked him in the eye. It was after we had agreed to meet up and I wanted him to know that I do like causal sex and I was not looking for exclusivity. Jamel nodded and looked at me, saying nothing as he sipped his wine. His face was unreadable; I couldn't tell if he was shocked or annoyed. I sipped my wine and stared right back.

Jamel broke the silence. "What kind of work did you do as a Corporal?" I didn't fight the change of subject. We talked about our military experiences, our units, and growing up with military dads. Different, but similar, because while his dad was strict, my dad was an abusive asshole. *Is an abusive asshole.* We talked about friends we made and people we lost. I told him about losing Vinnie. It didn't hurt to talk about him like that.

"We honor his memory every day with Vinnie's Vet Buddies, me and four others. It was his dream. He told us that when he got back after that last tour he was going to start a crisis line for vets, call it Vet Buddies where veterans could call in anonymously, just to talk to another vet who gets it. The line was for those who couldn't or didn't want to go to the VA. Vets that were sitting there moments away from eating their gun and needed someone to talk them off the ledge."

I tapped the phone I had put on the table. "The five of us made it happen for him. I'm on call tonight, just in case someone can't pick up the phone in their region. The call automatically gets forwarded to me."

Jamel was in awe. "Connor, that's the most amazing thing I've ever heard. You are amazing."

I shrugged. "It's not just me. We live in different parts of the country, so we all take a section. I take calls from New York to Maine. Joe is in New Jersey and takes everything west of there to Illinois. Samantha, we call her Sammie, is in Mississippi, so she takes the south from the Carolinas to Florida and across to Texas, right along the Mason-Dixon line. Benjin's in Michigan. He takes the rest of the Midwest to Idaho. And Taylor is from Oregon but lives in San Bernardino, so he takes the west coast states. And we all take Texas because Vinnie was from Houston. But callers can reach any of us because we set it up that way on the website. We have the main number and individual numbers listed with our ranks, regions, ages, religion, race, and gender."

"So, if someone might feel more comfortable talking to someone who looks like them, or of the same gender, or shares a religion, they can," he deduced.

"Exactly. If a black person in Connecticut wants to talk to someone, they shouldn't be restricted to just me. Maybe what they are going through is something Joe can understand or Sammie as the only female with us."

"That's thoughtful," Jamel said.

"It was all Vinnie's idea, his plan. We just brought it to life for him."

"A black person can talk to a black person; A woman can talk to a woman; What about a gay person?"

Thankfully, the waiter came with our food. I said, "We haven't gotten that far yet." We started digging in and Jamel was right. The pasta melted in my mouth,

❤❤❤ CHAPTER 3 ❤❤❤

and I had never tasted Alfredo that rich before. We kept talking.

"So just the five of you cover the whole U.S. of A.?" he asked.

"Well, the others have volunteers, but I don't have anyone volunteering for me."

"Why?"

I shrugged again. "Don't know. I haven't found the right one yet, I guess. They have to fill out an application and do a 20-page questionnaire, then the group discusses and decides together. We've declined two in my region already. The first one was just weird, and the second had severe PTSD. I liked him, but we didn't want him triggered by other people's stories. Sammie has four volunteers because she's in the South, where the majority of our calls are from, and she needed more men on her team. Joe has one under him, and Benjin and Taylor each have two. We just launched the line a little over a year ago, so maybe more people will want to volunteer. For now, I don't have anyone under me."

"I'll sign up and be under you. It's a great thing you're doing, and I would like to be a part of it," he said, seriously.

I smiled at him. "You want to be under me?" He knew I was not talking about VVB anymore. He smiled back, and we stared at each other for a few moments.

He cleared his throat. "How do I volunteer?"

"You go to the website and fill out the form." I spelled out the URL. "I won't be part of the vetting process because we know each other. The other four will decide, and if they can't, I give my vote if it goes 2-2. My vote would be a yes, by the way."

"I think Vinnie would be very proud of what you are all doing in his honor. He must have been a great guy."

I nodded and ignored the lump forming in my throat. "We all cover Vinnie's home state to honor his dream for everyone in Texas that seeks help. We want to kill the veteran suicide rate that keeps going up. And yes, Vinnie was an amazing person. Beautiful, easy-going, and loving toward others. He was the kinda person that everyone loved. His death was unfair to the world. He had a big heart and made everyone laugh. He made you feel like you were the luckiest person in the world when you were with him, that you could do anything, be anything. He was just full of life. He was loved, and everyone loved him."

Jamel heard what I had not said. "Including you. You loved him."

His gray eyes watched me with concern. I hesitated, then nodded, the lump in my throat getting bigger. He asked softly, "How long were you together?"

I didn't want to think of Vinnie that way. I tried to only think of him as my best friend, as a best friend to all of us. Because he was. But with me, he was so much more. But once again, I found myself opening up to a man I barely knew.

"Nineteen months. Until the day he died." I absentmindedly touched the inside of my right wrist.

"Did you have plans to stay together after you came home?"

♥♥♥ CHAPTER 3 ♥♥♥

I shook my head. "No. He was married and had a son before going on his second tour right before he died. But Vinnie was from a very conservative family like me, and he could never be who he was. Instead, he married his high school sweetheart and started a family."

"So he was your last relationship."

I nodded.

"And he was your only relationship."

I nodded again at his statements because they weren't questions.

"And then he died."

I nodded a third time. "Hidden IED took him out. He died in my arms."

Jamel paused and said very sincerely, "I'm sorry, Connor."

I can't feel this right now. I shrugged again. "It's okay. We were all close to him. The six of us did everything together. When he died, we all knew that we were going to make this happen for him." I took another swallow of wine and looked away.

"I'm sorry you lost your first love that way."

Unsure how to feel, I turned to stare at Jamel. Feelings I kept bottled up for years now threatened to spill over, and I wasn't sure how to handle it. I tried to keep my voice even.

"Thank you. I'm okay now. I keep in contact with Bethany, his widow, a few times a year. I send money for Leo, their son. Less now than what I used to do. But she knows she can call me for anything, and I will be there for her, day or night, for the rest of her life. It was hard for her for a long time, but she's better now.

She just got a boyfriend, a nice boring accountant. It's her first relationship since Vinnie died. I'm happy for her that she is moving on, so I call her less now."

"Did she know?" he asked.

"Not at first, no. Not for many months, but then she figured it out. We would be on the phone for hours swapping stories about Vinnie, and one day she asked if I loved him the way she loved him. She wasn't mad. She was glad that we both loved him and that he died in the arms of someone who truly loved him. He deserved that. He deserved all the love this world could have given him."

Jamel watched me in silence. I wanted to turn away but didn't. He took a sip of his wine, leaned back, and said, "I would like to date you."

"Isn't that what we're doing?" I raised my eyebrow in amusement.

He smiled. "Yes. And I would like to keep dating you. Take you out on more dates and get to know you better. Can I date you, Connor?"

"Yes," I said without thinking. Then I thought about it and it was a no-brainer. I wanted to keep seeing Jamel, regardless of whether we fucked that night.

"I've been invited to a boat ride on Saturday night. My friend Dante is turning 30, and he invited a small group of us to celebrate with him on The Spirit of Providence. My ticket allows me to bring a plus one. Will you be my plus one on Saturday night?"

"I would be honored," I replied. I took another bite of my food. "You were right. This is really good pasta."

"They make it fresh every morning."

Chapter 3

We started talking about food, which led to him telling me about him and his Army family living in different European countries, Italy being his favorite. He spoke of cuisines he had eaten and the cultures he'd experienced. He told me about working for his dad's company, Jones Maintenance and Construction, LLC. His father, an Army Major, hires ex-convicts that are serious about a fresh start and gives them good and honest work so they can get on their feet. He runs his business and employees like he ran his unit and soldiers in the Army. But Jamel wanted to have something of his own, so he learned a trade and became an electrician. He got his contracting license and built his own business. I told him I had been working for Comcast since I got home from the service. It was nowhere near as impressive as what he was doing, but he seemed genuinely interested in my job and me.

We sat there for over two hours. When the check came, Jamel didn't let the waiter put it on the table. He took the check, and without looking at the total, he handed his card and the check back to the waiter.

"C'mon. Let me pay at least half."

He shook his head. "I asked you out. When you take me out, you pay. Since we're dating now."

I smiled at him. The waiter returned and brought the receipt, and Jamel left a $20 tip so I knew it was an expensive meal.

"Are you ready?" Jamel asked. I nodded yes. We walked out to the parking lot, and Jamel pointed to a cherry red Ford F150. "I'm right here."

I pointed to my light gray Infiniti Q50. "I'm right behind you." He turned, and I took the opportunity to walk right up on him. By the time he turned around, I was an inch away from his face.

I whispered, "You're not going to take me home?"

He closed the gap by a centimeter. I could feel his breath on my lips as I heard him say, "No."

"You really don't have casual sex?" I asked curiously, my lips brushing against his.

"I said I don't *like* to have casual sex. I didn't say I don't ever do it," he breathed on my lips.

"But not with me right now?"

He moved back slightly and gently ran his fingers through my hair and traced the side of my neck, across my shoulder, and down the arm of my fall leather jacket. When he reached my wrist, he held it. I was hard and tingling all over. He leaned into my neck, his light face stubble grazing my cheek, and whispered in my ear, "I said I want to date you, not just fuck you."

I leaned in and whispered back, "Don't people who date fuck too?"

"Yes," he said. "But not right away. Not yet."

He brushed his moist lips against the length of my neck before standing straight and letting go of my wrist. "Thank you for coming to dinner with me. I had a good time with you. I'll see you Saturday. The boat leaves at 10 pm, so don't miss it. Oh, and dress up. Dante likes flare. Good night, Connor."

I had a hard-on watching him drive off in his monster truck. I said I would date him, I didn't say I wouldn't fuck anyone else. I texted Lex on my way to my car.

❤❤❤ CHAPTER 3 ❤❤❤

It was unseasonably warm for October. Jamel was waiting for me at the docks at 9:40 pm. He had said to dress flashy, but that's not me. I wore simple khaki pants, a light blue button-down shirt, and a dark blue blazer to match my blue and cream Dockers. Jamel had on dark gray slacks, a black choker, and a metallic mauve shirt with the top two buttons open, revealing his chest hair. He walked up to me, kissed my cheek, and held his hand out to me.

"You're ready?" he asked.

I hesitated because I'm not a hand-holder. But Jamel's confidence made me reconsider my position.

"Yes." I took Jamel's hand and let him lead me onto the boat to his friends' table.

There were twelve people at the dinner. Though I was far from the only white guy on the boat, I was the only white guy at the table. He introduced me to seven of the twelve guests, including Dante. The rest were plus ones he didn't know.

Dante was a handsome, light-skinned guy, certainly liked flare. He wore a full three-piece, dark purple, pin-stripe suit, a fedora, cane, and gold-linked pocket watch. Dante looked like he stepped out of the 1920s. He also had on full makeup—two shades of purple eyeshadow, blushed cheeks, long eyelashes, and drawn-in eyebrows. He looked fabulous.

"Connor, yes, I've heard about you. You've made an impression on my boy here." Dante drooled every word and was already drunk. He leaned in and hugged me and I halfheartedly hugged him back, pulling away first. Jamel looked at me and shrugged as if to say, Just roll with it.

Dante's dates were Blaine, a male, and Jocasta, a female. Apparently, he liked them both and couldn't choose. I was pretty sure he would be fucking them both that night. Other than Dante, Jamel's close friends were Shawn, a transgender female, and Chantel, Shawn's long-time girlfriend, dating back to before Shawn's transition. They were raising Chantel's daughter together. It made me think of my friend Jack and Ethan. Ethan had a son from his previous marriage, and he and Jack were raising EJ together. Being the only white guy at the table, I was uncomfortable at first. I relaxed once I realized the Who-is-this-white-boy-and-why-is-he-here-in-our-space comments were not on the way.

Dante asked, "When the music starts, you are going to dance with me. Aren't you, Connor?"

I laughed. "I'm not much of a dancer, but I can two-step with the best of them."

"Okay good, because that's the least you can do since you didn't bring me a present!"

My eyes went wide. "I'm sorry. I didn't know..." I trailed off and looked at Jamel, who was amused.

"Don't pay him any mind. No one brought him a present," he said.

Dante responded, "Yes, you did. You brought me Connor." He winked at me, and I went a little red. I can be as flirty and forward as anyone, but men being openly and aggressively flirty with me makes me shy. It also makes my dick swell. The truth is, if Jamel weren't in the picture, I would have fucked Dante. It's who I am.

❤❤❤ CHAPTER 3 ❤❤❤

Jamel, who had draped his arm over the back of my chair, said smoothly, "Can't have him. He's all mine tonight." Then he winked at me. I liked his speed better.

I asked Jamel how he knew Dante. He explained, "He's been one of my best friends for a long time. We grew up together, and he came out when he was 11. Even after moving out of the country with my family, Dante and I stayed in contact. He's always been openly gay, flamboyant, and unapologetic about who he is. I wish I had had his strength when I was a teen."

I thought about Jack again. Jack's strength and courage were what I wished I had had as a kid, but I didn't share that with Jamel. Instead, I smiled. "It's eerie how much we have in common."

"What else do we have in common?" he asked. I smiled and drank. *I didn't come here to talk.*

Dinner was buffet-style, and the wide range of drinks was never-ending. I debated getting drunk, so Jamel would have to take me home. But I decided against it. I wanted to be fully lucid the first time, which I hoped was tonight. It was only day three, and the dating shit was getting old.

The music was a combination of pop, dance, and techno from the '80s to the new millennium. The dance floor was packed. I had never done a Spirit cruise around the harbor. I was having fun, and Dante caught up with me on the dance floor. He grabbed, flipped, dipped, and twerked all over me while Jamel watched and laughed.

I finally escaped when the music changed to slow jams from the '80s. I sat next to Jamel, who leaned in and said, "You have a couple of moves there, Con."

"I haven't seen your moves yet, Mel. You plan on leaving me out there?"

The music changed, and Phil Collins's song "In The Air Tonight" started playing. He stood up, reached for my hand, and led me back to the dance floor. With one hand, he played with the back of my air and placed his other arm around my waist. I wrapped both my arms around his waist and interlocked my fingers. We were close, but not as close as I wanted. The chorus was eerily fitting, almost like a prediction for what was to come: *I feel it coming in the air tonight... been waiting for this moment all my life.*

We stared into each other's eyes for a while. Jamel spoke first. "Your eyes are the color of blue topaz. My birthstone."

"So, you're a Scorpio," I deduced.

"I could be a Sagittarius."

"No, you're a Scorpio. Early November. Scorpios are sexy, intentionally and unintentionally. When's your birthday?"

He smiled. "November 17th When is yours?"

Wow. Fucking ... wow. I smiled back. "July 17th."

His mouth dropped. "Holy shit, Connor. A Cancer? And the same date? You're like my perfect match."

"Good. You're going to take me home tonight?"

He smiled again. "No."

"Why not?"

"I told you why."

"Because you want to get to know me."

"Yes."

"But not fuck me."

"Not yet."

♥♥♥ Chapter 3 ♥♥♥

"Why don't you want to fuck me? Isn't that part of getting to know me? The best part." I smiled widely.

He laughed. "One. I want to get to know you before I fuck you. I never said I wouldn't fuck you. Two. The best part of you is here." He removed his hand from my neck and touched the center of my chest. "I've known you all of three days, and I unquestionably know that about you."

He kept it there as he looked into my eyes. I realized we weren't dancing anymore as the drums in this classic song came in, and I once again felt like I could drown in all that silver he was giving me. He was also making me feel all mushy inside with his words. But this feeling was fleeting, I knew this.

"I'm not going to fall in love with you, Jamel," I told him honestly.

"I don't want you to fall in love with me," he replied. "I just want you to know that you deserve to be treated with love and respect."

Jamel's hands moved up to my neck. He caressed my cheeks with his thumbs and moved his face close to mine.

"Don't settle for experiences. Be unforgettable to someone. Because you, Connor McIntyre, are unforgettable. Like the color of your eyes, a true blue topaz gem is beautiful, strong and rare. You are all of those things. I know it. I want you to know it too." He moved my head down and kissed my forehead. Then he left me on the dance floor as the music changed again.

I kinda avoided him after that. I hung out and danced with his friends, and drank more than I should have. After about an hour I went on the top deck to catch some air. It was a cooler night than I thought it was and I needed it to clear my head. I liked that the top deck was pretty much empty, save for a few couples. I wished I had brought my pack of smokes on board. I could have used a drag.

I felt all the feels I hadn't felt in a long time, and I wasn't sure I liked having feelings for someone I barely knew. I didn't know why Jamel's words got to me so much. *I don't settle for experiences. I want these experiences. I don't fuck around to feel good about myself. I fuck around because I enjoy it. No strings attached. No emotional commitments. It makes things simpler, easier. And it's not like I can actually take someone home. When I want love and respect, I find my Lovie. When I want dick, I get dick. He doesn't get it. He's just one more person that doesn't get me.* I pulled out my phone and called someone who did.

It was after midnight, but of course, she answered.

"Connor, you okay?" Afia's soft voice came through after the first ring. It was as if she'd been expecting my call. I could hear her shuffling, and I knew she was heading somewhere with more privacy. She was probably in Ty's bed, but she left it to talk to me.

"Yeah, Lovie, just wanted to make sure you're okay."

She heard right through my bullshit. "Yeah, okay. How's the date with Jamel going?"

"It's fine. We're having a good time." I held onto the railing and looked out into the night sky.

"But?"

"But. I don't know about this. It feels too..."

Chapter 3

"Attached? I know you don't like feeling attached to someone. You like him, don't you?"

"I wouldn't know because he won't fuck me."

She laughed. "Connor, you don't need to fuck him to know if you like him!"

"Maybe you don't, but I do."

"I think you like this one. And I think it's a little scary for you to actually like someone for a change."

"I think the only person I like is you."

"Well, you're going to have to share me because I really like someone else, and he really likes me."

"Ugh, you're breaking my heart," I groaned.

"We knew this day was coming."

"What day is that?" I asked, but I already knew what she was going to say.

"The day that one of us would find someone and be in a real relationship. It was supposed to be you first."

"Nah. It was always going to be you first. You deserve to be loved fully."

"You deserved to be loved fully too."

"I am loved. By you."

"Shut up. You know what I mean."

"I know. But you know that's not going to happen. I need to—" I felt his arm around my back, and I turned around. Jamel gently took the phone from me.

"Afia," he said first.

I heard her talking, and I said, "It could have been another lover. Someone who wants to fuck me tonight. You're lucky I called her."

I don't know what made me say it. I kinda regretted it but not really. The look Jamel gave me was a mix of anger and lust. I could already tell he works very hard not to show his emotions. *Maybe I can push his buttons.*

Without taking his eyes off me, Jamel said to Lovie, "Afia, bye. Your boyfriend is mine tonight." Jamel hung up on her while she was still talking and put my phone in his pocket.

I turned back to the railing and said, "She's going to cuss you out for that."

"I can handle it."

I felt him move to stand behind me, but I didn't turn around. He felt around my back and put his hands next to mine on the railing. He was close but not close enough for me to tell if he was hard. I shifted my waist back to check, and he was. I leaned back and rested my shoulder blades against his chest. We were pretty much the same height, so my ears ended up on his cheek. His stubble was scratchy and sexy. I wanted to lick his face.

He moved his hands on top of mine. I looked down and was mesmerized by my pale white fingers mixed in with his long brown ones. We stood that way for a while without talking. A wind blew, and I shivered. He pulled his entire body closer to me, and it felt safe. Something I rarely feel with anyone except Afia. That's what made me turn around and face him.

Slowly and intentionally, we pressed our lips together and closed our eyes. I wrapped my arms around his waist and felt his rock solid body mass, and he wrapped his arms around me. We kissed slowly. He swallowed my thin lips with his full ones, and his tongue got lost in my mouth. We grounded our bodies together, and his groin traced the length of me.

♥♥♥ CHAPTER 3 ♥♥♥

The heat overtook me, and I started moving faster against him. I realized that I was way drunker than I had thought. That was the only explanation for why I was losing control. He let me practically fuck him with our clothes on. His hands moved down to my ass, and he pressed me against him tighter, encouraging me to keep going while he sucked my lips and tongue. I started to moan involuntarily. I knew I was fucked, but I couldn't stop. Before long, I started cumming in my boxer briefs, cum seeping down my leg. I fell against Jamel's broad shoulders, and he hugged me as I caught my breath. I should have pulled away, but I didn't want to. Instead, I did the opposite and rested my head on his shoulder, closed my eyes, and let him hold me. It felt good to be held.

We stayed that way for a little longer as we felt the boat docking. Then I whispered, "Please take me home, Mel."

He said, "Okay."

He took off my jacket and folded it around my waist to hide my cum stain. He kissed my lips sweetly, took my hand, and led me down the stairs outside instead of through the boat to his friends to say goodnight. We were among the first to deboard. Jamel led me to my car and pulled out my keys and wallet from my coat pocket. He looked at my driver's license.

Drunk and confused, I asked, "What are you doing?"

"I'm taking you home, Connor."

What!? "Take me to *your* home, Jamel." *How the fuck was that not clear!?*

"Get in the car," he said fatherly. "You're drunk. You can't drive. Let me take you home."

I was about to protest until he said, "I will call Afia right back and have her tell you instead. Since you listen to her more than you do anyone else in your life."

I went and sat in the passenger side of my car, annoyed as fuck. Annoyed with how he thought he knew me well enough to know I only listen to Lovie. Annoyed that he wouldn't fuck me. Annoyed at how vulnerable he had made me feel. Annoyed that he wouldn't. Just. Fuck. Me. He pulled out of the space and headed west toward Rockville.

I started feeling sleepy, but right before I closed my eyes, I said, "I don't think I want to date you anymore."

This asshole laughed at me but didn't say anything else. It took a little over twenty minutes to get home, and I ended up falling asleep. Jamel shook me awake. I looked up, and I was right in front of my house. All the lights were off, so I wasn't worried someone would see us. Maybe I just didn't give a fuck. He parked on the street, and I jumped out, still annoyed. I started walking to the detached garage's side door, but I stopped because *Where the fuck are my keys?*

Jamel was right behind me. He used my key to open my front door and followed me up the stairs to open up the main door. He looked around at my studio apartment as I plopped on the bed. He had said nothing since we left, and frankly, I didn't understand why he came up if he wasn't going to fuck me. But I was tired and just wanted to go to sleep. I felt him take off all my clothes, including my underwear, thinking, *maybe he is going to fuck me or at least suck my cock.* Then I felt him wipe my middle section and

❤❤❤ CHAPTER 3 ❤❤❤

leg down with a warm washcloth and put a fresh pair of underwear on me.

I mumbled something about him staying to fuck me, and when I felt him slide into bed next to me and wrap his arms around me, I thought he had understood me. But when I leaned my back into his chest and felt his hard cock on my bottom, he made no moves. And I was too tired to seduce him. *Maybe in the morning,* I thought as I fell asleep with him holding me, forgetting that I had never had a man sleep in my apartment before.

But in the morning, I woke up in bed alone with my keys, wallet, and phone on my nightstand.

CHAPTER 4

WE'RE JUST ... DATING?

Sammie called me. "Hey, you got one."

"Got one what?"

"A VVB volunteer request. Sergeant Jamel J. Jones."

I resisted the urge to roll my eyes, not that she could see it anyway. "Yeah, I know who that is. You're gonna have to vet him without me."

It had been over a week since I had seen him last. He called the first two days, and I just didn't answer because I didn't have anything to say. I was angry with him for treating me with respect and not taking advantage of my drunkenness, instead of treating me like the cum slut I wanted to be with him. I ended up fucking Lex three times the previous week. But I felt like shit because I thought about Jamel every single time and pretended I was fucking him instead. *This dude is under my skin.*

She must have heard it all in my voice. "Why, did you fuck him?" she asked knowingly.

"No," I said bitterly.

♥♥♥ CHAPTER 4 ♥♥♥

"Oh, but you want to?"

"Shut the fuck up, Sammie."

She laughed heartily, then said, "Okay, well he sounds like a pretty solid dude just from his questionnaire. Benj is going to interview him this week. I'll let you know at the next meeting what we decide."

"Okay, cool. How's your week going?"

We formally check in with each other once a month to talk about the program, stats, and complicated issues. We also informally check in a few times a month to ensure we take care of ourselves and avoid secondhand trauma. Sammie was our point person for that. And once a year, we plan a trip to see each other and make sure we were really doing okay. But we find reasons to call or see each other during the week. In the three years since we left the Marines, I've seen all of them in person at least three times.

"I'm okay. I got a lot going on but… I'm okay. I met a new guy, and it's early, so it might not go anywhere. But he's potential. He's bisexual and a nice, boring teacher."

"Good. You need nice and boring. You deserve it after that last train wreck."

"And you? Still fucking and sucking your way through New England?"

"Pretty much and still happy doing it," I said as Jamel flashed in my head.

"Settle down, Connor. Find a good man and adopt some babies. You'll be happy doing that too."

"Now, you sound like Afia."

"Good. That means I'm saying all the right things."

"Bye, Sammie." This time I did roll my eyes. "See you on the first of the month."

"Bye, Corporal."

I hung up and thought about Jamel again. *Fuck it.* I waited until my lunch break and called him. He answered right away. "Connor."

Something about the way he said my name made my heart pound. "Hey, Jamel."

He said, "I'm glad you called me. I've been thinking about you every day."

"Me too. But probably for different reasons." He chuckled, and I remembered his lips on mine. Suddenly, I wanted to see him, be near him, taste him, touch him, badly. "You're working today?"

"Yeah, I'm in Pawtucket, inspecting a house over here. I should be back in a few hours. Why? Do you want to meet up tonight?"

"Yes."

"Okay. Come over to my house. I'm making dinner for my family. Bring Afia. She knows where we live."

That made me feel relieved in a way and he knew it. "Okay. I'll call her right now."

"Okay, great. Hey, Connor? I'm really glad you called me. I've been thinking about you. Every day."

I smiled. "You said that already."

"Yeah? I must really mean it then."

Afia picked me up in her blue Subaru hours later, and we headed back over to North Providence, the Allendale section, to the Jones family residence. Apparently, Jamel lived in the downstairs apartment, and Ty, his brothers, and parents live upstairs. Afia

❤❤❤ CHAPTER 4 ❤❤❤

talked nonstop about how happy she was that I wasn't giving up on Jamel being the one for me.

"I can just feel it, you know? Like me and Ty. Like, how crazy would it be if we end up being related through marriage?"

I looked at her skeptically. "Calm down Lovie, it's been two dates, and the last one ended badly."

"I think the last one ended beautifully. You're just too much of a dumb ass right now to see that. Hmph!" She made me smile.

Afia pulled up to a three-story, 2000 square feet home that looked like a remodeled 1950s home. It probably was seeing how they are a family of contractors. We went up to the door and there were two bells. She rang the top one, and Ty answered the door.

"Hey Fifi," he called her as he kissed her on the lips.

I tried to glare at her because he was calling her by the pet name only her father calls her, but as expected, she ignored me and leaned in to kiss her man again. Ty smiled at her lovingly, then reached his hand out to shake mine. I shook his hand, but I held it a bit tight. He smiled at that too, then took Afia's hand and led her inside the vestibule with stairs on the left and a door to the right. He started going up the stairs when the door opened. Jamel was standing there looking like he smelled of fresh flowers after a rainstorm.

"Connor."

He said my name and watched me with those gray eyes of his like I was the only one standing there. He held his hands open, and I found himself walking toward him. He reached through my open jacket and pulled me against his body, and I wrapped my arms around him thinking, *When did I become this person who wants to be held?* He did, indeed, smell like he just came from the shower. I leaned into his neck with my eyes closed and sighed. I'm usually the taller one so it was nice not to be for a change.

Then I remembered we were not alone. I stepped back, and Jamel let me go. I looked around and saw Tyrell with both his eyebrows raised at his brother. Afia had a shit-eating grin that made me want to slap and hug her at the same time.

Jamel said to Tyrell, "Tell Ma to check the chicken. I'll be up in a minute." And just like that he took my hand and pulled me into his home.

It looked like a standard one-bedroom apartment. The living room and kitchen area were connected and a small table for four separated the spaces. The bathroom was next to the laundry closet and there was a closed door to my right, which must have been his bedroom. We stood in the living room and talked.

"How you been?" he started. He was standing so close to me.

"I'm good. Working. Keeping busy." I wondered if he'd hold me again.

"Yeah, same." We were watching each other, silently. Longingly.

"I see you applied for Vinnie's Vet Buddies as a volunteer," I stated.

"Yeah, I did."

"I hope you didn't do that just for me. We take it seriously."

Chapter 4

"Not at all. I told you I was going to volunteer before anything happened between us. I'm taking it seriously too."

"Is something happening between us?" I asked him. Just being around him made my dick swell and my heart pound.

"I don't know, Connor. Is there?"

I sighed and looked around the room. "I want to be with you," Jamel said plainly. I turned back to look at him as he spoke. "I want to be with you and see if this could be something real for the both of us."

I was kinda speechless at his frankness. "How do you know that after you just met me two weeks ago and two dates later?"

"Because I do. And I know I want more."

"But you don't want to fuck me?"

He let a moment pass. "Are you still sleeping with someone else?" he asked.

"C'mon, man," I said dismissively, rolling my eyes.

"Are you? Fucking other people?"

I looked at him defiantly. "Yes."

"Then why does it matter whether I'm fucking you or not if you're fucking other people?" he asked.

"So you're going to what, let me keep fucking other people while we figure out if we like each other or not?"

"No."

"Then what then?" The conversation was beginning to frustrate me.

"I want to be with you exclusively. But I want you to want that too."

"And how would I know that if we haven't fucked yet?"

He blinked at me three times. "Are you serious right now? The only way you know if you want to be with someone is if you're fucking them? Because you've been fucking around for a while without a real partner, so I don't see how that logic is working for you. So maybe you should try something different." I opened my mouth to retort, then closed it.

He looked at me intently. "How many other people are you with right now?"

"Just the one." Something about him made me always want to be honest with him.

"Stop fucking him," he said seriously, and I laughed out loud. He moved toward me slowly, and I stopped laughing as he backed me up against the nearest wall.

"Does he make you feel like how I make you feel when he's close to you like this?" he asked quietly. His lips were next to mine, and I could feel his breath on them.

"No." I gasped, my heart pounding loudly.

"Are you his dom or his sub? Top or his bottom? Or switch."

"Both. But I'm the dom—" He quickly spun me around and held my hands above my head against the wall before I could blink.

"What the fuck, Jamel!?" I yelled.

I knew he was stronger than me, but he showed me his strength by overpowering me. I tried to push back, but he leaned into me so I could feel how hard he was. He started grinding his very big, very hard cock against my ass in a circular motion. My equally hard cock was pressed against the wall, and I couldn't move.

♥♥♥ CHAPTER 4 ♥♥♥

He was using his strength on me, but his voice was even and calm as he spoke in my ear. "Is this what you want from me? Is this all you want from me? Holding you against the wall like this, slamming my dick into your ass, making you cum over and over again? Is this all you want from me, Connor? Because if that's all you want, you can have it right now, and I'll never bother you again. So what do you want? You want my dick, or do you want me?"

As much as I hated him overpowering me, I loved him overpowering me. But I knew if he didn't stop, I would cum in my pants again, and that could not happen. I used all of my strength to push him back with my body, and he let go of my hands.

"The fuck, Jamel!" I yelled at him again and pushed his chest with both hands.

He fell back a step but stood his ground. I opened his door and started walking out of his apartment when I heard him say quietly, "Is that all you want from me, Connor?"

I ended up in the vestibule leaning against the wall feeling horny as fuck and confused about having feelings for him. I closed my eyes and started thinking.

No one has ever made me feel the way he makes me, so I'm not sure why I'm fighting this so hard. It should be an easy decision. Except I do know. I'm scared. I'm scared of the intensity of these feelings and how vulnerable I am with him. I'm scared that it's not going to work out. I'm scared that it is going to work out. At the same time, I'm so tired of being scared of my feelings, tired of hiding how I feel from everyone around me. And I'm about to walk away from something that could be real because I can't get over myself. Afia is right; I am a dumb ass. I turned around and headed back into his apartment.

Jamel was standing there with his back turned from the door and hands on his head like he didn't know what he was doing either. The door creaked open, and he turned around and looked at me in surprise.

"No," I answered him. "It's not all I want from you."

The look on his face was like Christmas morning. He crossed the room quickly and pushed me back against the same wall. He grabbed my face and kissed me with urgency, and I rubbed my hands up his back, returning his urgent kisses. His lips forcefully sucked mine. It hurt, and I liked it.

He paused his kiss, looked at me with his gray eyes, and said, "Stop fucking him."

"Okay," I said. "But I don't know how to do any of this without…something to hold me over."

He kissed me again, softer this time, and reached down to my swollen cock. I sighed as he used one hand to drop my jeans and free my cock from my boxer briefs. He started stroking me and kissing me again and all I could do was hold on to his arms. He kissed me and sucked my neck hard and I knew he was leaving a bruise, marking his territory. He kissed me and stroked me and then reached his other hand between my legs and played with my testes. He kissed me and I loved the feel of his lips on my tongue and neck. He kissed me and I love his kisses.

He repeated, "Stop fucking him."

I could barely talk, so I nodded with my eyes closed and let him work me. He used my pre-cum as lube and

♥♥♥ Chapter 4 ♥♥♥

stroked me faster. He kissed my neck, and then went for my earlobe and sucked the bottom of it.

"Fuck! I'm going to cum," I told him.

"No, you're not. Not yet." He slowed down his stroking, and I died inside.

"Noooooooo, whyyyyyy?" I whined.

"You're not ready yet," he whispered in my ear. "Say it. You're not ready yet."

"I'm not ready yet. But I aaaaam."

"Shhhhh.....I'll let you know when you're ready." He was stroking me slow and kissing me deep. My penis was pulsing and aching in his hand. The skin was stretched so tight; I was like a steady faucet that wouldn't stop dripping.

"Am I ready now?" I asked when he finally let go of my lips. My eyes were wild. I looked like a drug addict, and he was my pusher but I didn't give a fuck. I had never let someone have full control over me before, and he was giving me all the reasons to submit. *I am all his right now.*

"Almost," he said. He went for my earlobe again, then stuck his tongue in my ear. I shuddered and moaned loudly, almost toppling over.

"Oooh, you like that," he teased me.

"Am I ready now?" I asked again, ignoring his comment. The torture needed to stop.

"One second." He went for the bottom of my earlobe again. It felt so good, it took me a second to realize he had let a finger escape from cupping my balls and had slipped a digit inside my hole.

"Ooooooooh fuuuuuuuuck meeeeeee," I moaned. *He just did one of my moves, dammit!*

"Lift your shirt up," he ordered as he pulled his finger out and released my nuts. I don't know how I did it, but I pulled my shirt up, holding the bottom part between my chin and neck. He began stroking me faster. He stepped back a bit and leaned down. He licked my right nipple with his long tongue, then he licked my left, making me shiver again. I moaned and heard him say, "Now you're ready." Then he bit the fuck out of my left nipple.

I let out a loud moan, and I kept moaning as I came all over my abs, his shirt, and his hands. I fell onto him. He let go of my cock and held me up.

"I got you, Con. I got you," he said sweetly.

He held me with one hand and licked my cum clean off his other hand, so he could hold me with both hands. He wrapped both hands around me and said, "End it. Stop fucking him."

I nodded profusely. "Done." And I meant it.

Jamel kissed the tip of my nose and leaned me against the wall, then took off his shirt and cleaned me up with it. He had this tuft of curly black hair right between his pecs that I couldn't wait to run my fingers through and a tattoo I couldn't fully make out because he was so close to me.

"I'm going to go change," he said. "Don't go upstairs without me." *Pfff, as if I had legs right now to move even if I wanted to.* He kissed my lips softly before he walked away.

He went into his room and closed the door. I stuffed myself back in my pants and leaned against the wall, trying to gain some semblance of myself. I heard Jamel huffing, and I knew exactly what he was doing

Chapter 4

because it was what I would be doing. I walked over to the bedroom door, and I could hear him more clearly.

I slowly opened the door. He was standing there, his cock poking out the hole of his dark blue boxer briefs. One foot was on the edge of the bed, and the other was on the floor, and he was beating his manhood ferociously. He looked at me as I came in, but he did not stop or slow down. My eyes went to his monster dick. I'm a good eight and a half to nine inches fully hard. He was definitely ten. And thick. All I wanted to do was get on my knees and put his dick in my mouth.

I started walking toward him, and he held his free hand up to stop me. "No," he said sternly.

I stopped and watched. His legs were like a Greek god statue, toned and muscular all the way up to his ass. His skin was the perfect shade of dark brown. He had a couple of tattoos, including a huge tattoo of a lion's arm that stretched down from the top of his shoulder to where the lion's paw laid over his right pec, like he was carrying a lion on his back. It was the sexiest thing I had ever seen. My eyes traveled back down. His penis was just a few shades darker than the rest of his body, but the head had more pink in it, starting from the circumcision line up to the head. I got hard watching his long fingers move fast over his cock, like I hadn't just cum like an open geyser less than five minutes earlier.

"Look at me," he said.

I realized I had been staring at his penis for a while. I looked into his eyes and held his gaze. I watched him scrunch his face and breathe through his mouth erratically. I only broke eye contact when he looked down.

I followed his gaze. He kept stroking and erupted silently all over his bed. Ropes of cum shot a whole foot out of him over and over again. He slowed down, squeezed the last bit out, then absentmindedly tasted his fingers. I smiled at him. *He's like my sexual soulmate.*

He didn't say a word as he grabbed his old shirt to clean himself off. He took another black t-shirt from the drawer and a pair of black track pants. After getting dressed, he walked over to me, took my hand silently, and led me upstairs for dinner.

♥

~~~November 2009~~~

It was November 1st at 11:02pm, and I was the last to log on to the video call that Friday. We schedule calls late East coast time so Taylor could join us after his kids go to bed on the West. He had the youngest kids of the group, a two-year-old and a five-year-old. Joe had the oldest kids, eleven and fifteen.

"Hey, Connor." They all greeted me in intervals.

"Hey, y'all. Sammie, you cut your hair again?"

"Yeah, I did." She ran her hands through her very short cut, like she was still in the military. I might have been the only one in the group that knew she was transitioning, but she had yet to confirm it with me. I only knew because we talked about it a few months after leaving the Marines. Three years later, she had more arm definition, a deeper voice, and shorter hair.

♥♥♥ CHAPTER 4 ♥♥♥

She still liked and dated men, she just wanted to do it as a man, her true self, she told me.

"You look good," I told her.

She appreciated the compliment from someone who was into men and it made her smile. "Thanks. Oh, Connor! We met a few days ago and we approved Jamel Jones as your volunteer. We think he'll do well."

I know I'm gonna get roasted for this. "Sooooo, full disclosure. Jamel and I are kinda ... dating now." I cringed, then smiled.

Benjin rolled his eyes. "Oh c'mon, Connor!"

Sammie yelled, "I knew you fucked him!"

"Dude. Did you really fuck him?" Taylor asked.

"We really need to have a rule around this now," Benj said. "It's getting out of hand."

"Oh, shut the fuck up, Benj. You're just mad that your volunteer didn't want to fuck you," Sammie said, and Taylor and I cackled.

Joe, the ever-present one that keeps us on track, said, "Can we get back to the Vets, please?"

"I haven't fucked him yet, seriously! We're just ... dating?" They all laughed at my question. I continued, chuckling at their reaction, "It's been two weeks."

Taylor kept laughing. "Two weeks, and you haven't fucked him yet!? This is a world record."

"We all know that's not going to last too much longer," said Sammie.

"This is a disaster waiting to happen." Taylor couldn't stop laughing. "Who else are you fucking in the meantime, Connor?"

"No one, man. I'm dry as a desert right now."

"Holy shit!" Taylor laughed out loud.

"Dude, I'm just saying, why didn't you tell us that when we got his app?" Benj asked, shaking his head.

"Because we weren't dating then, not exclusively."

"You really haven't fucked him yet? Because I've seen his picture, and I would fuck him. And I'm as straight as a board," said Taylor.

"Guys, the Vet stats." Joe tried again.

"It's not from lack of trying," I confessed. "Trust me."

Sammy laughed. "Oh, we're sure of that. We know your track record. You must be losing it."

I feigned offense. "Hey, I'm not that bad. You make it sound like I fuck everything that moves."

"Not everything. Only the ones with a big dick," Taylor said. Sammie snorted, and Benj shook his head again.

"Okay, I am kinda stressing out about it," I admitted.

"Okay, so no fucking, but what about the other stuff?" Taylor asked. "Blowing? Mutual jerking? Frotting? A little nipple play? Finger in the butt? Anything?"

I sighed. "No blowing but a little of everything else."

"Holy shit, not even blowing?" Benj asked incredulously. "You must be dying inside." He joined in on the laughter.

"I hate talking to all of you," I said amusingly.

Sammie said to the others, "It's because he really likes this one. I can tell. Connor'll hold out until he gives up the ass or takes his."

"Guuuuuuyssss?" Joe tried one more time.

"Alright, well, just make sure you and your boyfriend's lack of cumming doesn't mess up what we got going on here," said Taylor.

"It won't. He's very mature."

❤❤❤ CHAPTER 4 ❤❤❤

Benj agreed. "Yeah he is, I could tell from the interview I did with him."

It took me a second to process what Taylor had said. "Wait, does this mean he's my boyfriend, for real?"

Sammie laughed at me. "Yes, stupid. Dating someone exclusively usually means you're together to get closer. It's typical of relationships, but you wouldn't know that, having never been in one."

"Wait, you have never been in a relationship?" Taylor asked seriously.

Benj interjected before I could respond, "Fuck no. My Abbie in kindergarten has had more actual boyfriends than this fucker."

Joe said louder, "Can we talk about the Vets, please?"

Usually, I would have followed Joe's lead, but I wanted to clarify something. "I've been in relationships. It hasn't been that bad." *Knowing that it really kinda has.*

"Dude, it's that bad," Sammie said. "It's awful the way you throw your schlong around."

Taylor said, "I can't believe you haven't been in an adult relationship before!" He laughed again.

"I've been in an adult relationship," I said quietly.

Sammie laughed, "Nope, he hasn't."

Benj laughed and said, "No, not since Vin…." The laughter died out and everyone averted their eyes.

I blew out some air to shake off the awkwardness and said in a clear, firm voice, "Nope. Not since Vinnie."

They all looked at me. It wasn't a secret between the six of us. When we were stationed together, everyone in the group had caught Vinnie and me together. Several times. We didn't talk about it then for obvious military reasons. And we don't talk about it now, mostly to protect my feelings, I know. But I wanted them to know that I was okay, because I was.

Sammie spoke first. "Well. Just make sure Jamel knows he has some big ass shoes to fill."

I nodded. "He knows, Sammie. He knows." I rubbed the tattoo on my right wrist with my left thumb.

Joe interrupted the silence. "Can we talk about the Vets now?"

♥

Jamel had texted me during our meeting and I called him back at almost one in the morning. He immediately answered like he had been expecting me.

"I have a proposition for you," he said.

"What's up?"

"So this weekend kind of sucks, doesn't it? You worked and had a meeting tonight. And I'm working all day tomorrow."

"Yeah, but we planned to meet up Sunday, right?"

"Yeah, we did. But what do you think about taking the trip with me to Middletown tomorrow and hanging out with me while I'm on the job? I need to inspect, work on, and review permits for five houses. It will be an all-day ordeal. It's beautiful in Middleton, so you don't have to stay with me the whole time. And at least we'll be able to spend some time together."

I had a fleeting memory of being in Middletown, Aquidneck Island, for a weekend with a twink I had met on Facebook last year. He was from New Bedford so we agreed to meet there and made a whole weekend out of it. We did a lot of nasty things to each other, and

♥♥♥ CHAPTER 4 ♥♥♥

then I avoided his calls for the next couple of weeks. I wondered if Jamel and I would do nasty things to each other.

"Are we staying the night?" I asked him.

He paused then said, "I didn't think about it, but yeah, we just might. Pack a bag." I smiled widely. There was no getting out of not fucking me now. I was gonna make sure of that.

"Want me to pick you up?" he asked.

"No. I'll drive to your house, park on your street, then jump in your trunk."

❤ ❤ ❤ CHAPTER 5 ❤ ❤ ❤

JESUS CHRIST, WHO IS THIS PERSON I'M BECOMING?

We left early the next morning. It was a beautiful, sunny November day. Middletown was just an hour southeast of Providence, but it was like a whole other world on the island. We didn't talk much on the ride but weren't big talkers anyway. I wasn't talking because I was all in my head about the last couple of weeks.

I realized that I didn't hate what we were doing. As much as I hated not having actual intercourse—and believe me, I fucking hated that shit—I found myself enjoying Jamel's companionship and his affection for me. We had a lot in common, including similar personalities and humor. Jamel texted me every day just to say hi, or make a joke, or for no reason. It didn't matter because I started looking forward to his texts. I texted him randomly throughout the day too, sharing the funny and annoying parts of my day. And on the

Chapter 5

rare days that we didn't see each other, he would call to say goodnight.

Jamel wined and dined me, and I didn't hate it. We went out at least three times a week. When I chose the dates, we would end up at Dave and Busters, the batting cages, or the shooting range—all my favorite things. He didn't seem to mind. Because Jamel doesn't smoke, not even casually, I began smoking less frequently the more time we spent together. When I did light up, he would hand me a piece of gum afterward and then kiss me. That was his way of telling me he didn't like kissing me when I smoked. And because I was addicted to his kisses, I didn't smoke around him. I didn't bring a pack on this trip, preparing myself to eventually quit.

One day, Jamel asked me about my love language, and I had no idea what he was talking about. The next day, I went online and took the love languages quiz. Turns out my love language is Words of Affirmation. That was surprising because I thought it was going to be Physical Touch considering how much I love to be physical with others. But nope, it wasn't even number two. It was number three, behind Acts of Service. The more I thought about my results, the more I understood them. Because my dad and brother told me I was shit most of my life, I gravitated toward people who affirm my good qualities. People Like Afia, Winter, and Mina. Like Jack and Vinnie.

When I told him he smiled and shared his results, in order: Quality time, Physical Touch, and Acts of Service. It made sense why he wanted to date me before we slept together. It also made sense why he always held my hand. *Which, fuck, I don't hate that either.* I quickly got used to the warm, firm touch of his hands. We didn't touch in public, but we found reasons to touch each other when we were alone. Words of Affection was last on his list. He preferred to show feelings and wanted the same in return.

I loved kissing him. He loved to make me cum by fingering me and biting my nipples simultaneously. It's amazingly erotic, even though he stays fully clothed. We make out a lot, touch each other, and cum together, but we don't have intercourse. It's been three weeks of torture. I'd never gone that long without fucking. And no matter how late it got, he didn't let me spend the night. I tried not to object or complain too much. Our running joke consists of me randomly asking, "Are you going to fuck me now?" and he smiles and says no—but it made me wonder if he was holding out for himself or me. *It is probably both*, I reasoned within myself. Maybe he didn't want to be attached either, and that made me hold back as well. Maybe it was for the best that we weren't having sex.

But now we were on our way to a beautiful island and staying in a hotel together. Sex was finally on the horizon and for the first time in a very long time, I was the nervous one. I was prepared though: I had 12 packs of condoms, three bottles of lube, anal beads, dick rings, and butt plugs in my duffle bag, because why the fuck not? But I was still anxious. My mouth watered thinking of the shape and size of his dick and I was ready to tame that beast. *But what if I don't measure up for him?* Feeling sexually insecure was new for me.

❤❤❤ Chapter 5 ❤❤❤

We drove over to a construction site where townhomes were being built. Jamel looked sexy in his light-colored jean shirt, dark blue work jeans, and brown Timberland work boots. He was wearing a fully equipped tool belt that hung off his hips. He told me to dress down, so I chose an old blue long-sleeved t-shirt and blue jeans.

He explained, "They had hired electricians, but they were shortcutting the work, and the contractors didn't know it until the city inspectors came around and cited them. Naturally, the contractors fired that group, but then they had to get someone to review the work already done before the reinspection. The person that cited them, Joel, is an Army friend of mine and gave them my card, along with a few others. The contractors chose me mostly because I do all the work myself, so they aren't paying multiple guys to come out. But also because I do excellent work and get great reviews on Yelp and Google."

He handed me his circuit tester and put me to work immediately. I helped him check every electric outlet in the first house and if an outlet wasn't grounded, Jamel opened it and fixed it. He also made sure the wire lines weren't too close to the plumbing or other pipes. We spent nearly two hours on the first house. The second one was better, and we were there for forty-five minutes tops.

We took a break halfway through the third house and went toward the beach to grab some food. We split fish tacos and crab cakes and talked. He said, "You can stay here if you want and hang out on the beach. I have more houses to do, and the next one is the one that they got a bunch of citations on. I'm going to be there a while."

"I came to spend time with you, so that's what I'm going to do. And honestly, this stuff is fascinating. I deal with simple installations. This is more intricate, and I'm learning a lot."

He asked, "Is there any career you want to pursue? Because I don't think Comcast is your lifetime gig."

I laughed. "No, it's not, but it pays the bills."

"What bills? You live with your parents!" He laughed.

I chuckled. "I pay rent and utilities to my dad."

"Seriously? For the garage?"

"Don't you pay your dad rent for your basement apartment?"

"No, I put money toward the mortgage. The basement water tank and gas tank are in my name. I pay those bills myself."

"Oh. That makes more sense. But again, your dad is structured, and my dad is an asshole."

"Why do you stay there? Why don't you just get your own place?"

"I honestly didn't seriously start thinking about it until last year. When I got back, I just needed to be around familiar people. Not necessarily my family but my hometown, you know?" He nodded. "I know exactly how you felt."

"I just forgot how toxic they are, especially my brother Matty. But my rule was, if I'm paying for the space then it's my space. A month after I got back I had Afia in there and my asshole brother comes in, makes himself at home, and made Afia so uncomfortable with his remarks about her looks and her

Chapter 5

body, how she is all grown up and got childbearing hips, stupid shit like that. The next day I changed the locks and he's not allowed in my apartment, ever. Last summer, I put a deadbolt with a one-way lock inside. That way, even if someone has the key, no one can come up if I'm up there. So it's all good."

"But you can't have who you want over to spend the night."

"Afia spends the night."

"You're not sleeping with Afia, though. Wait, are you sleeping with Afia?" His eyebrow went up.

I laughed easily. "No." *No one knows about our slip-up, not even the other tribe members, and I will never tell.*

"But you have in the past." It wasn't a question.

I gave him the simple answer, "She was my girlfriend in high school for a bit, so..." I shrugged. *Gotta change this subject.* "She's falling in love with your brother now."

"I know," he said. "And I know he's already in love. He told me. Afia is it for him."

I breathed out air through my nose. Lovie can't be it for him because that would be the end for her and me. Jamel noticed my mood change. "You're not ready to let her go," he stated.

"I'll never let her go." And I meant that.

"Hmmm... We'll see." He smiled at me, and I didn't smile back. He smartly changed the subject. "So you didn't answer me. Is there anything you want to do, career-wise?"

"Honestly, all my energy is put into Vet Buddies. I'm hoping to get enough sponsors and donors so we can get paid for doing the work that makes us happy and keeps us grounded. Comcast pays the bills, but VVB is my passion right now." He nodded in understanding.

The waiter came with our check, and I grabbed it before he could.

"I invited you here," Jamel said.

"And you paid the last time. It's my turn." I gave the waiter my card without looking at the bill. It was my Act of Service to him.

After I paid the check, we went outside into the afternoon sun. We walked back to the site slowly, and I purposely bumped his arm a few times. Maybe I wanted him to hold my hand. As if he could read my mind, he reached over and took my hand and interlaced his fingers with mine. I had never held hands with a man in broad daylight, like a regular, normal couple. It made me nervous at first, but it felt good. Safe. Jamel made me feel safe no matter where we were. I could lean on him, tell him all my secrets, and they would be safe with him. And just like that I wasn't nervous about us anymore.

I turned to face him on the sidewalk of a beachy residential neighborhood, the kind of neighborhood where kids played in the front yard, people walked their dogs, and old people sat on their front porch rocking chairs and drank iced tea or lemonade. Okay, none of that was actually happening, it was pretty deserted for early November, but it could have been crowded and I wouldn't have cared. I faced him and I reached for his other hand and entwined our fingers. I brought both hands up between us, leaned in close, and said, "Thank you."

❤❤❤ CHAPTER 5 ❤❤❤

"For what?" He looked surprised at my public display of affection.

"For treating me with love and respect. For making me feel special and safe. For being everything that I needed when I didn't even know I needed it."

Jamel smiled a little, let go of one of my hands, and caressed the nape of my neck. At the same time, we closed our eyes and pressed our lips together. I reached up with both arms around his neck. I usually didn't do that because I always felt it was a little feminine. But feminine or not, I needed to be in his arms. Once again, he gave me what I needed. He wrapped his arms around me and pulled me real close against him as he tongued me slowly, sensually. I was surprised that my boner was gradual, not raging. And I was sad when he pulled away first.

Jamel put his forehead on mine and said, "You are special. And you will always be safe with me. No matter what happens between us, I'll protect you from here on out. You got me?"

I nodded, and we kissed. He held my hand all the way back to the site.

❤

We checked into the Quality Inn around 7pm. When we got upstairs, I didn't pounce on him, and he didn't immediately reach for me either and throw me on the bed. He put his bag down and said, "I'm going to take a shower. Order dinner? Either room service or take out. Your choice."

He went into the bathroom and closed the door. I had no idea if he wanted me to join him. But Jamel was pretty straightforward. If he wanted me there, he would have said so. Instead, I went back out and picked up dinner from the local seafood spot and two bottles of wine. On the way back, I decided that I wouldn't pursue it. If we were going to fuck, it was going to happen naturally. He gives me what I need, so if it's quality time he needed, that's what I would give him, liberally. And if we didn't have sex that night, I would have been okay with it.

Jesus Christ, who is this person I'm becoming?

When I got back, Jamel was on his tablet, sitting on the king-sized bed, wearing dark gray sweatpants and a white t-shirt. He looked like a chocolate snack. He came over to grab the bags and kissed me on my cheek. His ears were still a little wet from the shower, and I resisted the urge to lick him.

"Thank you. I'm going to take a shower too," I said.

"Okay." He brushed past me with his hand across my back. His touch sent shivers through my spine as I walked to the bathroom.

I stripped my clothes off and got in the shower, turning the water to boiling hot and letting it flow over my body. My unused penis was aching. The all-day sensual touching had me carrying a semi-hard-on all day. My sex drive is naturally really high, but I didn't want a substitute. I didn't even want to jerk off. I just wanted him. That was different for me; He was changing me. I stood under the water for at least ten minutes, switched it to lukewarm, and actually started

♥♥♥ CHAPTER 5 ♥♥♥

to wash myself. I wrapped the bottom half of my body in a towel and stepped out of the bathroom.

When I came out, Jamel glanced up, looked down at his tablet, then slowly glanced up again. I watched him eye-fucking me the same way he did when we first met, with his eyes glossing over my full black panther tattoo. Though I was not as muscular as Jamel, I'm athletic with definition and he noticed.

I started laughing. "See something you like?" I playfully flexed a bicep.

He smiled. "I like everything about you, Connor."

He watched me but made no move to come closer. I sat at the edge of the bed with my back turned to him to put on body lotion and get dressed. I stood up to slip on my blue sweatpants without underwear and grabbed a white t-shirt. My hair was still wet from the shower. I had started to dry my head when I heard him shift behind me. He took the towel from my hands and ran his fingers through the dampness, massaging my scalp. That was his Act of Service to me.

"Thanks for agreeing to come today. I really like spending time with you," he said.

"Thanks for inviting me to come along. There is no other place I'd rather be."

He leaned my head back and gave me a soft upside-down kiss. "Let's eat."

Jamel hopped off the bed and went toward the table which he had set up with food on plates and plastic cups of wine. We sat, ate, finished a bottle of Moscato, opened the bottle of Pinot, and talked about nothing and everything. After a while, I grabbed the TV remote and put on HBO, the only movie channel they had, and we watched one movie end and another begin. I got up, moved to the bed, and stretched out on my back, letting him see my hard on, but I didn't look at him. He got up, turned off the light, moved to lay next to me, and rubbed my cock over my sweatpants.

YES! "Are you going to fuck me now?" I said smiling.

He smiled. "No."

"Fuck Jamel, fuck fuck fuck!!!" I screamed at him, and he started laughing, making me laugh.

Then he said, "Maybe later. I just want to do this for now."

He slipped down my sweatpants to expose my flesh and held the base of my penis. I watched him move between my legs, bend over, and wrap his thick beautiful lips around the head of my cock. I could feel him suck me slowly. My breath was caught in my throat. He moved his lips a little way down, and I felt his tongue circle the underside of my head. A noise—a cross between a moan and a gasp—escaped me. He traveled down slowly until his lips were at the bottom of my shaft. His thin mustache hair tickled my naked skin and it was the most beautiful thing I had ever seen. He slowly pulled back to the head and looked at me with those sexy gray eyes and my dick in his mouth, and I changed my mind because this was the most beautiful thing I'd ever seen.

I called his name breathlessly, "Jamel." I was fucking panting like a dog needing water.

Then he attacked my penis like it was the meal he had been waiting for. He played with my balls and sucked me off, deep-throating, without a hint of a gag, every time he went down. I watched my dick disappear

Chapter 5

in his warm, wet mouth, and all I could do was hold onto his head and moan loudly. I did not last long at all, maybe four minutes before my insides started to seize up. In the middle of my moaning, I somehow told him, "oooooocoooomingooooooh." He heard me because he pushed my dick as far into his throat as he could and held it there. I could feel my cum leave my balls, travel through my slit, and shoot directly down his esophagus with his throat muscles swallowing me repeatedly.

When I finally stopped cumming, he got off of me and slid my now limp penis back in my sweatpants. He crawled over me but didn't lay down. He held himself up by his arms and lowered to kiss me, pressed up, and lowered to kiss me again. He was doing push-ups over me, and I laughed as he did four more.

"At ease, soldier," I told him, and he laughed, falling next to me.

I turned to face him, and he instinctively wrapped his arms around me. Then he put one leg between mine and the other leg over mine, and I got lost in him. I could feel his hardness against me. With my face in his chest, I said, "Let me blow you."

"Maybe later," said Jamel. "I just wanted to do it for you without anything in return."

I didn't say anything as the term Acts of Service came to mind. I just let him hold me until I fell asleep in his arms.

Sometime in the middle of the night, I woke up still in his embrace with the TV watching us. I rolled away from him to turn off the TV and use the bathroom. When I came back, he was awake, watching me and lying on his back. The curtains were open, the light from the streetlamp outside revealed the hunger in his eyes. I took off my shirt and crawled on top of him, laying my slimmer frame between his meaty thighs. We kissed softly as I took off his shirt and ran my hands through his curly black chest hair, licking his nipples and kissing him seriously.

We moved together, rolling around the bed, touching and kissing each other all over. He used his hands to pull my pants down as far as he could, then put his foot between my legs to push my clothes the rest of the way down. I sat up and pulled the pants off my ankles, then pulled his sweats off. He was also not wearing any underwear, which made me happy; he wanted this to happen as much as I did. I came back up between his legs and saw him holding himself. I gently took his enormous cock from him, and it was as massive as it had ever been. I relaxed my throat and completely swallowed him in one motion. His baritone moan immediately sent shivers down my spine to my dick. *This is going to be everything.*

I took my time and gave him the best blow job I'd ever given, complete with deep-throating, humming, licking, throat swallowing, gagging, saliva spitting, tongue flicking, and head twisting. He moaned loudly, grabbed my hair roughly but let me have full control over him. I rolled his balls between my fingers and tasted his salty pre-cum in my mouth. I could feel how close he was.

Then I heard it, the Tetris ringtone. I pulled off his dick and jumped up as it plopped back against his skin.

♥♥♥ CHAPTER 5 ♥♥♥

He literally growled at me, but I still ran to my bag and pulled out the flip phone.

I took a deep breath, exhaled, opened it, and said as calmly as I could, "Hi, this is Connor. How are you doing right now?" Then I listened.

I could hear Jamel panting from the bed, but I blocked him out. Because Steve was on the phone, hurting badly. His wife left him that night and took his four-year-old daughter with her. I asked about their fight, and after fifteen minutes, Steve eventually got around to it: he hit her for the third time, which for her, was the last time. I didn't scold or chastise him for hitting his wife. I listened to him tell me how short his fuse had been since he came back last year and that he had never been this person.

I stood by the window and asked him if he understood what PTSD was and let him yell at me about how everyone keeps talking to him having trauma, and he was sick as shit of hearing it. I asked him instead to imagine driving his favorite car but driving it with his foot on the gas and brake at the same time. Jamel was shuffling behind me, but I didn't turn around. Instead, I gave Steve my full and undivided attention. I gave different analogies of PTSD until he understood how the war changed us, and as much as we want to go back to the old us, the old us is gone, and we need to figure out who this new person was. He asked me how I did it. I told him that I'm still learning who I am three years later.

Jamel came to stand to the side of me. At first, I didn't look at him. Then I realized he was fully dressed, handing me my clothes and charger. I mouthed "Thank you" to him and put on my clothes with the phone on my shoulder. He plugged the charger in the outlet closest to me, so my phone could charge while I talked. Jamel had also put a chair behind me, then he backed away and faded into the background. I sat as Steve talked about his experiences in Baghdad. Things he had seen and done. He asked me about my experiences. I shared some that related to his and correlated them with trauma.

I asked him what was the best thing in his life at the moment. He told me it was his daughter, Emiline. We spent the next hour talking about Emiline, and I watched the sunrise with Steve on the phone. Jamel slid a cup of coffee on the table next to me, and I took it without looking at him. Steve asked me if I had kids. I told him I didn't. He told me to get on it, and we laughed.

I asked again, "How are you doing right now, Steve?"

And he told me, "I'm better now."

"Do you want some resources in your area? No pressure, I just want to give you some things and someone to follow up with." I would have said okay and left it alone if he had said no.

But he said, "As long as it's not the VA, I've been there already."

I gave him the number to Menergy, an organization that runs therapeutic groups for men who have committed domestic violence. I also referred him to a trauma-informed male therapist in Massachusetts who uses Skype, and a meditation app I sometimes use. I told him to call back any time, day or night. He thanked me. Two hours later, we hung up.

♥ ♥ ♥ CHAPTER 5 ♥ ♥ ♥

♥

I swiveled my chair around to see Jamel lying at the bottom of the bed, watching me. I asked, "Can I borrow your tablet? I just want to record the call." He got up and handed it to me wordlessly. I logged into the system, recorded Steve's first name and area code, checked off the subjects we talked about, and wrote a brief paragraph about the call.

I put the tablet on the table, looked at Jamel, smiled, then cringed and said, "Sorry?"

He laughed loudly and stood up. "C'mere."

I stood up and went into his open arms. We stood there for a moment holding each other, and he gave me the Words of Affirmation I needed, filling up my depleted cup. He kissed my cheeks and head with every word, saying, "You were amazing, warm, loving, patient, intelligent, kind, empathetic. You're the best kind of person. Beautiful, selfless, and giving. I'm so grateful that someone like you wants to be with me."

I wanted to say so much back to him about how I felt about him, but instead I leaned into his shoulder and neck a bit more and asked, "You want to have sex now?"

He laughed and said, "Do *you* want to have sex now?"

"No. Take me home. *Your* home." Just so we were clear on whose home I wanted to be in. We packed our bags and got on the road.

"So, nope, still no actual fucking," I told my tribe that Wednesday. They were all pretty much open-mouthed as I told them about my weekend.

Winter shook her head furiously and said, "I don't understand why you didn't just fuck right afterward."

I couldn't explain it to her, but Afia did. "No, it's not what Connor needed. He needed to feel safe and secure and cared for after dealing with someone else's emotional issues."

"Okaaaay, but you could have felt safe and secure in his arms and on his dick, I'm just saying," Mina said, making us all giggle like we do.

Winter asked, "But even when you went back to his house? No sex?"

"No, we just sat on his couch and talked a bit about the call. Then, because technically he's my volunteer, we started talking about the logistics of VVB, and I did a little initial training and took him through the modules. Then it was five o'clock, and I needed to get home, shower, and change for Sunday dinner. Plus, it was nice just being with him."

"Oh my God, Connor, you're in a real fucking relationship. This is awesome. And I'm kind of surprised you aren't freaking out more," Mina said.

"I should be freaking out more, but... but I'm not. I don't know, y'all. I've never felt this way about anyone before. I met him a month ago. A month. That's not a long time to be feeling this strong for someone," I admitted to them.

"Well, it's just two months for me and Ty, and I know I love him," Afia said.

I narrowed my eyes at her. "Calm down, Lovie. Nobody said anything about love. I just really like him. I like spending time with him even though he hasn't plowed me yet. I could understand if he had, then I

Chapter 5

would have a reason to want to be around him. But this is new for me. I'm more freaked out about if it actually happens, and I'm not sure why." I sighed.

"Well," Mina started, "Could it be that you're afraid that once it actually happens, or after it happens a few times, the magic of Jamel will wear off on you?"

"That's true," agreed Winter. "You guys are building toward the mountain top, and once you reach there, there isn't anywhere else to go but down."

I groaned. "Well, I didn't think about it like that, so thanks for giving me something else to be worried about."

"That's not going to happen," Afia said confidently. "Jamel won't let that happen. Just because you've crossed a new level in your relationship doesn't mean it all goes downhill. There are more levels to cross."

Winter looked skeptical. "Like what? I love yous? Marriage? Kids? Connor doesn't want that."

"Connor does want that!" Afia retorted.

"Yeah? You see Connor as the family man type? No offense Con, but you know that's not you."

Winter had a point. I'm definitely not having kids. And gay marriage? I'd have to come out of the closet fully for that, so, nah. But Afia looked so hurt that there was something that we didn't have in common, so I said, "I know there are more levels to reach after sex and maybe one day I will want all those things. Except kids. But it could be that I have some fears about the dynamics of our relationship changing after that. I like how we are with each other right now. Everything is easy and fun, and sex complicates things, and I don't like complicated. I have enough complications in my life. I don't need another one."

"Well, you won't know until you do it. Have you seen each other since Sunday?" Winter asked.

"Yeah, we had dinner last night, but we won't see each other again until Saturday night. He's working on a house all day today, Thursday and Friday with his dad and Ty, and I have an installation on Saturday morning."

"I think you're going to fuck on Saturday," Mina declared. "I think you both know you've waited long enough for it, and it's going to be epic."

I smiled at Mina. Then Afia said, "And then you're going to wake up the next day and be the same people you were the day before. Because nothing is going to change about your relationship except you will be closer. So don't worry." She touched my hand. Mina touched my other hand. Winter rolled her eyes, but she touched my hand on top of Afia's. *I love all three of these women*.

Mina let go first and said, "Okay, my turn. So I accidentally on purpose joined a private Facebook group of couples looking for a third..."

CHAPTER 6

WE'LL JUST BE SCARED SHITLESS TOGETHER.

Mel and I made pizza from scratch that following Saturday. He had only done it once before with some Army buddies. It had come out pretty good then, so he wanted to try it with me. He was definitely a better cook than I am, but that's mostly because I never really tried to cook. I get three meals plus snacks where I was at home. But it was fun learning to cook with him. We touched and kissed and played with our food as it was cooking. It was turning out to be a perfect night.

Then the night went to shit.

Afia and Ty knocked on the door that evening, and I realized that since the first time we all had had dinner with his family, I hadn't been around Afia and her boyfriend. The four of us ate pizza and drank liquor, and I watched my Lovie be very affectionate with someone else that wasn't me. I didn't like it. It was weird for me to be in a room with her and for her not to be affectionate with me by kissing me, holding me, sitting on my lap, or snuggling in my arms.

So, what do I do when I start to feel uncomfortable about my feelings? I drink a little more than I should and let my mouth say inappropriate things.

I started making snide comments like, "Ty can't handle a woman like Afia. She can be wild if you know what to do." Afia punched me hard after that comment. I also found myself pulling out of Mel's embraces. He took the hint and stopped trying. He sat back and watched me get a little drunk and make a fool of myself.

When Tyrell called my Afia, Fifi, I said coldly, "No one calls her Fifi but her father. Not even me."

"Well, I do," Ty said and kissed her neck as she sat in his lap. "I guess I'm just as important to her as her dad."

I scoffed. "You've known her for five minutes. Her dog is more important to her than you are."

"Shut the fuck up, Connor," she said annoyed, and I laughed her off.

I kept going. "I'm just saying. You two look comfortable but don't get too comfortable. I'll be coming to get my girl back real soon." I winked at him and she glared at me.

"She's not your girl," Ty said coldly. "For the last three years all you did was keep her from being with someone else that could really love her. But that ended the day I came into her life. You don't get to use her anymore for your own selfish reasons."

"What!?" *What the fuck? What the fuck has Afia been telling him?*

♥♥♥ CHAPTER 6 ♥♥♥

The look on Afia's face was a mix of shock and guilt. "I never said that, Connor!" She turned to Ty angrily. "Why would you say that!?"

"Because it's true," he said factually.

"What's true?" I asked hotly.

"This fake-ass friendship y'all got. It's all one-sided. You take everything from her and give her nothing in return. You're a fucking cornball, and you're about to lose the only person that ever gave a shit about you, to me."

Jamel called his name quietly, "Tyrell. Don't."

But fuck that. Now I'm pissed, and ready to beat the shit out of my boyfriend's brother. "Shut the fuck up, Tyrell. You don't know me, and you don't know shit about our relationship!" My words were falling together.

"You don't have a relationship, dawg. You never did."

I cocked my head to the side mockingly. "Yeah? I guess she doesn't tell you everything, does she? Guess you're not as close as you think." I smirked. She turned to me with a deadly stare. I knew I had fucked up, but I locked eyes with her anyway.

"What does that mean?" Ty asked. "You two were fucking, for real?" He tensed up.

She stood up slowly off his lap and said to Ty first, "I am not fucking Connor. Connor is GAAAAAY!" She yelled the word. Then she turned to me, clapping her hands at every other word like she does when she's really angry.

"You're gay, Connor. You're fucking gay! You're not even bisexual anymore. You don't like tits and licking clits and female cum because you're FUCKING GAY!"

I leaned back on the couch and let her yell at me because she was finally paying me some attention. "I love you, Connor. I love you so much, but I need you to know that I can love you and still be in love with someone else. You don't own me, and you certainly don't own my heart. So please stop being a complete DICKHEAD to the man I love before you actually do lose me in your life."

My heart cracked from her even considering it. I could never lose Afia.

Ty smirked, winked at me, and touched Afia's arm. She pulled away forcefully and snapped at him, "And you, what the fuck is wrong with you!? I told you Connor is the most important thing to me, and you act like an asshole to match his assholeness. And for what? You thought you were somehow defending me? Because he's right: you have no idea the extent of our relationship. How we have taken care of each other for the last ten years of our lives. So if you ever in your fucking life come for MY Connor again, I will not just end this relationship—I will end YOU."

She grabbed her sneakers and left the apartment, and Ty ran out after her. I heard them arguing in the vestibule, the door slam, then it opened and and slam again. I figured she left first and he followed.

I looked around to see Jamel at the table quietly watching me. "What, you gonna yell at me too?" I said, rolling my eyes at him.

He said quietly, "I don't understand why you don't let her go. Especially since you have someone in your life now."

Chapter 6

"Let her go where? She's never going anywhere. She's going to always be in my life, by my side."

"Why? Do you love her?"

"Yes! Duh."

"You know what I'm asking, Connor. Are you in love with her? Do you want to be with her?"

I opened my mouth then closed it. Jamel continued, "Because I don't think you are in love with her or want to be with her. I think she is familiar and comfortable to you, and for some reason, you think she's the only one capable of loving you. And that's why you're afraid to let her go."

"Okay, Oprah." I scoffed.

He was staring at me, and I couldn't tell if he was upset or sad, so I went over to him and straddled his legs. He let me, but he didn't touch me. I wrapped my arms around his neck and said, "Are you going to fuck me now? Since I'm gay and all." I smiled, but he didn't.

"No," he said.

I cocked my head to the side. "Are you sure you're gay? Because this dry spell does not seem to be affecting you the way it's affecting me."

"It's affecting me. But your emotional health is what's affecting me more."

"What the fuck does that mean?" I leaned back, annoyed.

"Get off me, Connor. We're not fucking tonight."

"Oooh, but we were so clooooose last week. Can't we just start all oooooover?" I whined and started gyrating on him. I moved my hand to touch his groin, but he grabbed my wrist and stopped me firmly.

"No," he said calmly.

I was so pissed and a little drunk, or maybe more than a little because my words were falling together. "What the fuck why is it so hard for me to fuck my boyfriend nobody wants to fuck me what the fuuuuuk!?"

He watched me for a moment. "Get. Off. Me."

I huffed and kinda rolled off him. "I'm going the fuck home. I'm going to take care of it myself."

I went to grab my shoes, and he quickly got up and grabbed my keys off the entrance table. "You're drunk. You're not driving anywhere. Go lay down," he ordered.

And then I became really pissed that he thought he could control me. "Are you going to fuck me?"

"No."

"Then I'm not staying here. What the fuck!" I yelled at him, trying to put on my shoes.

He looked like he wanted to grab me but didn't. Instead, he said, "So when you're hurting emotionally you turn to numb it either with alcohol or sex. Or both."

What the entire fuck is he talking about? "I'm not hurting emotionally. I just want dick, and you refused to give it to me. So, I'm kinda done with this shit now." *I don't know why it's taking me so long to put on my damn shoes.*

"You're afraid she is leaving you behind. That you'll lose the only person you think really gives a shit about you."

"She *is* the only person that really gives a shit about me," I mumbled as I finally got one shoe on.

"I give a shit about you," he said quietly.

"Not the way Lovie does," I said factually. I got my other shoe on.

"Because you won't let me."

♥♥♥ Chapter 6 ♥♥♥

"Because you won't fuck me!" I yelled at him.

"Is that really what this is about?"

"Yes! We are two grown-ass men doing teenage shit because you won't just do it already. And I'm sick of begging when I could get dick anywhere." I grabbed my coat and put it on.

His eyes flashed in anger, but I didn't give a shit. I was ready for him to get mad at least once and show some desire for me. Then we could have make-up sex. *This fucker never yells, and that is not normal.*

Instead, he stayed ridiculously calm and said, "And why would I give myself to someone who's just going to take it for granted? Who, despite how I feel about him, tells me how he could 'get dick anywhere'? I have real feelings here, Connor, for you. But I still don't know how real your feelings are for me and—"

I couldn't believe that shit just came out of his mouth! I ran up and pushed him, making him stumble backward.

"Are you fucking serious?" I said incredulously.

I kept pushing him while yelling at him, and he kept falling backward but didn't move to grab me. "You think I've been spending all my time with you, falling into your fucking arms all the time because this is fun for me? It's not! It's fucking scary the way I feel about you!" I tried to push him a few more times, but he finally caught my arm.

I yanked it from him and said, "You know why I can't let Lovie go? Because she is the only person who knows who I am. And I'm not talking about being gay. I'm talking about all of me. She really knows me. My hopes. My dreams. My fears. She knows my thoughts before I think them because she thinks them too. We're so different on the outside, but we're exactly alike on the inside. If it wasn't for her, I would be one of them—a fucking racist asshole. But she plucked me right out of their hands by being who she is, and she has never let me go. She's my family because I don't have one! You're asking me to let the one person I consider family go?"

I started crying like a fucking dumb ass. "Lovie will always love me and never fucking leave me. You have no idea how many times I wished I wasn't gay, and I could just love her the way she deserves to be loved. But I can't... I can't... I can't give her what she needs, what she deserves; a lover, a husband, a father to her children. So, I give her everything else of me. My time, my shoulder, even my life if she needed it. She's a part of me in ways you could never understand." I sniffed and wiped my tears. "But sometimes ... when I'm with you, and you say things to me or do things for me ... when you hold me... And I think, he just might. He might want to love me and never leave me just like Lovie. He might want to be my family too. He just might replace her in my life as my everything. And that's a real fucking scary thought."

I sniffed a few times. "So, in case you didn't know how I was feeling about you. That's how."

He came closer and said softly, "I don't want to replace her. I just want you to give her room to breathe and let me in too."

I wanted to. I wanted to so badly at that moment. But I couldn't allow myself to feel and end up losing someone I cared deeply about. And even with that

Chapter 6

thought, I wasn't sure if that someone was Afia or Jamel. Maybe it was both. But it was all too much at that moment, so I gave myself an out.

I sniffed, kept my face hard, then asked, "Are you gonna fuck me now?"

But I knew the answer. In that exact moment I had a drunken clarity: He was 100% right. I use alcohol and sex, so I don't have to feel. He knew it too. He knew either way I was leaving and never coming back. It was just a matter of whether he was going to get something out of it.

He clasped his hands in front of his face like he was saying a prayer, closed his eyes, took a deep breath, exhaled, opened his eyes, and shook his head.

I nodded. "Bye, Mel." I turned around and left his house.

It was close to midnight on Saturday, but people were still out in the streets. I lit a cigarette, walked for a bit, then caught a ridiculously expensive cab back to Rockville. I figured I'd somehow get my car in the morning or ask Afia to get it for me. I didn't have my keys, but I kept a spare in the garage behind the corkboard, so I grabbed that first. Then I went upstairs, put my phone and my wallet on the nightstand, stripped naked, and got in my bed. I thought of Jamel and started jerking off, remembering that blow job he gave me just a week before. It didn't take long for my cock to start pumping cum all over me. I reached down for the shirt I was wearing earlier and wiped myself down, then closed my eyes. I didn't know how I was going to feel in the morning about walking out on Jamel the way I did, but I was pretty sure it was going to hurt like a bitch. But at the moment, I was numb and just needed to sleep and forget. *I will deal with my aching heart tomorrow.*

♥

My phone buzzed me awake, and I looked at the time. It was 4:17am, and Jamel was texting me multiple long texts. By the time I finished one, the next one had already come. My heart became a puddle of emotions as I read each one:

[Jamel: You're probably not awake, so I guess you will see this in the morning. The day I met you I just thought you were a regular white guy that liked to hang around and sleep with black people. But after that first week we hung out and we talked a little about the things you have been through and the things that fulfills your life, I knew you were something special. And you are. I call you amazing because your heart is so big and you care about people around you so much that you would do anything for them. That's a rare quality. I call you beautiful because while you are handsome, when you are happy and relaxed, your eyes and your smile light up the whole room. And that is the most beautiful thing to me, your happiness.]

[Jamel: You are Special. Beautiful. Amazing. I've tried to tell you and show you every moment we're together. Because you deserve to know it, to believe it. Not because I want to take Afia's place in your life. You're right, I could never love you the way Afia loves you.

Chapter 6

No one can. And if that's what you're waiting on to let her go or find love for yourself, then you've set yourself up nicely to never find that thing in your life that you want, need, and deserve, all in one. But you need to know, just like Vinnie, you too deserve all the love this world could ever give you.]

[Jamel: I'm sorry that I've been holding sex over your head for so long. I just really wanted you to know how much more you are worth to me. But also, if I'm honest, since you shared your fears, I would like to share some of my fears too. I started feeling really strong feelings for you really fast, and that was scary. That IS scary. So a part of me thought that if I bedded you a little too early, you would cut and run and I would be just another nameless face you've had that one time. I want to be so much more than that to you.]

[Jamel: It's not that I don't want to fuck you. God knows I wanted to fuck you from the moment I saw you at the pharmacy. You allude sex with your eyes alone. It's that now that I know you, your big heart, your ingenious mind, your tough spirit and a bit of that gentle soul that you've shown me so far, I don't want to just fuck you anymore. I want to make love to you. You told me on day three that you weren't going to fall in love with me and I was OK with that then. But now I think I'm falling for you and I'm no longer OK with it.]

[Jamel: Because like I keep trying to show you, you deserve to have someone fall in love with you and give you their all, and you deserve to be able to fall in love and give your all as well and feel safe while doing it. And the scary part for me is, I want to be that person for you. I want to give you all of me and get all of you in return. And I've never wanted to do that with anyone else as much as I want to with you. That shit terrifies me. So maybe, a little, not fucking you, not letting you fuck me, was my way of holding myself back as well.]

[Jamel: So here's the deal. If neither of us is ready to conquer our fears, then we can just be friends. You can go back to fucking whomever you like, and I will go back to my solitary life and fall all the way back from wanting to spend time with you. And maybe one day we'll come together again when we're ready. And maybe we won't. But we'll feel good about the decision we've made because we'll make it together. Or. You could come back to my house and let me make love to you the way I've been envisioning it for the last couple of weeks and we'll just be scared shitless together. It's completely your choice.]

[Connor: Fuck, Jamel. My heart feels like it's going to come out of my chest. I don't know if I'm one hundred percent ready for what you're offering me. But I know I don't want to just be friends. And I know my feelings are just as strong for you as you feel for me. And I know I don't want to make love to anybody else but you. And if we're doing it together, then maybe it's not so scary, right? So give me a few minutes to call a cab, I'm coming back over.]

Chapter 6

[Jamel: Don't call a cab. I'm still sitting in your car outside your house. I'm going to take you home with me.]

I went to the window to look, and my car was in the driveway. I thought of my love languages: Words of Affirmation? Check, and I have the texts to prove it. Acts of Service? Check. How thoughtful of him to drive my car back to Rockville, so, in the morning, I wouldn't have to explain why I didn't have it. Physical Touch? *That's about to be checked right now.*

[Connor: No. Come upstairs. Now.]

[Jamel: Are you sure? I don't want to out you or cause any problems for you with your family.]

[Connor: Are you coming up or not?]

I watched him walk out of my car and come toward the side door. I met him at the bottom of the stairs and opened the door even though he had my keys. He looked at me lovingly, then looked me up and down lustfully when he realized I was naked. He closed the front door, and I reached behind him and locked the deadbolt. I took his hand to lead him upstairs and closed my main door. I started to strip him one article of clothing at a time, starting with his sneakers and working my way up. We weren't talking because there was nothing left to say. When we were finally both naked, he pulled me close to him by my ass cheeks, and we hungrily kissed as I wrapped my arms around his neck. Somehow, I was slowly falling backward on the bed to lay down and it was okay. *Because he's got me.*

He spent a lot of time kissing my lips, sucking my tongue and neck, and kissing me down to my nipples. I knew he was leaving hickies on my pale white skin again. The hair on my body is very light and fine until you get to my groin, then it's a dirty blond forest down there. Typically, I manscape. I did for last weekend, but it had been a week, and the forest was growing back. He didn't seem to mind, though. He sniffed and kissed my stubbly groin before he kissed his way up my cock. His mouth finally made its way around it. It was like heaven the way his lips looked around my dick, the way my entire cock effortlessly disappeared into his mouth.

After a few sucks, he came off me with his lips and replaced them with his hand. He used the other hand to push the back of my thigh up gently. His mouth made its way down past my balls to my hole and his tongue was like a paintbrush, creating the Sistine Chapel. He was there for a while, licking inside, outside, and all around. He came up to suck each testicle succulently and deep-throated me a few more times before returning to the epicenter of my arousal and began painting the Mona Lisa. He could have stayed down there forever, and I let him know so by my moans and trembling.

He moved up and looked at me, and I knew he was looking for supplies. I pointed to my nightstand and smiled. He opened the bottom drawer and found all he'd ever need for a wild night: colorful condoms in different sizes, several types of lube, toys, buttplugs,

♥♥♥ Chapter 6 ♥♥♥

balls, dildos, and vibrators of every shape and size. He gave a deep throaty laugh. I sat up to kiss him.

He leaned toward my ear and said, "We'll keep it simple for now." Then he nipped my ear.

He took out a clear, water-based anal lubricant and a Magnum X. I stretched my legs out wide and laid down again, not taking my eyes off him. He looked at me with so much lust, but his only response was a quiet, "Shit."

Jamel added an unreasonable amount of lube to his fingers and reached down to stroke the outside of my hole. He added more lube to his fingers and put two fingers inside me. When he found my nub, my eyes rolled back, and I moaned loudly. He let me go so he could roll the condom on and add lube to the outside of it. He leaned over as I closed my legs around his back. He kissed the tip of my nose, then nuzzled his wide nose with my long one and I loved it. He kissed me slow and deep like he did the first time, and I melted into him. I was paying so much attention to his amazing kisses that it wasn't until I felt the pressure of my ring pulling apart that I realized he was slowly entering me.

I moaned and whimpered in his mouth as I felt the pain of his length, weight, and girth go through me. My back tried to arch its way up, but his rock-solid body held me in place. He leaned into my neck and whispered, "I'm almost there. Just let me get there. Hold on to me, okay? I got you."

I realized I had been grabbing the bed and not him, so I wrapped my arms around his neck again and dug my heels into his lower back. He was so big. It felt like forever before his pubic hair was touching my ass. When he got it all in, he asked, "Are you okay?"

I'm not going to lie to myself. The combination of his cock size and not having had a cock up in me in a while made it painful. The last time I had sex with Lex, I was fucking him as a consolation prize. It was the same night Jamel told me to end it with Lex. I hadn't been fucked since the week Jamel and I met, over a month. I had to breathe through it and let myself adjust to him.

But I lied to him and said, "Yes. I'm okay. Just give me a few seconds, then move, slowly at first." He followed my instructions, moving slowly back and forth until the pain gave way to immense jolts of pleasure. I had never felt so full in all my life and got lost in the intensity of his silver eyes. After a bit, I groaned to him, "Faster."

I fucked up by telling him to move faster because when he did, I thought I would pass out every time his big dick slid against my prostate. When he pulled back, I thought I would cry at the emptiness even though he hadn't completely left me. I dug my nails into that space where his neck ends and his back begins, and I let out the moan I save for a really good fuck. Then he leaned up and put my legs on his shoulders so he could hold onto my thighs and fuck me. I moved my hands down to his muscled ass to help guide him, not that he needed it.

Thank God the garage is detached because I would have woken up the whole house the way I was moaning and talking shit: "Fucking hell… this big … fucking cock… don't stop… Fuck don't … ever stop … fucking me … with this … monster … fucking …

Chapter 6

cock.... fucking holy shiiiiiit.... don't ever ... fucking stop ... fucking meeeeee..."

He held my legs to the sides of him so he could get closer, breathing, grunting, and sweating on me as I held onto his back. His dog tags were hanging off his sweaty chest onto mine. Between the beating he was giving my prostate and the squeeze of my dick between our abs, I didn't stand a chance. I exploded cum between us as he switched up his stroke to grind against my insides for the next minute or so. I swear I blacked out for a second. Then he pulled out, and again, I almost cried at the emptiness. He turned me on my stomach, put a pillow underneath me, spread my cheeks, and began to slowly and gently lick my beet red, sensitive hole and balls again. He used one finger to tease me in between his soft licks. I punched the bed, moaning loudly from pleasure.

He added more lube to me and entered me again. I sighed from satisfaction. He laid on top of me, kissing the back of my neck, and went back to how he started, with slow, long deep strokes. His hands were everywhere; he would run his hand through my hair, pull it roughly, then massage my scalp gently. He lifted his hand slightly, trailed it down my back until he reached the deep groove right above my ass, and lay his palm there to arch me more and push in deeper. He ran his hands up my back to my hair, lay down and start again, kissing the back of my neck, all the while never changing his stroke. I cried out over and over again as he buried himself even deeper and moaned. His baritone mmmm's sent shivers throughout my body.

After a while of slow grinding, he began pounding me harder than before, fucking me senselessly. I lost all of my senses. My words were incoherent, and my eyes kept rolling around. I could only hear his grunting and the slapping sound of his thighs hitting my ass. And I smelled only us, that animalistic funk that happens in a closed room with no ventilation. His pounding became less rhythmic, and I knew he was close. I dug my nails into the bed as I felt my second orgasm of the night rise. I squeezed my rectum as I came again. He slammed into me two more times, then froze and groaned loudly. I felt him ejaculate but disappointingly couldn't feel it inside me because of the condom.

Jamel slowly regained consciousness and looked down at me, trying to focus his eyes. He leaned down as I turned my head to see him. He nuzzled his nose against mine again, kissed me slowly, and tongued me deeply as he pulled out. I felt so empty that I had no idea how I'd been functioning without his dick inside me. When he was completely out, he sat up, took off his protection. I thought he was going to lay down, but then he started stroking himself.

He looked at me and laughed. "Fuck, I'm still horny."

"Let me ride." My eyes were wide and full of lust.

He moved to his back, and I got up to grab another condom and more lube. When we were both ready, he held himself straight, and I sat on his chest and pushed back on the head. I winced a bit but allowed myself to feel all of him as I made my way to his lap. Once again, our bond was complete. He moved his hand to my hips as I placed both palms flat on either side of him, and we just looked at each other. I smiled first,

♥♥♥ CHAPTER 6 ♥♥♥

and he followed. I began to move, and I watched his eyes flutter. I leaned down, and we kissed and moved together. Jamel filled me up in a way that I had never been filled before. Every time I went down on him, my entire body shivered. We had both already cum, so we knew we would last longer.

I wanted to try something new, something I learned from my previous lover. I held onto his shoulders. I began to wine my hips as if I were dancing reggae. Jamel grabbed my skin tighter and moaned, "Hoooooooly shiiiiiiiiit." I could tell he was not used to talking during sex, and I knew I was doing something right.

I kept moving in a circular motion, and my lover's baritone voice got a bit higher and a lot louder with every breath he made. His head twisted around like the exorcist. I felt what Lex had felt when he did this to me; the feeling of how I twisted my insides against him grazing my walls, and grinded him against my prostate was indescribable. I was glad I had never returned the favor with Lex. This was all for Mel. I moved my fingers to his hairy pecs, already wet with my cum and his sweat. I mixed in my new drip of pre-cum and moved faster while I talked shit about how he loved the feel of me riding his cock. Somehow, I managed to move just my hips up and down on him, which drove him wild as he thrusted to meet me. And just like that, my white ass learned to twerk.

We fucked for a while and held onto each other as we moved into climax together. Mel came first, drawing out my name, "Coooooonooooor," as he pressed his thumbs into my hips. Again, I could feel his cum moving up his cock as he pulsed. That was enough for me to jizz all over him again, hands-free for the third time in two hours.

I eased up to release him from inside of me, took the condom off him, and moved to lay next to him. He instinctively pulled me back into him and held me, kissing my head, hair, and face.

Jamel started to laugh. "You're so animated in bed. I fucking love it."

"Oh yeah? You like my dirty talk?"

"It's more like sexy encouragement," he said amusingly.

I chuckled. "And that was me tame. Now I know not to hold back anymore."

I snuggled deeper into the area between his shoulder and chest, yawned, and closed my eyes. I threw my arm over his torso as he rubbed my back. Everything about it feels so damn right.

"You're so beautiful, so special, and so amazing. I feel so lucky to have you right now," he murmured in my hair. "I won't hold back anymore if you won't."

"I guess we'll be scared shitless together now," I muttered as comfort and sleep took over me.

CHAPTER 7

AND SUDDENLY I WAS GOOD WITH THAT.

My phone went off again way earlier than it should have. Jamel grunted, grabbed the phone, handed it to me, mumbled, "Afia," and turned back over to sleep, one hand draped across my midsection.

I rubbed my eyes and answered, "Lovie, I'm so sorry."

"Answer the door, Connor. I've been knocking for five minutes already, and I know you're there because I see your car."

I groaned and rolled out of bed, saying to him, "She's coming upstairs." I went to my dresser and pulled out a pair of sweatpants and a tank top to put on.

"You want me to go?" he asked groggily.

"For Afia? Of course not. But you may want to, you know, put on underwear."

He laughed, yawned, and reached for his clothes on the floor as I opened the main door to head downstairs. Afia was standing at the front door in a long-sleeved dark orange ankle-length dress that hugged all her curves, a silk orange, black and silver scarf around her neck, and her favorite knee-high black boots. She was ready for church.

I said automatically, "I'm so sorry for being a dickhead."

"I know," she said. "That's why you're going to apologize to Ty. And apologize to Mel for whatever you said after I left. Ty said he was pretty distraught when he got back to the house last night."

I smiled at her as I closed the door behind her. I whispered, "Mel accepted my apology over and over again in the middle of the night. He's upstairs."

Her eyes went wide. "Holy shit, finally!" Then she whispered, "Aaaaand?"

"Mina was right. It was epic."

"Yay!" She hugged me, then said, "And it's not over. There is so much more coming. You just wait. Oh, I'm so happy for you, Connor! You deserve this happiness."

I hugged her tighter. "You do too, Lovie. That's why I'm so sorry. I feel like shit. I won't come between your happiness again, ever. If it's Ty, then it's Ty. I will make nice with him."

"Thank you," she whispered into my neck. We held each other for a moment, knowing we would be doing this less and less. I let her go first, took her hand, and led her upstairs.

Jamel was sitting on the bed with his running pants back on. She smiled when she saw him, then said, "You need to open up a window or two or all of them. It smells like straight sex in this bitch."

❤❤❤ Chapter 7 ❤❤❤

He laughed loudly. I shoved her playfully but then went to open up the nearest window. A cold blast cooled my skin, and I realized how hot it had been. I opened up another window and lit the vanilla incense stick I used to cover up my smoking.

Afia sat on the couch in front of the TV. "Connor, your parents just left for Mass, so you have about an hour and a half before they get back. I was going to my church at ten o'clock, but Mel, I don't see your truck. How are you getting home?"

"I was just going to jump in a cab again," Jamel said.

She shook her head. "I'll take you home and go to your church at 11am instead. You're giving me a good reason to see Ty." They smiled at each other, and he nodded a thank you.

Then he asked me, "Do you mind if I take a shower here?"

"Not at all. Extra towels are behind the door."

He grabbed his t-shirt and went into the bathroom. I went to sit next to Afia, and she crawled into my lap like always, wrapped her arms around me, and let me hold her. Then she handed me her phone with Ty's number already on the call section. "Now, Connor."

I resisted the urge to roll my eyes and pressed send. Ty answered, "Connor?"

"Yeah, how did you know?"

"She told me she was going to have you call me from her phone about an hour ago."

I smiled. "Of course she did. Soooo, listen. I was really drunk last night and said a lot of stupid shit to get under your skin. I'm sorry about that."

"Yeah, I also said a lot of stupid shit. Afia is right. I don't know the extent of your friendship. She explained some of it to me last night, and I got it. You've always had her back. So, I'm sorry too."

"So we're cool?"

"Yeah, but listen. I just want you to know I'm not taking her from you. I mean, not in the way you think. Y'all are like family. So, in the same way I don't think about you taking my brother away from me, I don't want you to think I'm taking her away from you. I just want to love on her, you know? Cuz I do. I love her."

"Yeah, Ty, I know you do. And she loves you too. It's all my insecurities coming out, and you were right about some of it. I have been selfish about her, and I won't do that anymore. I want her to be happy. And you make her happy."

"She makes *me* happy. She's an amazing girl."

"She sure is," I said as I smiled at her.

"Is Jamel with you? I can't find him," he asked.

"Yeah, he's here. Lovie… Afia is giving him a ride home soon, so you'll see them both."

"Okay, cool, cool," he responded. I handed the phone back to Afia.

While still snuggling in my lap, she said to Ty, "Thank you. I love you." I heard him say, "I love you too," and "see you soon." They hung up.

She turned to me and said, into my shoulder, "Thank you. I love you."

"I love you too."

She continued to snuggle on me as Jamel came out of the bathroom fully dressed. He sat on the other end

Chapter 7

of the couch, and Afia began to move off me. Jamel said, "It's okay. Stay." She slowly laid back down.

I looked over at him and smiled. We were quiet for a moment as Jamel watched Afia and me. Afia began to talk. "Our relationship isn't one-sided, Jamel. I protect Connor because Connor has always protected me. When I started high school in Rockville, it was awful. I was one of ten black students and the only one in my year. I know you know how it is Mel, growing up being the only black face in a sea of white ones. Rockville is very small and very white, with hidden racism everywhere. For the first month of high school, I got pushed around and teased about everything from my natural hair to my brown skin. One day, I was coming off the field from my last gym period, and a group of girls cornered me, saying they just wanted to see my hair. At first, it was fine, but they were yanking it and pulling on me and telling me it felt like grass and Brillo Pads. Stupid shit. They had me in a circle and wouldn't let me out. They just kept pulling my hair, pulling me to the ground. The baseball team was coming out to start practice, and they all saw it, but they all walked past and ignored it. Except for a sophomore named Connor. He stopped and came over and asked them what the fuck did they think they were doing."

Afia kept going, "Olivia, the main bitch said, 'We're just fucking with the darkie,' and smiled. Connor said, 'How would you feel if someone pulled on your hair, you stupid cunt bitch?' She got mad and went over to slap him, I guess, but he reached behind her and pulled the shit out of her ponytail, wrapping it around his hand and bringing her to her knees, making her cry. And he told her, 'If I ever see you fuck with ... what's your name?' I'm like, Afia. He continued, 'If I ever see you fuck with Afia again, I'm going to rip this dry horse shit right out of your head. That goes for all of you. Leave Afia the fuck alone. Forever.'"

I smiled at that memory. "I hated that bitch. I hate bullies," I said. I held her a bit tighter because I knew she needed it.

She continued talking to Jamel. "So they left, and Connor asked if I was okay, and I said yes and he said 'okay, how are you getting home?' And I realized that they kept me there long enough that I missed the bus, so I said 'I don't know.' And he said, 'wait for me, I will walk you.' So I waited on the bench for baseball practice to be over, and he walked with me the two miles to the other side of Rockville. We became friends on that walk. After that, no one messed with me, and I mean no one. I found out that Connor was the popular kid from town, and he got respect. He sent the word out that I was his little sister, and no one was to fuck with me, ever. I watched the black and brown friends that I made get pushed into walls, 'nigger' written on their lockers, clothes bleached and trashed, get beat up, but not one person even looked at me wrong, whether I was with Connor or not. He saved me that day and protected me until he graduated the year before me, and by that time, there was no one to fuck with me anyway."

"When he told me he was bisexual, I knew I had to protect him too. I know what kind of family he has, and if it ever got back to them, even rumored, his father is a fucking maniac and would physically hurt him. Do

Chapter 7

you know why Connor doesn't like to be hugged or why he'll pull out of a hug first? Because when he got in trouble, his father used to put him in a straitjacket and cave his chest in, then make him stand in the corner for hours with it on, while the family had to ignore him."

I had to stop her before she revealed too much. "Stop talking, Lovie," I murmured.

"No, Connor, he needs to know. He needs to know why you are the way you are sometimes. Why you don't like being attached. Why you push people away."

"I didn't realize he doesn't like to be hugged," Jamel said. "He always lets me hold him."

She smiled at him. "And that's a good thing, a really good thing. Because the only other person that he lets hold him is me. Which is why I do, every chance I get, so he knows he's loved." She squeezed my midsection, and I squeezed her back.

She sat up a little and looked at Jamel. "I protect him now the way I do because he protected me fiercely back then and still does when racist shit happens to me. No one has ever done that for me, to this day, except Connor. He never, not one time, asked me to pretend to be his girlfriend. But one day he got into a fight in the hall—"

"Fuck no, not that story!" I cringed.

"Shut up, Connor. He got into a fight in the hallway with Kurt Littles, who told the whole school Connor tried to touch his dick. It was getting around fast, and by fifth period, they met in the hallway and started fighting. Connor was beating the shit out of Kurt, but Kurt kept saying it, and everyone was watching. Even after the school police came and handcuffed them both, Kurt kept screaming how Connor wanted his dick and I know Connor was getting embarrassed. Jack, our other friend, and Connor's ex at the time, was standing next to me and said, 'I wish I could help him, or just go up to him and tell him it's going to be okay. Or distract people, you know? Save him from all of this, anything.' Jack was the only kid at our school that was Out."

Huh? I didn't know that. "Wait, you never told me Jack said that to you."

"Oh, I didn't? Well, it initially wasn't my idea to do it. He said it, and I told him, I'll do it for you. I'll save him."

"What did you do?" ask Jamel.

"I went up to Connor with his black eye and blood running down his nose, handcuffed and against the wall. I wrapped my arms around him, and I looked into his eyes. He knew what I was going to do right before I did it, and he let me. I tongue kissed him and rubbed his dick in front of everyone, students, teachers, the principal, the police, everybody, like we had been kissing and fucking around with each other all that time. I kept going until the police pulled him away. Then I turned to Kurt and said, 'Nobody wants your little dick, Kurt. Connor is straight, trust me, I know.'"

I laughed. "They called him Little Dick Kurt for the rest of the school year until we graduated." Jamel laughed with Afia and me as we cackled.

He asked, "So you pretended to be his girlfriend after that?"

We exchanged looks and laughed. "Well, technically, he had a girlfriend, Winter. But honestly, I forgot

Chapter 7

all about her because the only reason he ended up with Winter was because Jack broke up with him like a month before that because Connor wouldn't come out of the closet. So no, I couldn't pretend to be his girlfriend yet because his real girlfriend found out about me kissing him and telling everyone that I was fucking him and, she literally beat the shit out of me the next day."

Jamel's mouth dropped. "Holy shit."

"Yep, she took an ass whipping for me and will never let me forget it to this day," I said sheepishly.

Jamel laughed, then asked, "Wait, aren't you all friends now?" He knew about my tribe.

Afia said, "Oh yeah, she's my best friend now. We hang out more than I do with Mina. But that's how she introduced herself to me, with her fist in my mouth."

We started to giggle like we do. It wasn't funny at all then but ten years later it's kinda funny now.

I told Jamel, "I was on a week-long suspension, so I didn't find out until the day after. I had to bring them both to my house to straighten everything out. I told Winter the truth about me and that Afia was just protecting my reputation. We all became friends after that. And instead of Winter being my girlfriend, Afia became my girlfriend for the next four months until I graduated, which honestly made more sense because we were always together. But Winter and I had to have a public fight about it first."

"Wow," was all Jamel said. I looked over to him and smiled, and he smiled back.

"So, now you know," Afia said. "Now you know the type of person Connor is, why we're so close, and why we still protect each other."

He nodded. "Every time I learn more about Connor, it just makes me happy to have someone like him in my life."

Jamel and I watched each other over Afia's head, and she noticed. She got up and ordered, "Go."

I rolled my eyes playfully. I moved over to Jamel, and he stretched one leg on the couch so I could sit between his legs. I kissed his lips softly, then turned around and pushed back against his chest. He wrapped his arms around me as I drew my knees up to my chest. He kissed my head and sighed. Or maybe I sighed. Maybe we both did. *This must be how Lovie feels when I hold her. And now when Tyrell holds her. Being in my lover's arms is everything.*

Afia sat back down and told Jamel, "I tried to explain some of this to Ty, and I think he gets it, but I have a feeling you get it more. So, if Ty's still struggling with my friendship with Connor, please help him because I will never give Connor up. He's the one person in my life that would do anything for me, and I would do anything for him. He's part of my family, so he will always be in my life, no matter what. And anyone that tries to make me choose will lose to him. I know that sounds crazy but it's just the way it is."

I heard her, and I had pretty much told Jamel the same thing the night before. But I said, "Choose Ty, Lovie. He loves you and will also do anything for you. He loves you. He can make you happy in ways I can't. Choose Ty."

♥♥♥ CHAPTER 7 ♥♥♥

She shook her head, but Jamel said, "I'll make sure Ty never makes you choose. For everyone's sake here." She smiled at him, and he held me tighter. It was so weird for me seeing Afia over on the other end of the couch without me, but she looked so happy to see me happy that I let it go.

Jamel said, "One question, Connor: Did you really try to touch Kurt Little's dick?"

"I sure fucking did. I didn't try, I *did*. We were in the locker room taking showers, and I glanced over the half wall once, and he caught me. So he came over to my stall gyrating and kept taunting me. 'You like my dick Connor, want my dick Connor, want to suck my dick Connor?' I gave him one warning. I said, 'If you come any closer, I'm going to cup your balls and jerk your dick.' He didn't listen. The moment he stepped into my shower and got close, I pulled him all the way in, gyrated against him on the wall, then stroked his dick a few times. He moaned like a bitch in heat. I got his pre-cum on my hands and licked it, then I let him go. After that, he ran screaming from the locker room."

Afia cackled, and Jamel's mouth dropped open. "Holy shit, Connor. You're a sexual predator!"

I asked innocently, "Is it the lion's fault that the sheep willingly entered its lair?"

Afia snorted, and Jamel let out the throaty laugh he reserves for when something is hilarious. For an hour, Afia and I shared more high school stories with Jamel. Then, someone banged on my front door.

I heard my father's voice. "CONNOR. Open the door. Now!"

I froze. Afia's eyes went wide for a second, then she said calmly, "It's okay. I brought Mel over here, and we're leaving together. Okay? Okay?" She held my gaze until I nodded.

She pulled me to a standing position. I was trembling, so she put her arms around me to steady me as my father yelled again. "CONNOR. OPEN THE DOOR."

Jamel was unsure of what to do. He stood up and tried to caress my back, but I pulled away from him and went downstairs to answer the door. My father is an inch or two taller than me but might as well be a foot taller than me. He is broad-chested and heavy-handed.

I opened the door, and he said, "You missed Mass."

I swallowed. "Yes, sir. I have company, sir."

"I know, I see Afia's car. She was here all night, wasn't she? You two were loud. We heard some noises coming from here." My heart almost came out of my chest. "What did I tell you about fornicating in my house?"

I mumbled and kept my eyes down. "I'm sorry, sir. It won't happen again, sir."

He grunted and moved past me to go upstairs. I followed behind him, unsure of how he would react to seeing Afia and Jamel in my apartment. I stood behind him with my head slightly bowed to avoid everyone's eye contact, even Afia's. Jamel was fully dressed with his coat and shoes on, looking like he had just stopped by with Afia.

My dad paused at Jamel's presence but did not acknowledge him at first. He said sternly, "Afia. Good

Chapter 7

morning. If you come by, you make sure you come into the house and greet everyone first."

"Yes, Mr. McIntyre," she replied respectfully. "I was on my way to do so, but I saw you all left for church."

"Shouldn't you be on your way to your church as well?" He looked at his watch. It was after 10:30am.

"Yes, we are on our way," she said. Then, she grabbed my boyfriend's arm. "Please meet my friend, Jamel Jones. Sergeant Jamel Jones."

Jamel reached his hand out for a shake. "Pleased to meet you, sir."

Dad eyed him a bit suspiciously but took his hand. "Sergeant. What branch?"

"Army, first infantry. Four tours in Afghanistan," he told him. Dad's branch was Army, so he relaxed just a little. My father's ranking, Staff Sergeant, is one step above Jamel's, and when my father told him, I could see Jamel do the mental shift in his head that occurs when meeting a superior officer.

My father grilled Jamel quickly about his unit and duties. Jamel was wearing his dog tags too, which was a plus. Later, I asked Jamel why he wore his dog tags to my house because he wasn't wearing them earlier in the evening; they typically hung off his dresser mirror. He said he felt like he was going to war for my heart and needed luck. I guess it worked.

"So what brings you by to meet my son? Are you going to enlist him back?" he asked.

Jamel said very easily, "No, I'm working alongside Connor in the Vinnie's Vet Buddies organization."

"You mean the hobby he has that keeps him from getting a real career?" my dad asked.

Fuck him for that.

Jamel glanced at me, then back to my father. "Actually, sir, I think it's a really great thing for us. I'm sure you remember how hard it was for our men coming out of 'Nam, and I know firsthand how hard it is coming out of the Middle East now. It's things like Connor's hotline that keep our vets sane and grounded and help them know they aren't alone. The fact that he and his unit put so much time and effort into it is what makes it great. Your son is brilliant, and I'm happy to be a part of it, sir." Jamel made eye contact and held his hands behind his back respectfully as he talked, and I lifted my head a bit higher.

Dad surprisingly nodded in agreement. Or maybe just acknowledging what Jamel had said. Either way—shocking.

Afia looked at me and held my gaze for a moment. "Connor, sweetie, we have to go."

"Are you coming by later?" I asked her, my eyes pleading.

She walked up to me and hugged me. "Yes. I will be here." I hugged her back, and it was painful when she let me go. She said to my dad, "Have a good day, Mr. McIntyre." And then motioned for Jamel to follow her out.

Jamel looked at me like he didn't want to leave, or maybe he saw the fear and desperation in my eyes. But I got myself together, and I gave him a slight head nod toward the door.

He went to shake my dad's hand again. "Good to meet you, Staff Sergeant McIntyre."

Chapter 7

Jamel turned to me and touched my shoulder, giving it a slight squeeze. "I'll give you a call, Corporal."

I nodded, and Jamel followed Afia downstairs and out the front door. When the door closed, I leaned against the wall and waited.

My dad started, "This place looks and smells like shit. Clean it up."

I looked around, and the only thing out of order was my unmade bed and a couch pillow that ended up on the floor. But I nodded anyway. "Yes, sir."

He berated me about sleeping with Afia in his home, how much of a sexually immoral deviant I was, and how I continue to bring her into my sinful ways and let her sinful nature infect me with her biblical sin of Ham. *Fuck him for that.*

But then he said, "It's time to let her go because you'll never be serious about that girl. It's time to find a pure girl to settle down and marry." *Pure meant white. Fuck him for that too.*

I looked him in the eye and said, "If I wanted to be with a black person, wouldn't that be my business?"

I knew it was coming, and I let it happen anyway. He swung out and punched me on the side of my head, then grabbed me by my shirt and slammed me against the wall.

He spit as he said, "Bed that wench all you want, but you aren't bringing a nigger into my family, giving her the McIntyre name. I will kill you, her, and whatever nigger babies you have."

My father, a walking contradiction of morals. I looked him in the eye and said, "Sir, yes sir." Anything more would have led to him pummeling me with his fists.

He let me go, and as he walked out, he said, "Dinner is at six."

"Yes sir, we'll be there."

Two days later, Jamel texted me.

[Jamel: You're still getting off in five minutes at 4:30pm?]

[Connor: Yes. Want me to meet you somewhere for dinner?]

[Jamel: Can you leave your car in the lot overnight?]

[Connor: Yeah I guess. Nobody will mess with it. Why?]

[Jamel: I'm picking you up. I'm already outside.]

[Connor: OK. Are we going somewhere?]

[Jamel: No. I just want to pick you up and take you home. My home. And I'll take you to work in the morning.]

I texted back OK, unsure of why he was picking me up. We hadn't seen each other the day before because I had to work, so I kenw he wanted to spend some quality time with me, and I hoped that would include him fucking me again. I headed down quickly, and his cherry red pick-up was right out front. He

❤❤❤ CHAPTER 7 ❤❤❤

pulled off as soon as I got in and took the road to his house. I didn't say anything, waiting for him to explain.

"I've been thinking about you all day. So I'm taking you home with me tonight. I picked up food from Boston Market already because I'm not cooking. All I want is you. All of you. All night." He said all this without taking his eyes off the road. *Sir yes sir!*

It only took fifteen minutes to get to his house from where I work in West Warwick, and I was already spouting a bulge. When we parked on his block, I went to open the door. He took my arm to pull me toward him, leaned over, and tongue-fucked my mouth.

After a few moments of intense kissing, he released me and said, "Wait."

He came out of the car to open up my car door, and I laughed. "Was that really necessary?"

"Yes," he smiled, then took my hand and half-ran us inside the house to his downstairs apartment. He said, "My parents are out tonight having dinner with some friends. Ty is with Afia, and Lavell has a study group for midterms. It's just us for the next couple of hours."

He opened the door. His apartment was dark with an orangey glow. All the curtains were closed, and there were lit scented candles everywhere—Three on the table, two on the living room coffee table, and two on the kitchen counter. I couldn't tell yet how many were in his bedroom. I was shocked. It was some real romantic shit that nobody had ever done for me. I turned to look at him, and he had a sly smile on his face.

"You know this isn't necessary, right? I was going to give you ass tonight anyway," I told him with a wink.

He smiled a bit and pulled me close. He kissed my lips, making his way to my cheek, my neck, then to the bottom of my earlobe, and whispered, "It's necessary because you're worth it. And you're not going to give me ass tonight. I'm going to give you mine."

Holy shit! I let all the air out of my lungs as he picked my chin up and looked me in the eyes. I don't know why I thought I'd have to wait a bit longer or work a little harder for my typical top, take-charge boyfriend to be my bottom. I had miscalculated a lot about him and the nature of our relationship. He wanted all of me, so he was giving me all of him. And suddenly I was good with that—giving him all of me.

I bit my lower lip and said to him plainly, "I'm going to bang your fucking back out."

He smiled. "I wouldn't expect anything less." He kissed me gently on the lips. "Shower first."

We stripped in the living room, and he led me to the bathroom, which also had candles. I had never been in his shower before, so I was like a kid in a candy store going through his grooming products. I picked up his blue loofah with the handle hanging on the shower caddy, raised an eyebrow, and said, "Yeah?"

He laughed. "I like to exfoliate." I chuckled back. He said, "I have extras if you want one. I just change out the pouf from the handle. What do you use?"

I shrugged. "A bar of soap and a washcloth to scrub a couple of times a week."

He nodded. "Well, I'm about to change your life, Corporal, sir. I'm going to pouf you all over, and by the time I'm done, you're going to want one yourself. Trust

♥♥♥ CHAPTER 7 ♥♥♥

me." He poured his ocean-scented Head & Shoulders body wash on it and proceeded to exfoliate my skin.

"Tell me about your tattoos, starting with this one," he said. He scrubbed my large black panther with the red outline that covers the entire left side of my body.

"I got it months after I enlisted, after basic training. Taylor has a cheetah on his right, because he's left-handed, and mine is on my left. The tattoo represents strength, honor, valor, wisdom, and power. We thought it would make us ferocious over there."

"And did it?"

"I think so. We certainly thought it did, at least."

"Hmmm... It's very sexy. Especially the way it folds into the side of your abs. Beautiful."

I smiled as I raised my other arm for him to scrub my pits. "Well, yeah, that too."

"And your cross?" he asked as he turned me around. I have a small black cross on my right shoulder blade with white, cursive letters: PS7326.

I recited the verse for him, "My flesh and my heart fail, but God is the strength of my heart and my portion forever. Psalms 73, verse 26."

He nodded and smiled. "That's a good one. And your wrist?"

I have a tattoo of a wrist band on my right wrist with the letters VB hanging off it on the inside. I looked down and rubbed the letters with my left thumb. That used to be a secret signal to say "I love you" when others were around. Now I do it to remind myself that someone loved me once.

I told Jamel the truth. "Vinnie and I got matching tattoos. His said, 'CM.' Mine say, 'VB.' For Vincent Barrone. But now it just means Vet Buddies."

He nodded, then said nonchalantly, "Or it could mean both."

If I were to pinpoint the exact moment I started to actively fall in love with this man, it would be right then. The fact that he readily accepted that Vinnie would always be a part of me made my heart burst. But I said nothing about how I was feeling.

Instead, I told him, "I've been thinking of getting another one. A colorful phoenix across my back."

"That would be fitting for you," he said.

I have to admit I didn't hate the loofah thing. My mom and sisters use them, but I had never thought to use one.

"You're turn," I told him as I turned him around and used a fresh loofah, without the handle because I wanted my hands to graze his body with my fingertips. "Tell me about your tattoos." I started to scrub him down.

He told me, "The lion paw, my biggest tattoo, represents my need to lead and protect others around me. Strength. Bravery. Justice. It's me. Being the oldest, I just fell into that role. I got it before I enlisted. The compass on my left forearm reminds me to always look for direction. I also got that one before I enlisted. I considered going into the Navy for a moment. The scorpion on my right shoulder is my zodiac sign, and the cross on my left shoulder with the words 'Psalms 103' is my faith. I haven't thought about another one, but I won't rule it out."

Chapter 7

"Um-hmm," I said as I rinsed him off, got on my knees and put his monster cock in my mouth. He gasped and held my head. I bobbed on him while fingering him with my soapy hands. I had him just where I wanted him, at the mercy of my mouth and tongue. This time, no call would get in the way. I had never missed a call, but I was willing to at that moment.

He said between groans, "Fuck... I'm ... gonna ... cum ... down ... your ... throat..."

He started face-fucking me. I felt his ass cheeks clench in my hands as he groaned and unloaded all my mouth. His cum was salty, with a hint of sweetness in it, and I greedily swallowed.

I stood up and said, "Now we're ready. Let's go."

I brought him to his room; it was as lavender and vanilla scented as the rest of the house. As he laid down on his belly, I took the massage oil he had on his dresser and massaged his muscles from his shoulder blades to his thighs. We moved in silence. I put on a condom, lifted his bottom, and put my tongue in his puckered hole. My lover shivered in my hands. I dragged my tongue around his anus, kissed and sucked his perfectly round balls that I kissed and sucked, and made my way up again. My sweet tooth relished putting my face in all that chocolate.

After a nice, long rim job, I lubed him up, put a pillow underneath him, and slowly entered his ridiculously tight and hairy hole from behind. He wasn't an anal virgin, but he was close to it. Jamel really didn't do casual sex, and the only sex he did have was with him as a top. That was clear from his tightness and groaning as I made my way down to his prostate.

I leaned over and put my tongue in his ear. I moved incredibly slow at first and increased speed little by little, listening to him moan deeply. I rose myself up on my knees and thrusted repeatedly into the sweet ass in front of me, elated that it was all mine. I moaned along with him, moving faster, switching up strokes, and eventually pounding the fuck out of him. Then he started breathing out my name in a whisper with intense need and lust. My heart and cock burst as I gave Jamel all of me.

When I had regained my senses, I moved off him and onto my back. Jamel did what he does best. He pulled me toward him, his leaking dick against my belly as I melted into him and let his tongue play with my ear. I was not done. I reached between us and pulled off the condom, then I moved him onto his back and laid against him, kissing him, grinding my body against his until I became hard again. Then I put on a fresh condom, slid between his legs, and entered my lover once more. I nuzzled my nose with his, just as he had done with me, and we kissed before I began to move inside of him. He moaned and groaned as I made love to my man the second time, telling him how I make him feel while fucking him. He trapped me between his muscled thighs and wrapped his arms around my back and agreed, calling my name sweetly and softly and stroking himself until we came together.

We fell asleep, woke up, ate dinner in bed, and made love again, with me entering him face to face. He wasn't kidding when he said he wanted me all night. I was happy to oblige, even though I was concerned about the soreness he'd feel in the morning. But he

Chapter 7

wouldn't hear of it. He kept saying to me, "I want all of you." Of course, in the middle of the night, I ended up reverse-riding him and neither of us minded the break in our sexual agreement that it would be his turn that day. It was the perfect night.

In the morning, we showered together, then I blew and swallowed him again right before we left the house without it reciprocated. I was happy to have the taste of him on my tongue as I went about my day.

CHAPTER 8

Look who's attached now?

~~~Winter 2009~~~

The holidays came and went, and Jamel and I became inseparable. Afia became my cover story, as Jamel called it, for a whole new reason: So I could spend time with Jamel away from my home. For his 29th birthday the following weekend in November, I took Jamel back to the Quality Inn in Middletown, and we made up for last time by fucking like rabbits for 48 hours. A week later, after my family's Thanksgiving dinner, I spent the rest of the night with Jamel and his family.

While family wasn't something I liked to be around, it was different with his wonderful, fun, and open family. I quickly grew to love all of them. Jamel's Dad, Major Wendel Jones, was a no-nonsense guy and saw the world in terms of black and white, not unlike my father. The Major never abbreviated names; Jamel was always Jamel, never Mel. He was also not a big talker, and

Chapter 8

he demanded respect, obedience, and compliance from his boys at all times, regardless of how old they were. I easily fell in line, addressed him as "Sir" at all times, knew when to shut up when he spoke, and was mindful of how much I cursed when he was around.

Despite his sternness, the Major was very open and accepting of his son being gay. He told me, "Being black is hard enough. Being gay is hard enough. But to be black and gay in this country was going to be a life full of pain and hardship. I wanted Jamel to know he could always come home for acceptance and refuge." He wasn't warm and fuzzy, but I desperately wished he was my dad.

In contrast, Jamel's mother, Denita, was the warmest person alive. She had the same gray eyes as Jamel and Tyrell and a heavy southern accent, like Sammie. She was ten years younger than her husband and was his complete opposite. He was dark-skinned color; she was light-skinned. He was tall; she was very short. He was quiet and reserved; she was loud and made jokes all the time, even inappropriate ones about sex that made her sons blush. Surprisingly, the Major never scolded her for it, at least not in front of their children. The Major didn't show any affection; she showed her kids nothing but affection. She said "I love you" in the middle of conversations and gave her sons random hugs. It was always funny to see those hugs because she wasn't any bigger than 5'2, and her sons were at least 5'10. Denita would hug midsections or wait until her sons were sitting before giving them neck hugs out of nowhere.

She was also the first person to make a joke about my race. The third time I had dinner with the whole family, the week after Thanksgiving, she asked us, "So y'all together now? For real?"

I looked at him for an answer, and he simply said, "Yes, ma'am."

And she said, "Hmph. I always knew at least one of my sons was going to bring home a whitey. And you're just about the whitest whitey I've ever seen." She burst out in loud laughter, making everyone, including the Major, laugh. After that, I started receiving Mama Denita's random hugs too.

I also got along with all of Jamel's brothers. Even Ty and I grew into a cordial relationship, although not exactly an outright friendship. During the holidays, I met Jamel's brother Donell who was part of Phi Beta Sigma and took his fraternity very seriously. We smoked pot and talked about white privilege and black consciousness, two things I had never really thought about. But Donny impressed on me that I needed to if I was serious about being in a relationship with a proud, gay, black man. He showed me how I had been using my privilege to protect Afia all along.

I met Lavell at the first dinner I had with the family. He was, indeed, a nerd, or a Blerd as his brothers called him. We bonded over Marvel comic books. Lavell had hundreds of them, including many first editions. I found myself hanging out in this 17-year-old's room a lot, because teenagers are awesome.

Three of the brothers had nicknames, Ty, Mel, and Donny, but Lavell was just Lavell, just like his father. Lavell made it very clear that he would not "Barry"

Chapter 8

up his name like President Obama, who was his idol, did in his early years. Lavell was going to MIT to study Engineering. He planned to lead the global community on climate change, and I had no doubt he would be the one to do it.

Even though Lavell didn't like politics as a career path, he was very much into debating politics. The whole family was, and no one had qualms about letting their opinions be known. It was a complete change from my house, where the only opinion was my father's, and there was no deviating from that. But the Jones family would argue about everything. Music, movies, shows, politics, race, religion, sex, gender, and relationships. You name it, they argued about it, loudly and lovingly. The Major, who was not a loud person in general, and Jamel, who was very much like his dad, would join in at a much quieter tone too, but just as passionately. But I loved the loudness and grew to love the screaming matches over the dinner table. I even joined in on a few myself.

The best part was seeing Afia all the time. She and Ty were inseparable. We hadn't double-dated since the last attempt ended in disaster. But we would still meet up for family dinners and events. If either Afia or I were going over to the Jones residence, we would ride together. I would be downstairs with Mel, and she'd be upstairs with Ty. Or one of us would get there and find that the other was already there. I got used to seeing Ty and Afia together and loved how happy he made her, how he treated her and took care of her, like the amazing woman that she is. He was her perfect match.

I also introduced Jamel to my tribe, my crew, my family. He came to one of our Wednesday tribe meetings, and Winter and Mina held no punches when asking him why he waited so long to mount me and other questions: Did Jamel understand who I was? Had he accepted all of me? Would he run at the first sign of trouble? He held his own with them, and I was impressed. But he didn't stay long because Winter and Mina told him he had to leave so we could talk shit about him and compliment the size of his dick. I fell in love with his family, and he grew to love mine as well.

Jamel and I still went out on dates at least twice a week and did all our favorite things, but our quality time now included sensual and mind-blowing sex. Maybe it was mind blowing because I actually cared about him and he cared about me, so we spent time wanting to please each other to the max, but regardless, the sex was amazing. We were versatile, but I was happily a bottom for him more often because I could not get enough of his cock. The way it felt when he was inside of me was ecstasy. I had never felt that way with any partner before, not even Vinnie, who I also cared about deeply. It was not always making love, though. Sometimes we'd be roughhousing and cumming all on each other's faces and bodies and licking each other up. That was amazing too. No matter how we fucked, we always had an epic time doing it.

Although every time we had epic sex, my favorite parts were the kissing before and the snuggling after. That surprised the shit out of me more than anything else about our relationship. Being in his arms made every wrong in the world right, and I longed to be

Chapter 8

in them all the time. We never said it, but we didn't need to. We knew that we were falling in love with each other.

♥

After Christmas dinner and spending time with Matty's kids, I casually left my house and drove over to Providence to see Jamel. I didn't tell him I was coming. We had exchanged presents the night before, so I knew he wouldn't be expecting me. I just showed up and rang the upstairs doorbell because that was where I assumed he would be.

Mama Denita answered the door. I started to say, "Merry Chri—" when she squealed, "You're here!" She pulled me into a huge hug. Then she half dragged me up the stairs yelling, "Jamel! Look who's here!"

She pulled me through a door off the kitchen that I had never been to. Jamel and his father were sitting in his father's office nursing drinks, and both looked at me when we came through the door. He had a look on his face like he wanted to smile but didn't. The Major, by contrast, looked amused at my arrival.

"Merry Christmas, Major Jones. Jamel," I greeted. His father raised his glass in acknowledgment.

Mel stood up and walked over to me. "Hey."

"Hey."

He stopped short of hugging me but then leaned in and kissed my cheek. "I didn't think I would see you today."

"I didn't think so either," I told him. "But I ... just wanted to stop by ... and see you." We were perfectly aware that his parents were listening.

He nodded. "Well, you can always do that, anytime day or night."

I nodded, then I started smiling, making him smile. I cleared my throat. "So, where is everyone?"

"Ty is with Afia, naturally."

"Naturally."

"Yeah, he left maybe an hour or so ago to go to her parent's house. Donny went to a frat party, and Lavell is upstairs Skyping with his pen pal friend in Cambodia. Yeah, don't ask."

I laughed. "Okay." I looked around and said, "Well, if you're busy—"

But the Major answered for him, "We're done here. Go entertain your friend, Jamel."

The Major stood up and pretty much shooed us out of his office. He went to the living room with his wife, and Jamel led me back out the main door and downstairs to his apartment. As soon as his door closed, Jamel turned, pulled me toward him, and put his lips on mine. I reached up to his neck with one hand and gently bit his top lip.

"Merry Christmas," he said. "This is a nice surprise. Everything okay?"

"Yeah, I just—" I wanted to tell him that I missed the shit out of him since the last time I saw him 24 hours ago, but as usual, I swallowed how I really felt. So I repeated, "I just wanted to stop by."

But I was getting attached, and he knew it. I hated being vulnerable, but I promised myself I wouldn't hold

❤ ❤ ❤ Chapter 8 ❤ ❤ ❤

back. I would act on how I felt and trust Jamel has me in his hands. As usual, Mel didn't hesitate to put my vulnerability at ease. He smiled at me, took my hand, and led me to his room.

He sat me on the bed, then walked over to the Bluetooth player and put on jazz music. He bent down to take off my sneakers, then stood up to turn off the light. He moved behind me to get on the bed and pulled me playfully backward into him. I giggled, sighed, and closed my eyes as I melted into his arms. We laid that way silently, listening to the music play softly in the background, his arm draped over me, his fingers entwined with mine on my chest, his breath in my hair. We were so close we could have been one person.

He broke the silence. "What do you want to do for New Year's Eve?"

I smiled. "This."

Even though my back was turned, I knew he was smiling too. "Okay, baby," he said softly.

It was the first time he called me baby. It was goofy and corny, and I loved it. But I didn't tell him. I just chuckled.

"Everything okay with you and your dad?" I asked.

"Yeah. We were talking about the business and his health. He'll be sixty next year, and I just want him to slow down a little bit. He already has one heart attack under him. But he won't slow down. Not until I'm ready to take the business over from him, is what he said. But I got my own business, and I'm waiting for Ty to get his plumbing license. So us taking over the company won't happen for another five years, at least. In the meantime, I'm going to join in on more contracting jobs with him, be his foreman, take some of the stress off him." I nodded my head in understanding.

Then he said, "He also asked me about you. You and I."

"Yeah? What did you tell him?"

"I told him that we're together. It's good. And it's serious."

I smiled and pushed myself closer into him as if that was possible. "And what did he say?"

"He said that I seem happy with you. I told him I am. He said okay."

I nodded. Then I said, "I am happy too. With you."

He kissed the back of my head. "Stay the night."

I smiled again. *Look who's attached now?* "Okay, baby," I responded.

I fell asleep in his arms, fully clothed. We didn't make love in the morning either, we just jerked each other until we came together.

On New Year's Eve, I again went over to his house, and we spent the night making love in his bedroom while the year changed. The next day, we didn't leave the apartment. We slept in, made breakfast, and got right back into bed.

We decided to find a movie to watch when I told him, "I don't watch war movies."

He said simply, "Okay." I love how I didn't even have to explain. Another military guy just gets it.

"I still do but not as much as I used to," he said. "But I did watch Inglorious Bastards because shit, Tarantino."

Chapter 8

I chuckled. "True, but even that I didn't watch."

"2012?" he offered.

"I saw it," I told him. "Avatar?"

"I saw it," he said, and I laughed. "Harry Potter?"

"Is that a joke?"

"No, actually. You never read the books?" he asked seriously.

"Um … noooo. Why the fuck would I read a kid's book?" I said and giggled.

Jamel shook his head in feigned disappointment. He went into the living room to his mini-shelf and returned with the first book of the series. "I'm about to change your life, Corporal, sir. Take care of it. And you don't get the second book until you return this one." He was so serious that he made me laugh again but I stuck the book in my bag.

We went back to find a movie to watch and settled on *Law Abiding Citizen*. Halfway through the movie, I thought about Jamel watching war movies. It's on the VVB questionnaire, and I was curious about his response.

"What's the last war movie you watched, and how did it affect you?" I asked him with my head on his shoulder.

He chuckled softly, knowing he had answered that question already. "*Miracle at St. Anna*," he told me. "And it gave me a lot of feelings, but in the end, it made me proud to be an African American soldier."

"Never heard of it. What's it about?" I asked curiously.

"Four black soldiers in an Italian village during World War II."

"That sounds interesting."

"You?" He turned the question around to me.

"*The Patriot.*"

He nodded. "It's a good one. One of my favs."

"What's your all-time favorite one that you can go back to?"

"*Glory*, probably."

"That movie is amazing," I agreed.

"Yeah, it is. But in front of my dad, I have to say *Platoon.*"

I laughed out loud. "Fuck, what is with military dads and that movie? My dad had me watching that shit at like age five."

He laughed and said, "Same." He was quiet for a moment, then said, "We can watch it together if you want."

"*Platoon?*" I asked incredulously.

"Fuck no!" He laughed. "*Miracle at St. Anna*. But only if it doesn't give you flashbacks or nightmares."

"It won't. I just haven't watched any war movies since I came home. No point in that. I got enough memories of the horrors of war. I don't need it glorified on the big screen."

"Was it all bad?" He kissed my head.

I played with his chest hair as I answered. "No. Not all bad. We did some good. Protected civilians."

"Same," he said. "We built schools and mosques. Built plumbing and electrical systems. If we made a difference in just one person, one family's life, then I'm okay with my part in it."

"Same," I said softly. "I don't know if it's a flashback, but I get stuck in a particularly bad memory

Chapter 8

sometimes. I typically can pull myself out of it. And I don't have nightmares. Dreams. But not nightmares. I spent the first couple of months dreaming of Vinnie every night. Like his ghost was haunting me. But it was comforting too, like he was still out there. Watching over me…." I trailed off. *I just keep spilling my guts bare to this man.*

"I get nightmares," he confessed as he rubbed my arm. I could tell that made him vulnerable to tell me that. He did that for me.

"What about?" I asked, still rubbing on his chest hair gently. I kissed the skin on him that was closest to my mouth. I wanted to make sure he felt as safe being open with me as I felt with him.

He hesitated, then said, "It … doesn't matter."

"It matters to me," I said softly.

He kissed my head again. "Different things. People I couldn't save mostly. I have a savior complex." He chuckled.

"Well, I must be a whole savior project for you," I joked.

"You're not my project," he said as he kissed my head a third time. "You're kind of saving me right now. Saving me from myself. From my loneliness…." He was quiet for a moment. Then said, "Anyway, I don't have them too often. Maybe once or twice a year. When I do, I write it down, my feelings, my guilt, my apologies. Then I burn it, and let it go. It's how I cope."

Wow. He is so emotionally mature, and here I've been, running from every feeling I've ever had other than feeling horny. I asked him, "If I'm lying next to you and you have a nightmare, do you want me to wake you?"

"Nooo," he said seriously. "Don't wake me. Just… I'll settle myself. After the tears fall."

He got quiet again. I moved from his shoulder to lay my head across his chest and stretched my arm over him.

"Okay, baby," I said softly. We continued to watch the movie in silence, but I knew he was reflecting on what he had just revealed and so was I.

"Hey, I'm going to Florida in April to see my cousins. Do you want to come with me?" he asked.

"Yes," I said automatically. *Anywhere he goes is where I want to be.*

After the holidays, I started spending full weekends at Mel's apartment from Friday after work to Sunday when I had to make my appearance for Sunday dinner. Even if I had to work on a Saturday, I would just go right back to Mel's place. Mel didn't spend the night at my apartment, but during the week, if we were both free, he would come over and hang out after work, and we'd cook together. Everyone assumed he was a military buddy I had met through Afia, and that we were just good friends. So him coming to my house in the afternoon and leaving later was not suspicious at all. But when he was there, we knew to keep sex to a minimum. We got so loud the first time, our sounds echoed outside my apartment toward the main house. He got a kick out of what my dad had said to me.

He was changing me. I felt it every day. I stopped smoking, which made Afia happy. It was a habit I picked up being with Vinnie. Jamel worked out three days a week, and I started exercising with him on the nights I

❤❤❤ Chapter 8 ❤❤❤

didn't work. We both appreciated the increased definition in my pecs. It felt good just being with one person consistently, happily. Unlike in the past, I wasn't bored, and I didn't want someone else. All I wanted was him. He was becoming my best friend, my lover, my everything. He was becoming what he said he would be, everything I want, need, and deserve.

❤

"Last order up for business: Our annual retreat," I said to my unit at our March 1st meeting.

"We're coming to you, right?" Sammie asked. She was completely bald. Taylor kept asking her if she had cancer before I told him officially to shut the fuck up.

"Yeah, it's fine, but I can't do it Labor Day weekend," I said. "One of my friends is getting married."

"Oh is it Afia? Is she marrying Ty?" Sammie asked excitedly.

"No, it's probably Jack and Ethan," said Joe.

Taylor said, "Yeah, Afia and Ty aren't ready for that yet."

"If it's Jack and Ethan, I hope Mina brings Sam to the wedding," said Benj.

Sammie agreed, "Yeah, they need to just make it official already."

Why the fuck do they know so much about my friends and their lives?

"Yeah, it's Jack and Ethan," I told them. "And they only invited a few people to the actual wedding. I was one of the honored guests. Let's move the retreat to August instead."

Sammie, Joe, and Taylor said okay, but Benj said, "Actually… I don't think I will be able to travel in August. I'll be on paternity leave starting in July."

"Paternity! Oh my God, Benj. Congratulations!" Sammie squealed. Even though it wasn't her normal squeal, her voice didn't reach high octaves anymore.

"Yeah, Benjin!? Is that how you tell us? Fucking congratulations, man!" Taylor yelled at him.

"Wow, yeah, congrats, Ben! I know how exciting this is for you," Joe said.

"Wait a fucking minute. July? Leslie has been pregnant this whole time, and you're just saying something now!?" Sammie yelled at him.

"You know why I wanted to wait," said Benj. "We just needed to make sure, you know?"

Yeah, we all knew. Benj and his wife had been trying to have a second child since he got back home. She had miscarriages within the first couple of weeks of two pregnancies. I was the only one who knew she was pregnant again because Benj had a call back in December from a vet whose wife was going through fertility treatments and had a miscarriage in the first trimester. The vet was trying to be strong for his wife but broke down on the phone with Benjin. Always the counselor, Benj walked him through the grief and loss and gave him some resources, then Benj then called me and broke down on the phone about how terrified he was about losing this one.

"It's all good, Benj. Congratulations, and send our congrats to Leslie as well," I said.

Joe had an idea. "Why don't we just go to you this year instead? That way you don't have to go anywhere.

Chapter 8

We can get hotel rooms in Dearborn, and you come out when you can."

"No, we can't do that," I said. "Benj is going to want that time with his family."

"Actually, that's not a bad idea," said Benj. "I would love it if you came to me instead. Meet Leslie and Abbie finally and this new baby girl that's coming."

"Yes!" Sammie said. "Let's do it."

"Alright, Benjin," I agreed. "I'll give my notes for the working day, and you plan the activities." I had bought a five-hour seminar on Motivational Interviewing, and we planned to do a whole day session on it to become better at counseling vets.

"Something on the Great Lakes," said Joe. "I've always wanted to go there."

"You got it, Joe," Benj said.

"Are you taking Jamel to the wedding, Connor?" Sammie asked.

"The wedding is invite only, no plus ones, so I'm going with Afia because she got the invite too," I said.

Taylor scoffed. "I just love how you're assuming Jamel is going to be around in September, Sammie. I'm still not convinced our boy here is actually going to keep this one around for that long," he said smugly.

"Shut the fuck up, Taylor," I said, annoyed.

"So you haven't cheated on him yet?" Taylor asked with his eyebrow raised.

"No, and fuck you."

"No, you haven't, or no not yet?" He laughed.

"I'm not going to fucking cheat on him. Shut the fuck up!" I snapped.

"Okay, okay. I'm just trying to see how serious you are. No need to get all testy." He smiled, and I gave him an icy glare.

Joe warned him, "The Corporal is about to put his foot through the computer and up your ass Taylor, so I think you really should shut the fuck up now."

Taylor threw his hands up in surrender. "Alright, I'm going to shut up now." He leaned back in his chair, still smiling like he knew something we all didn't.

It was quiet for a moment, then Sammie yelled, "Why do you have to be such a DICK all the time, Taylor!?"

I couldn't help but smile, and everyone chuckled. She sounded just like Vinnie.

Later that night, I thought about what Taylor had said. He was not completely wrong in thinking I wouldn't be faithful or want to stay with Jamel. My track record speaks for itself. Even though I have strong feelings for him, it is always in my head that I might wake up one day and not want to be with him anymore. Or more realistically, I will randomly meet someone else and want to fuck them instead. It has happened to me like that, especially when I feel like the other is getting too attached to me. That's why it was so easy to let go of Lex, I knew he had way more feelings for me than I did for him, and I didn't want that.

But it feels different with Jamel. It feels like he is who I'm supposed to be with. I want to be close to him and I want him to get closer to me. I know he will be around in September. I know we're going to spend every holiday this year together. I can't explain it, but I just see Jamel as a

♥♥♥ CHAPTER 8 ♥♥♥

fixture in my life, for the rest of my life. But I can't speak for him. Maybe one day, he will wake up and realize he doesn't want to be with me anymore.

My anxiety began to overwhelm me as I thought about all the men and women I had ghosted. The ones I ignored, hurt, or left behind who had strong feelings for me. Maybe this was the universe giving me karma, making me fall for someone only to have him leave me eventually. It was after 2am on a Tuesday, and I needed reassurance. I texted Jamel.

[Connor: You up?]

[Jamel: I wasn't but I am now. What's up?]

[Connor: Nothing. Just couldn't sleep.]

[Jamel: What are you thinking about?]

[Connor: You. Us.]

[Jamel: Yeah? What about me? Us?]

[Connor: We've just gotten really close in such a short period of time. And I'm okay with that. I just hope you're still okay with that too.]

A couple of seconds passed, and my heart clenched while I waited for his response. My phone rang in my hand instead. "Hey, Mel," I answered.

"Connor." His deep voice was husky and urgent. He paused then began to ask, "Are you having second tho—"

"No!" I cut him off. "I just wanted to make sure you weren't … that you still… still wanted this… me … I guess." I hated feeling that vulnerable.

"I still want this," he said. "But if you don't… I need you to tell me. If you aren't sure anymore…" He sighed. "I can handle honesty. I can't handle ambivalence." I heard the nervousness in his voice, nervous that I was starting this conversation to end our relationship. Somehow that made me feel better.

"I want this. I want us," I said confidently. "I'm not ambivalent. I just wanted to make sure *you* weren't ambivalent. Because that would really suck for me."

"No. I'm not. I still want to be with you every single day. I've gone from someone who rarely spends time with people outside my family to someone who wants to spend all my time with you, waking or sleeping. I don't see that changing any time soon. What about you?"

"Fuck, Jamel. I'm planning all our holidays for the rest of the year in my head."

He laughed his deep throaty laugh. "Well, I know what we're doing at the end of April. So what are we doing in May for Memorial Day?"

"Flight 93 National Memorial. I'm driving," I said automatically, and he laughed again.

"Fourth of July?"

"Jetties Beach, Nantucket."

"Columbus Day?"

"C'mon. We don't celebrate the beginning of the murder of Indigenous Americans." I scoffed.

Chapter 8

He laughed again. "Veteran's Day?"

"We put on our suits, go to the parade, and walk around town getting thanked for our service."

"Wow, you really do that? For what, an ego boost?"

I hesitated, then was honest. "Ah... Actually, it was more of me trolling for dick. People love a man in uniform, especially gay men." He laughed really loud, and that made me laugh.

"So you want me to cruise with you?" he asked amusingly.

"No, I just want you to be right by my side."

"Hmmm..." was his only response. Then he asked, "New Year's Eve?"

"Same thing we did last New Year's Eve and New Year's Day. Two of the best days of my life."

"Yeah, same." He was quiet for a moment, then he said, "I'm good with all these plans, Connor. I want to do all these things with you this year. But I get to plan next year. Deal?"

I smiled widely at that. "Deal," I said softly.

"Do you feel better about us? A little less scared shitless?" he asked. He knew. He figured out this conversation was more for my reassurance than about him.

I chuckled. "Yeah, Mel, a lot less. Thanks. And sorry for waking you up."

"Don't be. I'm here for you, day or night. I'm always going to be here for you," he said.

I smiled at that because I believed him. "Yeah. Same."

CHAPTER 9

I GET YOU BETTER NOW.

~~~Spring 2010~~~

Jamel and I took a few days off and drove to Miami for a long weekend in April. He has two female cousins from his mother's side of the family that share a condo down there, and he tries to see them at least once a year. When he asked me to join him on New Year's Eve I happily agreed. His method of travel is typically flying but I suggested we drive down instead. We looked it up and it was a twenty-two hour drive at least. North Carolina was about halfway down, so I suggested I drive for the first eleven hours, then we could spend the night around Wilmington. He would drive the next eleven hours, and we would stop every six hours or so for food, gas, and stretch. He happily agreed. Quality Time? Check.

We left Tuesday mid-morning and took my car. It was newer and had less than forty thousand miles

Chapter 9

on it. We started by listening to my iTunes, and he didn't seem to mind a little Blink 182 and Fall Out Boy mixed in with Nelly and Destiny's Child. Jamel took off his sandals, leaned the seat back, put his foot on the dashboard, and started reading on his Amazon Kindle. I kept glancing at his feet. Even the man's feet were beautiful. Long, brown on top, peach-colored and smooth on the bottom. Toes perfectly shaped. Nails perfectly trimmed. I'd never sucked anyone's toes before, but he made me want to. Jamel made me want to do a lot of things.

About forty minutes into the ride, I asked him, "What are you reading?"

"James Patterson's *I, Alex Cross*," he said without looking up.

"Wow, they're still making Alex Cross books? I used to read them when I was a kid."

"Same. I collected them as soon as they hit the stores. This just came out in November, and I haven't gotten a chance to read it yet."

"Yeah, why is that? I used to finish them in less than a week."

He finally looked at me and smiled. "Other things seem to be occupying all my free time." I smiled and nodded. "What books are you into right now?"

"You're going to laugh if I tell you," I said sheepishly.

"What? *Twilight*?" he asked amusingly.

I laughed. "NO! Not yet anyway." We both laughed. "So, what are you reading?"

"You probably never heard of it. *Catching Fire*. From *The Hunger Games* series."

"Nope. Never heard of it. Sounds interesting from the name. What's it about?" He turned his tablet off and turned to me.

"Oh, I didn't mean to stop you. You can go back to reading."

"I don't want to. I want to hear what interests you," he said sincerely. I glanced at him as he watched me. *I guess that's what this trip was about, right? Getting to know each other a little deeper.*

"Okay. Well, it's a dystopian novel. You know what that is, right?" He smiled sarcastically. "Yeah, okay, right. Well, it's a society that sends kids to this tournament called The Hunger Games to fight till the death until one survives, the Victor. It's so fucked up, like who wants to send their kids to die while the rest of the country starves? But you know, one day they picked the wrong kid, and her sister, Katniss, enters in her place and wins by defying the rules. Now their entire system is going to shit as people are rebelling against the government because they realize they can. It's also a love story, but I don't know if she ends up with Peeta or Gale. I hope it's Peeta, but it probably will be Gale."

"Soooo, *Twilight* without the vamps and wolves?" he asked with a smile.

"Shut up," I said, and he chuckled.

"I thought you don't read kid books?"

"It's not a kid book. It's Young Adult Fiction," I said seriously.

He laughed. "Yeah, okay."

"Shut uuuuup!" I whined, and he laughed again. "I know it's not as serious as Alex Cross."

♥♥♥ Chapter 9 ♥♥♥

"Actually, it sounds pretty good." He turned back on his Kindle and said, "I'm ordering it now. *Catching Fire?*"

"No, the first book is called *The Hunger Games*. *Catching Fire* is the second. I'm about halfway through it."

"Cool." He finished and turned to me again. "I like dystopian novels. The first book I ever really read was called *The Giver*."

My mouth dropped in shock. "Fuck, Mel! That's like my favorite book ever!"

He laughed. "Of course it is."

"I'm not kidding!" I practically yelled at him. "I almost lost my mind when Lovie sent me the next two books when I was in the Marines. I needed to know what the fuck happened to Jonas!"

He laughed. "I actually haven't read them so don't spoil it for me. I thought Jonas died."

"Aaaahhh!!" I yelled again and briefly put both hands on my head before grabbing the wheel again. "Don't ask me any questions if you don't want me to ruin it!"

He laughed again. "Okay, I won't. But *The Giver*, yeah, I feel like that book got me into reading. It was just fascinating to me that you had this world where everything was perfect, and no one saw color. But in actuality, it was pretty fucked up."

I shook my head but in agreement. "And it's like, once your eyes are open, you can't go back. Poor Jonas. Everyone thought he had this perfect life, but all he's doing is keeping secrets, even from those he loves. Secrets about what he's really doing with The Receiver, secrets about what's going on in his home, secretly hiding his feelings from everyone. It fucking sucks!"

I glanced over to see Jamel watching me intently, and I realized I was revealing a bit too much about myself.

"I always thought Jonas was pretty fucking brave and strong to survive all that," he said. I didn't say anything, and we were quiet for a moment. Then he said, "I'm also reading *Joker*. Since you like dystopia."

I love how he knows when to change the subject and not push too hard. He reads me so well. "What's that about?" I asked.

"It's an adult graphic novel about Batman's *The Joker*. It gets crazy."

"Like, *The Walking Dead* crazy?" Lavell introduced me to the graphic novel last year, and I'd been getting into them.

He laughed. "No Walkers. But death and mayhem, yes. Oh, I heard they are making the comics into a show. Let's watch that together when it comes out."

"They better not fuck up Rick Grimes, man," I said seriously. "I'll be pissed."

He laughed out loud. "Agreed."

We stopped in Maryland to get food and gas and to stretch. As soon as we crossed the Chesapeake Bay into Virginia, Jamel said, "Slow down. Obey the speed limit."

I scoffed at him. "Okay, *Dad*," I laughed. He didn't. "What?"

"Nothing. Just slow down. I don't want us to get stopped by the police."

♥♥♥ Chapter 9 ♥♥♥

"I have my veteran's card on me, and so do you. We'll be fine," I told him. He glanced at me through the corners of his eyes but didn't say anything. "*What?*"

"Can you just do me this favor and stay to the speed limit?" he asked quietly.

"Okay," I said. I thought he was annoyed with me, but he reached over, squeezed my thigh, and left his hand there.

We quietly listened to music for a while until Jamel broke the silence. "Tell me about Jack," he said out of the blue.

I looked at him, surprised. "Jack? Jack Frazier? My Jack?"

He chuckled. "I don't know a guy named Jack."

"Oh," I said, wondering where this was going. "What do you want to know?"

"Whatever you want to tell me about him." I didn't respond right away. He said, "You and Afia mention him a lot, and I know he's one of your best friends. And an ex." He gave me a knowing look.

It was my turn to chuckle. "We were kids." I sighed, then stayed silent for a long moment.

"Okay," he said, nonchalantly. He reclined the passenger seat and closed his eyes.

I smiled at him then started talking. He knew I would. "I found myself attracted to Jack even in middle school, but of course, I had no idea what it was about him that made me feel how I felt. I would see him in passing, but we never crossed paths until high school. When you meet him, you'll see. He's fucking gorgeous. Gorgeous jet-black hair, beautiful green eyes, perfect dimpled smile. He was gorgeous as a boy, and now he has this perfect manly, toned body to go with it. Not that I'm checking him out or anything."

I glanced at Jamel, who was watching me and smiling. "Right," he said sarcastically.

I laughed and continued talking. "Jack started at Rockville High the year behind me. He was quiet and kinda nerdy, so people thought he was soft. But when a varsity baseball player, Adam, tried to bully him in the lunchroom a month into the school year, he got on the table and slammed his metal tray into Adam's face and gave him a bloody nose. It was the best fucking thing I've ever seen. Nobody fucked with Jack after that."

Jamel laughed. "I like Jack already."

I laughed as well. "Jack is still kinda like that, principled and hot-tempered. It takes a lot to bring him there now, but when he snaps, he flips the fuck out. Anyway, by then, I knew I was attracted to him. He didn't have a lot of friends, but he hung out with this black girl in the library all the time. I never knew her name until that day on the field. Afia. Afia and I became friends, and Jack and I became cordial. But I was a jock, and I could tell he was wary of jocks. So I spent sophomore year watching him from afar or being close to him with Afia between us."

"So, did you save Afia that day on the field because you wanted to get closer to Jack?" Mel asked.

"Hmmm...You know, I never thought of it that way. It was more like, hey, that's Jack's friend, and I didn't want something bad to happen to Jack's friend. And I really did hate that bitch Olivia, so it was a no-brainer. But Afia is right. When I walked her home, we found out that we had a lot of things in common: Favorite

Chapter 9

movies, how much we loved the X-Men cartoon, we even made the same corny jokes. We sang Alanis Morrisette and Biggie Smalls songs almost the whole way. We knew all the lyrics. I had never hung out with any person of color before that, and I went home that day thinking she was the coolest chick ever. My dad used to say to us, nothing good comes from being with a colored. He literally still says the word colored like we're in the fucking 1950s. But after hanging out with Lovie, I thought, 'Shit, ain't nothing wrong with black people. My dad is just being a fucking dickhead about this, like everything else in his life.'"

Jamel chuckled. "I like Alanis Morrisette," he said.

I rolled my eyes. "Of course you do, Mel. You're the male version of my Lovie. I'm sure you like Notorious B.I.G. too."

"Why? Because I'm black?" he asked seriously.

My eyes went wide, and I started stuttering, "N— no... I was ... just... just sayin—"

"I'm fucking with you, baby. Of course, I like Biggie. I'm black!" He started laughing loudly as I shook my head.

"Asshole," I muttered with a smile.

He laughed and said, "Finish telling me about you and Jack."

I continued, "So the next summer Jack was hanging out with Sam's 17-year-old cousin from Europe, a biracial kid who was gay or bi, I think. By extension, he was hanging out with us without Afia: me, Sam, Rick, and Liam, the jocks. I knew from the way Jack looked at Sam's cousin. God, what was his name? Anyway, I knew that he was into him. But that wasn't confirmed until after the kid left. Jack came out to us right before the school year started. To this day, I still think it was the bravest thing I have ever seen. Jack has always been and will always be fearless."

"How'd he do it?"

"We were on his family's apple farm and started a firepit at night. We sat around talking about how we were all growing up and changing and that we weren't kids anymore. Henrietta, Brayden, and BJ were heading back to their colleges. Me, Mina, and Sam were going into our junior year, and Liam, Stacy, Afia, and Jack were going to be sophomores. Jack just came out with it. He said, 'I'm just glad I finally figured out who I am. I know I'm gay now, and I'm okay with it. I just hope you all are too.'

"We all just looked at him like, What the fuck? Stacy burst into tears and ran away. She had a major crush on him and thought he would eventually notice her, and now she knew he never would. BJ flipped out a bit, saying that Frenchie—that's what I called their cousin—Frenchie turned him out and into some kind of freak. But Jack was insistent that he had been attracted to boys for as long as he could remember. And that their cousin didn't do anything to him that he didn't specifically ask for or want. And he had no regrets about falling in love with a boy. I was fascinated. I asked him, 'So you're going to be kissing guys now?' He looked me in the eye and said, 'I'm only kissing the boys that want to kiss me.' Then he stared me down as if he knew."

Jamel laughed. "Uh-oh."

"Right? I don't know how the fuck he knew, but he knew. Probably all that time I was ogling him from

Chapter 9

afar, I wasn't as subtle as I thought. It scared the shit out of me. I laughed him off, told him, 'No guy in this town is going to kiss you. Better go after Frenchie.' I was an asshole." I shrugged and Jamel did not refute my assessment of my teenage self.

"But then school started, and I could only think of one thing: Jack. Jack is gay. Gorgeous Jack is into guys. Is Gorgeous Gay Jack into me? So, one day in the first week of school, I saw him walking home, and I ran up to walk with him. I asked him, 'So you're really gay?' He said yes. I asked, 'What's that like? Being gay? Having feelings for a boy?' He said, 'Same as having feelings for a girl. How do you feel when you're with Drea?' Andrea, my girlfriend at the time. I'm like, 'I don't know. I like her enough.' He laughed at me but didn't say anything else. I asked him, 'So what was it about Frenchie that you liked?' Oh, Chris! That was his name, because he corrected me right away. 'Chris,' he said. He said he liked Chris's hands more than anything else. Warm but strong and masculine. His arms. His biceps and triceps. Chris was a track star, so he had muscles. He liked Chris's collarbone and the way his Adam's apple moved when he talked. The shape of his pecs. The curve of his back muscles. That V shape at his groin."

"All the things you liked about boys too," Jamel said and winked at me. I smiled back and continued.

"I walked him home, and he told me all about his relationship with Chris and all the things they did together. Chris wouldn't break him in. He said Jack was too young, but he let Jack fuck him anytime he wanted to, which apparently was a lot. I had lost my virginity at like thirteen, so knowing that Jack wasn't a virgin either lit a fire in me. By the time we got to his porch, I knew I needed to kiss him, so I did. I just leaned over and put my lips on his. At first, he pulled away, shocked, but then he kissed me back. It excited and scared me how right it felt. Then I told him, 'I just wanted to see what that was like. I'm not a faggot.' He shoved me and told me that was my one and only pass, and that if I ever used that word around him again, he was going to punch me in the mouth. Then he went inside and slammed the door. Like I said, I was an asshole." I shrugged again.

"Sounds more like you were a confused kid," said Jamel.

"Maybe," I said quietly, thinking about that day. "The next day I went to his house, and his aunt let me in. I apologized to him and promised to never say that word again. We played video games for a while. Then I pounced and kissed him again, with tongue. This time, I knew to keep my mouth shut about how confused I was. So, that was our new routine. I would catch him in the bathroom or the locker room or an empty classroom and kiss him. I would walk him home a couple of times a week, when I didn't have baseball practice or something else going on. We'd go to his house and make out on his couch, groping each other. He never made a move first. It was always me pouncing on him."

"Like a lion catching his prey," Jamel said, and I laughed again.

"Then one day I was like fuck it. I told him to come to my house instead. Matty had moved out and married by that time, and the girls had dance class with mom, so I knew the house would be empty. We were

Chapter 9

making out on my bed, and I pushed his head down. He did not resist, almost like he was waiting for the go-ahead to take what we were doing a step further. He sucked me off, and it was the best blow job I had ever had up to that point. No girl had ever sucked me off like that. I returned the favor and as soon as he came in my mouth, the guilt and shame overwhelmed me. I said to him, 'I'm not gay. I just wanted this experience, and now it's over. Go home.' The look he gave me was heartbreaking. He left, and we ignored each other for weeks. See, still an asshole."

"I think," Jamel started, "You were a 16-year-old boy who was afraid of his feelings and afraid of his very homophobic father. That doesn't make you an asshole, Connor."

I was quiet for a moment. "Well, either way, him not talking to me was torture. I thought it was me ignoring him, but he avoided me like the plague. And if we were in the same space, he never looked at me, not once. To have those beautiful green eyes no longer see you, it cut me deep. I broke up with Drea, and I knew I had to get him back. A couple weeks later was Halloween, and they had a party at the farmhouse. I knew I would find a way to corner him. But he didn't come downstairs. Maybe he knew I was going to be there, or maybe he just didn't want to be bothered with anyone.

"Mina, Winter, and Stacy were guarding the stairs to keep guests out, but I convinced them to let me pass. I went to his room, and he was sitting on the bed with a big bowl full of popcorn, Doritos, and pretzels mixed together and a half-gallon of iced tea that he obviously stole from downstairs. He was watching the Halloween marathon. He looked at me, and my heart stopped. It was the first time he looked at me in weeks, and I missed him so much. We just stared at each other, then he said, 'If you're coming in, then come in and leave the door open.'"

I was getting lost in the memory of my first time with Jack, and Jamel let me. "So, I did. I took off my shoes and joined him on the bed. We barely spoke. We just watched Halloween II and ate junk food for the next hour. Then I couldn't help it. I kept watching his Adam's apple move and stared at his collarbone. I kissed him right there on his collarbone. He said, 'Stop.' I kissed his neck, and he said, 'Don't.' I turned his face to me to kiss him, and he allowed it for a minute or so. Then the kid said with tears in his eyes, 'You're not gay, right? This is just an experience. You're not really gay? Right?'

"So I got up, closed and locked the door, and showed him how gay I was."

"Wow," Jamel said. "Sounds like it was a good experience. Not everyone's first time is with someone they really care about. Now, who's one of the lucky ones?" He squeezed my leg, and I smiled at him again.

"I had three thoughts the whole time. One. I was definitely gay, at least bi. Two. My father is going to put a bullet in my head if he ever finds out. And three. Might as well die happy." I laughed out loud, and Jamel chuckled.

"We were together for a little over a year, until midway through my senior year. We broke up like five times in between. The only reason we never went

Chapter 9

anywhere is because I was scared to death of my father and couldn't come out the closet to be with him. When Jack finally caught on that he could never be with me publicly, he ended it with me and told me we would just be friends. He made sure we were still friends by calling me every day and hanging out once a week. Probably to make sure I didn't eat my father's gun over him breaking up with me, but still. Jack probably knows it even though I've never told him, but I fell in love with him hard."

"So, Jack was your first love, not Vinnie?"

I shrugged. "I guess he was."

"You and Jack never tried again? As adults?"

"Nah," I shook my head. "I needed his unhindered and consistent friendship more than anything else, and he knew it before I did. When we broke up, he made it clear we couldn't be together like that ever again, even if I came out. I graduated, turned eighteen in July, and entered the military, and we've been friends ever since. Although there *was* that one time when I came back after my first tour to take Afia to prom. Jack came with his boyfriend, some college guy in the same nursing program as Mina. I cornered Jack in the bathroom and kissed him like old times."

Jamel laughed out loud. "You really were a bit of a predator. You kind of still are."

I laughed. "Maybe a little. I just always knew how to go for what I want." I glanced over at him and smiled and nodded. "But I told him I would never do that again. When I came home, I only leaned on Jack and Afia about loving and losing Vinnie. I was grateful for his friendship that wasn't clouded by feelings. He was right."

"So, between Jack and Vinnie, you didn't have a relationship with anyone else?"

I shook my head slowly. "There was Jack, then Vinnie, then … everyone else."

Jamel's mouth opened slightly. "Ooooh. I get it now."

I looked at him. "Get what?"

He smiled at me. "You. I get you better now."

"What does that mean?"

He chuckled and squeezed my thigh again but didn't answer. Instead, he said, "I look forward to meeting him one day."

"You will. Actually, his birthday is Saturday, and he's turning twenty-five. I'm missing his annual birthday gathering at Red Rock to be here with you, so you should feel special," I said smugly.

"I do feel special, Connor. Thanks for suggesting the drive instead of flying. I have a feeling we are going to learn a lot about each other on this trip."

I put my hand on his thigh and left it there. "Next year, we'll go together. Promise."

He put his hand on top of mine and rubbed it. "It's a date."

It was already dark when we got to Carolina Beach in North Carolina. We were exhausted, so we crashed. Jamel woke me up when it was still dark and a bit chilly. We took two blankets out on the beach and spread one of them to sit on and watch the

Chapter 9

sunrise together. As usual, I was sitting between his legs, leaning back on his chest as I held the ends of the other blanket wrapped around us. At first, he wrapped his hands around me, across the belly. But then, as the first rays of light appeared, he reached down into my sweatpants and pulled my cock out. I slowly pulled my knees up and opened my legs a little wider.

He wordlessly stroked me, spitting on his hands for lube until my pre-cum became more than enough, then he jerked me faster. I saw colors in front of me as my eyes closed to slits and the sun rose before us. I could feel his hard dick on my back as he worked my member. I moaned liberally, the sound of the crashing waves drowning out my song. Soon, I began to feel my own internal waves. I didn't bother letting him know I was cumming. I just gasped and came all over his hands and my sweatpants. He moved his hand up through the blanket and put his fingers in my mouth to lick. Then he put his hand to his mouth and licked the rest.

I turned my head around to look at him. The sunlight reflected in his eyes made them look like the color of the Atlantic Ocean, and once again, I was drowning in them. We moved in simultaneously to kiss, our soft lips touching over and over again without tongue. I turned my whole body around, knelt in front of him, and kissed him with more passion, my tongue leading as I tasted his. I gave him the ends of the blanket and moved my head down to his groin, and he automatically closed the blanket around me. I pulled the top part of his sweatpants down and reached in to pull out his big black dick. It was already leaking, and I was hungry.

I worked him slow with my mouth, tongue, and lips, keeping my hands on his thighs for support. He never shaves down there, it's always soft and curly like his chest hair, and I love it. I relished having him in my mouth, filling it up like he fills up my other hole. I took him deeper and deeper until my lips hit his pubes, and I heard him moan. I pulled up to the head and deep-throated again. I continued to suck his dick until his balls tightened and his mushroom head swelled. I knew he was about to bust his load. I moved him up from my throat just a bit, ready for him.

He sighed out my name as he came in that way that drives me crazy, "Coooooonooooor." I let him fill my mouth and cheeks with his jizz.

I lifted my head and moved my face toward his. He was ready, he kissed me open-mouthed, and I deposited his cum on his tongue. He swallowed and tongued me slowly as I wrapped my arms around him. I pulled away because I couldn't find the words to express how happy I was. I knew elation was all over my face, and I wanted him to see it. He smiled at me widely, his joy reflected in his gray eyes. I wanted to tell him I loved him right then and there, but of course, I didn't. Instead, I turned sideways to sit fully on his lap, put my head on his shoulder, and put my arms around his neck. He wrapped his arms and the blanket around me, and we held each other for a while, the sun warming the sand around us.

♥

♥♥♥ CHAPTER 9 ♥♥♥

Jamel drove exactly the speed limit down to Miami, which I teased him about. If it was eighty, he did exactly eighty; If it was forty-five, he drove forty-five miles an hour. He put in his music playlist and started with Notorious B.I.G.'s "Hypnotize," making me laugh. Then he turned it down and said, "Wait, you don't sing the N word right?" He gave me a hard look.

I laughed out loud. "Noooo! Lovie put me in my place a long time ago. Plus, my dad says it enough for me to hate it. So, no. I don't ever use it, not even in a song." Of course, I didn't mention that my dad uses it in reference to Lovie, and that's really why I hated it so much. Jamel nodded, touched my face, smiled, then turned the volume back up.

After a couple of Biggie hits that we rapped together, I said, "Okay, give me one life-changing song for you."

"Hmmm... 'If I Ruled the World' by Nas. That whole album was life-changing for me as a teen. Everyone was into Jay-Z, but I was into Nas. He always spoke to me."

I was thoughtful. "Do I know that one?"

"I don't know Connor, do you?" he asked playfully.

He found it, and as soon as it started playing, I recognized it. It was one of Afia's favorite songs. Lovie would sing the Lauryn Hill part, but I never actually listened to it before. I watched Jamel sing silently and bob his head and it made me want to. I started listening to the lyrics and realized it was so like Mel with his so-called savior complex and black pride.

When the song ended, I told him, "It's perfect. It's so you."

He smiled, then asked, "What's yours?"

Instead of answering, I played it. As soon as the chords by "Somewhere I Belong" by Linkin Park came on, he smiled. "Oh, you know this one?" I playfully asked him.

"Not this song in particular. But everyone knows Linkin Park. They are universal. Especially since the mashup album *Collision Course*."

"I wish I had it."

"I have it. We'll play it next after this one. It's like, representative of us."

"Because I'm white?" I said seriously.

"Yes," he laughed. "You're white, and I'm black. We are like Chester and Jay-Z. Mashed up." He laughed again. I scoffed, then looked away from him, feigning annoyance. "Oh c'mon baby, you're not—"

"Shut the fuck up. I'll be your Chester, baby." I winked at him.

He laughed out loud. Then he said, "Hey, I'm missing the song. Start it over. I want to hear why this one is life-changing for you."

I smiled. He never missed a moment to show genuine interest in me. I started the song over, finding myself doing the same that he had done, closing my eyes, bobbing my head, and miming the lyrics to myself.

The song ended, and it was quiet for a moment. Then Jamel said, "Holy shit, Connor. You won."

I laughed. "I didn't know it was a competition."

"It wasn't. But if it was, you won. That was deep."

"Yours was deep too. Deep in a different way. It spoke to me about who you are, and how you see the world."

Chapter 9

"And you just told me a whole lot about you." He looked at me intently, then looked back at the road. "In a good way. Don't look so worried." I didn't realize I had a worried look on my face, so I tried to relax a bit.

He asked, "Okay, what's the song you have pumping on repeat right now?"

I laughed. "You're just going to think I'm some kinda sexaholic."

"I already think you're a sexaholic, so don't worry about that." He laughed, and I laughed with him. He asked, "What, Ginuwine's Pony?"

"No, but that was a hot song."

He laughed out loud, saying, "Maaaan, you were like ten years old when that song came out!"

"Twelve!" I yelled at him.

We continued in our fit of laughter, with tears rolling down our faces, as we sang the lyrics and started pony riding in our seats. We laughed so long I knew he had forgotten the question. So I said, "Okay, I'm going to play it for you but no judgment."

He raised his three fingers in the air and said, "Scouts honor."

I looked at him, surprised. "I was a boy scout. You were a boy scout?"

"C'mon. Have you met my dad? We were indoctrinated into service at age three," he said, and we both laughed again.

I played Kings of Leon's "Sex on Fire." He listened with a wide grin on his face.

When it was over, Jamel just nodded and said, "That was hot. And sexy. Like you." Then he reached over and squeezed my leg. I blushed.

"Your turn," I told him.

He kept one hand on the wheel and found his song, B.o.B's Airplanes. I loved it immediately, and I played it again.

♥

We stopped in Jacksonville to grab lunch and got back on the road. We quietly listened to his playlist, then I started the conversation. "So I feel like you know all about my past relationships, but I don't know about yours."

He smiled without looking at me. "What do you want to know?"

"Well, obviously I want to know about the white guy. I mean, was he as fine as me? I doubt it," I said, smirking.

He laughed a big laugh, looked at me, then back at the road. "Nicholas Fedella has dirty blond hair and blue eyes, so yes, like you but not quite. Nick is about six years older than me. He was my first experience. I met him through Henry. He and Henry were best friends from Atlanta, and Henry, who is black, liked to take an interest in the new black recruits, helping us navigate covert and overt racism in the military system. Nick was a nice, funny, and generous guy that everyone loved. When you talked about Vinnie, it reminded me of him. He just got along with everyone. Everyone loves Fedella, or Nicky is what we call him. He would allow people to set up hour-long sessions to call home from his room. We had our own little crew: Me, Henry, Will, and Nicky. Henry was straight, Will was obviously gay, but no one mentioned it, and I

Chapter 9

thought Nick was straight too. What I didn't know was that Nick also took an interest in the new recruits for a different reason."

I laughed. "Uh-oh."

"Yeah, I was really naive," he said, laughing with me. "Apparently, having them come into his room to talk to their loved ones was the way he cornered them. I was still in basic training, and he was getting deployed in a couple of days. One night, I had just finished talking to my mother. I turned around to leave, and he asked me flat out, 'Are you gay, Jamel?' I laughed and said, 'D.A.D.T.' He walked right on me and said, 'Good, don't tell,' and he kissed me and grabbed my dick at the same time. And let's just say he spent the next four days showing me the ropes until he deployed."

"Holy shit," I laughed. "You willingly entered the lion's den."

"I did. I had the tattoo, but I wasn't a lion then. I was like a lost sheep." We laughed at that. "But he taught me a lot about myself, my sexuality, and what I liked. Kind of like you, I had that "I'm definitely gay" realization afterward. I had never touched a woman, and it solidified what I already kind of knew. No woman could make me feel the way a man could. And that's when I told my mama. So, no regrets about my first time." I nodded in understanding. "I didn't mess around again until I completed my first tour and went home for a few weeks. That's when I met Theo." He sighed.

"First love?" I deduced.

"Yep. Theodore Ellis. I was 20-years-old and went to a gay bar in Providence for the first time. There were two black guys there: Him and me. He came and sat at my table saying, 'I guess this is where the Negroes sit.' He made me laugh. He bought the beers, and we started talking. He was twenty-three, a curator at one of the art galleries, and a sculpture artist with dreams of being in New York City. He was very interesting. Cultured. Worldly. He was always so sure of himself and what he wanted."

Jamel stopped talking for a moment and seemed lost in thought, or memory, just like I had been the day before. I said softly, "You don't have to talk about it if you don't want to."

"No, it's okay," he said. "We were just really close for a long time. Not just him and I, but our families were close too. Theo lived with my family for a while in the basement apartment, so when I came home for visits, that's where I would go. It was kind of set up.... for us."

"So, you were basically living together," I stated.

He nodded. "Yeah, we were. But with me being in the military, we didn't physically see each other often. Between the distance and moving from Libya to Afghanistan after 9/11, and with the imminent fear of my death all the time, it got to be too emotionally taxing for him. So when he got a job offer teaching Art History at a college in New York, he decided to take it. It wasn't what he wanted, but it was where he wanted to be. So ... we broke up."

"How long were you together?"

"Three years."

Wow. I didn't know what it felt like to be with one person for that long. Other than Afia, that is, and that

Chapter 9

didn't come close to what he had. I asked, "Do you still love him?"

He glanced at me. "Do you still love Vinnie?" I didn't answer. Instead, I looked down at my tattoo with Vinnie's initials, but I didn't rub it. Jamel said, "A part of me always will love him, but no, not in the same way I did. I'm grateful for what we had. It made me who I am today."

I liked his response because it fit both of us. "Do you keep in contact with him?" I asked.

He shook his head. "No, we both knew it would be hard to let go if we did. I haven't spoken to him or anyone in his family in six years, not since he broke up with me via Skype right before I deployed the third time. I haven't seen him in person in longer than six years."

"Damn. That must have really sucked."

"To say the least." He chuckled sarcastically. "I think Dante keeps in touch with him, but he'll never tell me. Theo and Ty were really close, so I wouldn't be surprised if Ty stays in touch with him too. But again, he'll never tell me. My dad always said he wasn't strong enough for me, and the Major is always right." Jamel was quiet after that.

"So, who was next?" I leaned back a little, interested to learn more about this man that I was becoming enamored with.

He looked at me, smiled widely, and then looked back at the road. "Nick."

"Holy shit! Back to the lion's den? You're a glutton for punishment." We both laughed. "How the fuck did that happen?" I asked.

"He was just there for me when I needed it. And I think I was the only thing that was real to him. At first, it was something to fill the void for the first few months, and then ... I still don't know until this day how it happened. We became best friends and lovers all in one. But Nicky was a free bird, so even though he loved me, his wandering dick was a little bit of an obstacle for us to really go anywhere." He laughed.

"Oh, you knew what you were getting yourself into," I chided him.

"I did," Mel admitted. "But Nick was comfortable and familiar, and we were both military guys, so the issues with my last relationship wouldn't be with this one. Anyway, after about a year and a half of us both sleeping with other people, I decided to end it and just be friends."

"Are you still friends?"

"Yep. I spoke to him last month. He just made Sergeant First Class. Nicky has a military career and will never leave the Army. Maybe you'll meet him one day. I haven't seen him in person since I left."

"So, should I be worried that you're best friends with someone you used to sleep with?" I winked at him.

He gave me a look. "I'm pretty sure you've slept with all of your best friends, male and female."

I laughed out loud. "Not ... *All*." But really, he wasn't wrong. If Sam or even Liam weren't completely straight, I would have slept with them in high school. He gave me a skeptical look again, and I laughed.

He continued, "So, after Nick and I ended it, I continued having other ... experiences, but nothing serious for a while until—"

Chapter 9

I cut him off and asked, "Did you fuck Dante?"

His eyes went wide. He laughed out loud, but he didn't look at me. "We ... fucked around once when we were really really high and drunk one night. We wanted to see what it was like. But it was really awkward in the morning, so we decided to never do it again. That was five years ago. How did you know?"

"I just guessed," I said. "Because I would have fucked Dante too if he was my best friend. And for the same reason, just to see what it was like. You're not as innocent as you want people to believe, Mel."

"I never said I was. I never once judged you for your choices. I've made similar choices in the past." This was true. He hadn't ever made me feel bad about my past slutty behavior. "I had a thing for Navy sailors for a while. Something about the way they smelled," he said, almost dreamily.

I nodded profusely. "Especially when they were all sweaty and riding top. I had a thing too, Seaman are sexy as shit," I agreed. He laughed a big laugh and winked at me. It was uncanny that we were even attracted to the same type of guys.

Jamel said, "Then the Major had his mini heart attack, and I decided to come home, even though I was close to making Staff Sergeant. It was more important to be home with my family."

"Hey, what does the Major say about me?" I asked curiously. "Am I strong enough for you?"

Jamel again smiled without looking at me and said, "The Major says that you're my perfect match."

I grinned with all my teeth. "I knew I loved that man." Jamel laughed out loud, reached over, and caressed my face before putting his hand back on the wheel. He had a look on his face I couldn't quite make out. "He said something else about me," I deduced. "What did he say?"

He did a show of pursing his lips together tightly, then said, "I'll tell you one day. Not today."

I groaned, and he laughed. "So, who was the next one you were serious about?" I asked.

"D'wayne Tucker. Dee was a guy that I met after I came home for good. We met in a grocery store parking lot of all places, trying to get into the same space. We had one date, slept together that first night, and he just never really went home after that. We were good together, but I always felt like something was missing, like he was unsure about me or about us settling down together. One day, I flat out asked him, and he admitted he didn't know if I was his forever. That he was seeing his ex on the side and was trying to weigh out the options. What was missing, I discovered, was his commitment to me. So, I took myself out of the equation."

"Wow. How long were you in a relationship before you found out?"

"About two years. I don't talk to him either."

"Wow," I said again.

I began to understand the type of person he was. Either he was very serious about a person or not serious at all. And given the choice, Jamel would rather be serious about a person. It made even more sense why he wouldn't fuck me in the beginning. If I had told him that night at his house that all I wanted was for him to fuck me, he would have fucked me and

Chapter 9

never spoke to me again no matter many times we ran into each other because of Afia's and Ty's relationship. When he said he wanted to date me that first night, what he was actually saying was that he wanted to keep me around for a while. Jamel had been serious about me from day one. I expected it to scare me, but it didn't. It actually comforted me that he had always wanted this relationship with me.

"I get you better now too," I told him and he chuckled. But then I did the math in my head, knowing he had only been home three years by the time we met. I asked, "When did it end?"

And he knew I had done the math, I could tell by the way he hesitated and glanced at me. "Last March." He let a moment pass, then said, "I was way over him by the time you and I met in the pharmacy. He made it easy by not automatically choosing me. I don't want to be with anyone who doesn't want to be with me. By the fall, I wasn't even looking for another partner. I just wanted to be alone for a while."

"I'm glad you changed your mind when you met me. All three of those losers had no idea what they had." I smiled at him, and he smiled back.

"I don't know, maybe it was me," Mel said. "Maybe my expectations were too high. But I just wanted someone who valued me and what I had to offer. People look at me and think because I'm kind of pretty and have a decent body I just want to have fun, but that's the opposite of what I want, and when I make that known, they tend to cut and run."

I scoffed at him. "Kinda pretty, Jamel? You know you're fucking hot, and your body is more than decent.

Cut your shit." He laughed out loud. "But you're also humble about it, which makes you more attractive. And you're so authentic and real, with an honest heart. So, you're gorgeous, but you're also really, really beautiful, inside and out. And if they cut and ran, good. Fuck 'em. It's their loss and my gain."

He reached over and squeezed my thigh and left it here. I took his hand and raised it to my mouth to kiss, then held it in my lap between my two hands.

He was silent for a moment, then said quietly, "You're kind of a free bird."

And again, he was not wrong. "I ... am ... but..." I wanted to be thoughtful in my response. "The thing about us free birds is that we're free because we don't have a home. So, when we find that place, that nice bird bath fountain with fresh water near a shady cedar tree with owners that built a little birdhouse and keep putting out bird seeds, we tend to start building a nest and want to stay." He chuckled. "And soooo, I kinda like this new place, and I want to stay awhile. A long while."

He didn't say anything, and we were quiet for a moment. I knew we were thinking the same thing, so I said it aloud. "Jamel, I don't want anyone else but you. Yes, this feeling is new for me, this ... wanting to be close to someone... Attached. And sometimes it's uncomfortable being vulnerable ... like right now. But honestly ... I can't explain it, but I know it's you and only you. The way you make me feel is... And it's not just the sex; it's everything. Everything about us just feels so right and I'd be a fucking idiot to screw this up. And I've never been known as an idiot. So, you know ...be

♥♥♥ Chapter 9 ♥♥♥

a little less scared shitless about us. Because I'm sure … about us. I'm not going no-fucking-where."

"Connor." He said my name quietly and sighed. He looked at me, and I stared back at him so he would know how serious I was. He squeezed my hand and watched the road again.

"Okay," he said.

"Okay." I squeezed his hand back, then kissed it again.

CHAPTER 10

ME. I NEEDED HIM.

I woke up to sunlight streaming through the curtain and the sound of seagulls. I was on my stomach, nestled in Jamel's armpit, with a view of his perfect nipple and individual strains of curly hair around it. I stared at it wanting to reach out and touch it, but also not wanting to disturb his peaceful sleep as he laid on his back. We had planned on keeping sex to a minimum while at his cousins' house. That was my idea, not his. But we got carried away horsing around naked, and somehow, I ended up with my knees in my chest while he pounded me until I exploded cum on both of us, then half off the bed with his hand on my face pushed into the mattress while he buried his dick in me until he pulled out and came on my back. I had crawled up the bed and fell asleep on my stomach, and he fell asleep laying half his body over me. At some point that night, he must have flipped over to his back.

The sheet covered only half of his body, and the sun shone across his brown skin and chiseled torso.

❤❤❤ Chapter 10 ❤❤❤

My cream-colored arm and shoulder were right up against his side. The contrast between his skin color and mine mesmerized me. We were so different on the outside, but so much alike on the inside. He made me feel happy, alive, safe, and cared for, and I couldn't imagine myself with anyone else, ever again. The whole world could end right now, and I wouldn't have noticed or cared, as long as I got to lay beside him just like that. And lay there I did, for a long time, watching the steady rise and fall of his chest. It dawned on me that the feeling I was feeling was contentment. And love. I leaned over to softly kiss his skin and sighed. Then I whispered my feelings to his sleeping body. After a while of listening to his breathing, I slowly moved away, put on a pair of shorts and a sleeveless t-shirt, and made my way to the common area of the large, three-bedroom condo.

We had made it to Miami by dinner hour on Wednesday evening, and Corrine and Xiomara were so welcoming. They were both older than Jamel, Xio by almost eight years and Corry by three. Xio was a lesbian, and although she and Jamel were already close, she and Jamel became even closer after he came out. When Xio came out, her family wasn't as understanding as Jamel's. So her aunt, Corry's mother and Mama Denita's first cousin, took her in and raised her. Xio and Corry weren't sisters, but they might as well have been with how much they looked alike. They had gray eyes like Jamel but were much lighter skinned and straight-haired. Xio looked like Jennifer Beals, and Corry looked like Alicia Keys. The women joked that most people thought they were Latinas like everyone else in Miami. They both work in the school district, Xio as an English teacher to ninth graders and Corry as a social worker and guidance counselor to middle schoolers, and they were on spring break.

Xio and Corry were sitting at the breakfast table in front of the open sliding doors leading to the balcony when I came out of the room. Because they were on the twelfth floor, the smell of the ocean was so strong, even though their condo was a few blocks from the beach.

"Well, I guess you boys finally decided to wake up after the ... *night* you had." Xio laughed.

"Good morning," I responded with a smile as Corry giggled. I sat at the table with them, and Corry instantly poured a cup of coffee and slid it over to me with the milk and sugar bowl.

"So Coooonooor," Xio sang my name. "Who *are* you? I mean, you just ... Appeared out of nowhere, sweeping my cousin off his feet. He *always* spends New Year's down here with us, but this time apparently he was spending it with ... *you*." She gave me a knowing look.

I smiled as I prepared my coffee. "Well, I met Jamel through my friend Afia who is dating Ty."

"Ty has a girlfriend? A serious one?" Corry was skeptical.

"Yes ... why? Is he not a serious guy?" I asked, unsmiling. If Tyrell was not as serious as my Lovie was about him, I would cut his fucking balls off.

"Oh no, he's serious when he wants to be," Corry said. "It's that he usually dates unserious girls and ends

Chapter 10

up heartbroken. So, is your friend serious about him?" she asked with her eyebrows raised.

Before I could answer, Xio cut in, "Um..*no*. I want to hear about Connor first. Then we can talk about Ty." She turned back to me. "So, who are you again?"

I took a sip of my Colombian-brewed coffee. "I'm Connor McIntyre. Irish Catholic. Born and raised in Rhode Island. I live in a garage apartment in my parent's home. I have one older brother and two younger sisters. I work for Comcast. And Jamel is my boyfriend." I took another sip. It was really good coffee.

"Hmmm," Xio said and leaned back. Of course, she was the more protective one of Jamel. "Mel does not take just anyone down here to meet us, so you must be something special."

"Well, he is something special to me, so I hope I am to him," I told her. She nodded. Then I said, "So Miami isn't where Mel comes to take his flings?" I grabbed a muffin off the table and took a bite.

"No, he knows better than that. You're the second person he's brought here."

I guessed who was the first. "So, Theo?"

They both looked at me intently. Corry asked, "He told you about Teddy?"

"Wait, did he call him Teddy or Theo?" Xio asked.

"Um ... Theo. First time I heard the name Teddy."

Xio looked relieved. "Okay, good. Yeah, Teddy ... Theo was the other one. We thought they were going to stay together, but they didn't, and it was for the best. Theo just liked to say that his boyfriend was a strong Army man. I don't think he ever really loved Mel."

Corry looked at her. "You never liked him."

"*Nope*, I didn't," she confirmed. "He always thought he was better than Mel because he went to college, and Mel didn't. Uncle Wendel didn't like him either. He said he was a *pussy* and Uncle Wendel is *always* right. You don't *leave* someone just because they don't fit into your grandiose plans. And you *definitely* don't leave a military guy because you're scared he *might* die. Theodore was an arrogant, *little*, pussy ass *bitch*."

I laughed out loud as Corry clutched her imaginary pearls. I loved how Xio emphasized words.

"Zeee-oooh!" Corry scolded while dragging out Xiomara's nickname. Corry turned back to me. "They just weren't right for each other. They really didn't have a whole lot in common except for being black and gay. But you know, opposites attract."

"Obviously," I said, raising my cup of coffee with a smile, making them both laugh.

"You're really cute, Connor. Like, really, really cute. Jamel is like my little brother. Don't *fuck* with my brother's heart, *okay*?" Xio said to me sternly.

"No, ma'am," I told her automatically. "I have nothing but honest intentions here."

"Good. Because Mel is a good guy and needs a good man in his life. He is also not very forgiving once his heart is broken. He'll walk away and not look back if you fuck this up, no matter how much it hurts him. *That* is your only warning."

Corry nodded in agreement with her cousin. "Okay," I replied. They started talking about the plans for the day with each other, but I was thinking about what they had just said.

❤❤❤ CHAPTER 10 ❤❤❤

"I really care about him," I blurted out. They both turned to look at me. "I won't hurt him. I won't betray him. I'll never cheat on him. I'll never leave him." The words just came tumbling out of me, and I felt myself growing red from embarrassment as they watched me intently with their matching gray eyes.

They turned to look at each other, then smiled. Corry turned to me first. "Well, I guess this means he's not reenlisting."

Wait, what? "Jamel is going back into the Army?"

"Was," Xio corrected me. "He's not now. I'm sure of it, which is probably why he never mentioned it to you. It was supposed to be this year. If he was still going, he would have mentioned it to me a long time ago. I guess *someone* is giving him a reason to *stay*." She smiled at me. "Honestly, I didn't even know you could do that once you officially retired."

"You can," I told her. "You just need to resign your pension and rejoin under an RE-1 code which I believe he has."

Corry giggled as Xio smirked at me and asked, "Are you in the Army too?"

"Marine Corps. But I'm out now. I'm not going back."

"Ooooooooh," they both said as Jamel came in from the hallway, wearing a simple tank top, light gray sweatpants, a silky white wave cap tied on his head to keep his hair waves in place, barefooted, stretching. *It is moments like these that I can't take my eyes off him. He's so fucking beautiful.* And he only had eyes for me as he walked right over and leaned down to kiss me softly on the lips before sitting down next to me, pulling his chair closer. He smelled of Listerine, day-old deodorant, and his natural musk. I loved it.

"Good morning," he said. "What are we talking about?" He grabbed a muffin from the table and took a bite. I was still looking at him. He looked at me and smiled.

"What?" he asked quietly.

"Nothing," I said quietly back at him.

He nodded slowly, leaned back, and put his arm around the back of my chair. I moved slightly back, so my neck touched his arm. I wordlessly handed him my cup of coffee and watched his lips form around the rim to take a sip. I finally tore my eyes from him to notice his cousins had casually left us at the table alone.

Corry took us sightseeing and to the beach every day, and Xio took us to gay clubs every night. When I was in the Marines, Vinnie, Sammie, Taylor, and I would sneak out and go to gay clubs when we were stateside, but it wasn't often. It was good to do it again and Jamel and I had a blast. It was freeing to be dancing, hugging, and kissing my lover in public for once.

The Saturday night after we came back from the club, and an exchange of blow jobs, we were lying head to feet staring at each other. I told him, as I massaged his foot, "I love your eyes so much. Everyone compliments me on my eyes, so it's nice for a change to be hypnotized by someone else's eyes."

He smiled at me while continuing to massage my foot. "Yeah? It's kind of a family heirloom. Not

Chapter 10

everyone gets them, but they get passed down to a couple of kids every generation. Ty and I are the only ones that have them from our mama."

"My whole family has the same color blue eyes, so I don't think there's anything special about them. But gray eyes against your brown skin is the sexiest thing to me. On a black person it isn't typical. That's why it's so interesting," I said.

"No, it's not typical. They came from my maternal great, great, great grandmother."

"Was one of her parents white?" I asked.

Jamel gave me a small smile. "Her mother, my great, great, great, great grandmother was raped by her slave owner, who had gray eyes."

My mouth fell into an O. *What a fucking idiot I am, drooling over eyes that were a result of slavery and tragedy.* "Of course. I'm sorry for asking dumb ass questions."

He patted my leg. "Don't be. And it's not a dumb ass question. It's a part of my family history, but not every black person has this history, so it's a legitimate question. My mother's family is from Florida, generationally. My great, great, great grandmother was born into slavery in 1862. She was white-passing most of her life until she got married."

"White-passing?"

"She was very light-skinned and straight-haired with gray eyes, like Xio and Corry, so most people assumed she was white. She decided if she wanted to correct them or not."

"Oooooh. Got it."

He continued, "She knew her history and married the blackest man she could find and started having babies. Twelve, in fact. My great, great grandfather was her last baby, and he was the only male with gray eyes. He passed them down to my great grandfather, who passed them to my grandmother, who passed them to my mama, who passed them to me. And if either I or Ty have kids, we'll pass them down too."

I was quiet for a moment. I didn't want to change the subject, but I wanted him to know. "Mel? I'm not having kids."

He paused, then said, "Okay."

I needed to make sure, so I asked, "Is it okay, though? And I know it's only been like six months and way too early to have this conversation. I get it, but I just wanted you to know. I'm not going to change my mind later on down the road."

"Okay," he said again.

"I mean, are you sure?" I asked again.

I didn't know why I was pressing the issue so hard at that moment. But I had thought long and hard about this for a long time. I loved being an uncle and hanging out with other people's kids, but I just didn't want to take on that kinda responsibility in my life, helping to mold and shape another human being in this world. It's not for me. There were plenty of people more equipped than I was to do it, namely those that didn't have my trauma history, so rather than try and fuck it up, I'd rather not do it at all.

I told him, "If you have a strong desire for a little person to call you Daddy one day, I get it. Not saying we have to break up today over it, but if it's a future you are thinking of with me, you won't have that. Not with me. I'm sorry."

Chapter 10

He shook his head. "It's not a dealbreaker for me, baby," Jamel said. "If I were the only boy, maybe I would feel more pressure to have them, but I feel no such pressure at all. My parents have three other boys and will have grandchildren with or without me. And Ty wants a lot of children. So, I'm good with not having kids."

I stared at him, my perfect match. Then I crawled up the bed to him for one of my favorite positions, my back toward him and his arms around me. He kissed the nape of my neck a few times, sniffed my hair, and entwined his fingers with mine.

We were quiet for a moment, then Jamel said, "Maybe I just want you to call me Daddy."

I double blinked. "Like fucking hell!" I scoffed.

He busted out laughing, making me laugh with him. He knew I would never call him 'Daddy.' He was lucky he got 'baby' out of me, and 'Daddy' was way goofier. We didn't talk again and fell asleep.

♥

On the way back to North Carolina that Sunday, I got my first real lesson of seeing racism in America through the eyes of a black man. I drove up I-95 in my typical heavy-footed fashion. Neither of us was paying attention as we talked and laughed about things that happened during our trip. We heard the whirl of the Georgian state trooper siren before we saw the patrol unit. Jamel looked at me, and I patted his thigh, understanding, but not really understanding, his apprehension.

"Relax," I told him as I pulled over. "We're good."

Jamel moved my hand off his thigh, put both his hands on his knees, sat up straighter, and looked straight ahead.

One officer went to the passenger side, and the other went to the driver's side as I rolled down the window. I gave him my best smile. "Afternoon, officer."

"License, registration, and insurance, please," the trooper said.

"Sure thing."

I leaned past Jamel, who had not moved a muscle, grabbed my documents from the glove compartment, lifted up to pull my wallet from my back pocket to take out my license, and handed the officer all three. He looked at my documents and said, "Do you know why I stopped you, son?"

"I think I was speeding a bit. Sorry about that," I said apologetically.

"You were. Ten miles over the speed limit. Where are you coming from?" he asked.

"Just hanging out with friends and family in Miami. Road trip with my friend here. We're stopping in North Carolina for the night before heading home to Rhode Island."

I turned toward Jamel to acknowledge him, and I saw Jamel glance at me through the corner of his eyes, then straight ahead again, but he said nothing.

Then the state trooper leaned a little to get a look at Jamel and said to him, "Do you have ID on you, boy?"

Boy? What the fuck? I looked up and gave the officer a dirty look.

Chapter 10

Mel said slowly and calmly, enunciating each word, "I am going to reach into my pocket for my wallet and pull it out, sir."

As he did, two things happened. I grabbed his arm to stop him from getting his wallet and said to the officer testily, "Why are you asking him for ID when it's my car, and I'm the one driving?"

At the same time, the officer on the passenger side unhooked his holster and put his hand on his gun. I knew I fucked up because of the look Jamel gave me: Pure fear.

The officer on my side also put his hand on his holster and said nastily, "I asked because I can. Is there a problem with your friend's identity, son?"

From my peripheral, I saw the other trooper move into position. His hand was still on his unhooked but holstered weapon. I was finally afraid. I had no idea what to do. *Ho. Lee. Shit.*

Jamel said quietly, "Connor. Let. Me. Go." I pulled my hand from around his bicep.

Jamel said again, "Officer, I am going into my wallet and pulling out my ID to hand to you, sir."

"Slowly, boy," he ordered.

There goes that word again. I was "son," but Jamel was "boy." I felt a burning anger in my chest. I wanted to snap the fuck out, but I knew this situation was bad for Jamel, and anything I would have said or done would have made it worse.

Jamel slowly raised up in his seat, pulled out his wallet, and grabbed his Rhode Island state ID. I said to him quietly, "Give him both." We looked at each other.

"Give him both your IDs, Sergeant," I said louder. I was determined that they show my man some respect.

Jamel pulled out his VA card, handed them both to me, and I handed them to the officer. He put his wallet on the dashboard and both hands back on his knees.

"Any weapons in the car?" he asked as he looked at Jamel's IDs.

"No, sir," we responded in chorus.

The officers moved back to their car. We sat in silence for a moment. I started, "Jamel—"

"Shut the fuck up, Connor," he said quietly and firmly, without looking at me.

So I did. We sat there in silence for about five minutes before the state troopers came back. The trooper on the passenger side was more relaxed with his hands on his sides, but his holster was still unbuttoned.

The officer on my side handed me back both my and Jamel's information and asked me, "Are you military, too, son?"

"Yes." I reached into my wallet and handed him my VA card. He asked what branch, and I told him Marine Corps. He said a couple of things about some of his family members being in the Army but directed his conversation to me, the Marine, not the actual Army guy. I kept my comments to short or one-word responses. I knew I had to get us both the fuck out of there and fast.

After a minute or so, he said, "You're free to go. Slow down and drive safe. And thank you for your service."

The officer on the other side said, "Thank you both." He tipped his hat toward my boyfriend. Mel did not respond back.

♥♥♥ CHAPTER 10 ♥♥♥

I put the car into drive and moved slowly back onto the road. We drove for a couple of minutes in silence, and then I started again, "Jamel—"

"Pull over," he ordered. As soon as I did, he turned to me and snapped, "Don't you ever endanger my life like that again."

I looked at him wide-eyed. "Endanger your life? How the fuck did I endanger your life?"

He took his seatbelt off to turn his whole body toward me. He said in a low voice, "Connor, they will use any excuse to shoot me point-blank in the head and justify it later. So, when you are in the car with me, driving or not, pretend you're a black man. Don't drive past the speed limit. Don't give more information than necessary. Don't argue with a cop. Don't *ever* make sudden movements. Any one of those things you did could have gotten me killed. If you don't see or understand that, then we're going to have a problem."

I sat there stunned. But I knew Jamel was right. Afia and I have had experiences of subtle racism, but typically, people back off once they see me. Like when we had to get her car repaired or waited to be seated at a restaurant. People would talk down to or get nasty with Afia, but once they saw me, they suddenly turned respectful. Afia and I had even gotten stopped by police a time or two. She would tense up and sit quietly, and the cops usually ignored her. No one had ever asked her for ID or required her to prove who she was when she was with me. No one called her "girl," and no one would dare belittle her in front of me. I understand now it was because she is a woman, and as a white man, I used my presumed authority to protect, defend, and fight for her when we were together.

"I'm sorry," I said. "You're right. I just thought—"

"I know what you thought," he cut me off. "You thought that they wouldn't mess with us because you're white, it's your car, and you're a veteran. And for the most part, you are right. But do you see how quickly they went for their guns? You can't be loose or reckless either. Be cognizant of how they see me, a big black man, even if I'm standing or sitting next to you. It's a traffic stop for you. It's life or death for me."

His words shook me to my core. I foolishly thought that the same privilege would extend to my relationship with Mel, but I realized that it wouldn't. Afia needed my whiteness to shield her, but Jamel would need more than that. He will always be seen not just through his skin color but also by his masculinity and size. He would need my intuition when these situations arise. And the best way I could protect him was not to put him in situations or further exasperate situations where people viewed him as a threat.

I took a deep breath and said, "I'll do better and be more aware of how people see you, especially when you're with me. I promise." He nodded, but I couldn't tell if he was still upset with me. He turned to stare out the front window.

"Jamel?" I called his name. I was hoping this didn't ruin the relationship we built over the last six months. I didn't know what I would do if he left me over this. I reached over and touched his thigh again. He put his hand on top of mine and looked at me.

"We're okay, Connor. Let's just go."

❤❤❤ CHAPTER 10 ❤❤❤

I hesitated, but then I slowly eased out to the road and kept to the speed limit.

❤

By sunset, we had returned to the same hotel in Carolina Beach. The rest of the ride was fine but quieter than the first couple of hours. I let Jamel read quietly for a long time, and he stared thoughtfully out the window at other times. But it was reassuring that he never let go of my hand. We held hands through the hotel and up to the room. When we got there, he dropped his bag near the front entrance.

"Order room service? I'm going to take a shower," he said, then turned and went into the bathroom and closed the door without waiting for a response. I sighed and lied on the bed, fully clothed. I wasn't sure his silence meant he wanted to be alone. I wasn't sure if anything I was doing or saying was right.

I ordered a couple of surf and turf dinners, then I decided to take a chance. I knocked on the bathroom door before I opened it. A blast of hot steam hit me, and I quickly closed the door. I could see Jamel's outline through the foggy glass door.

"Jamel?"

"Yeah, Connor?"

"I'm sorry."

He paused. "It's okay, Con. We're good."

"Are we? Because I feel like you're still mad at me."

He paused again, then said, "Come here."

I stripped and got in the shower with him. He moved over and pulled me closer to him under the rainfall showerhead. He kissed then nuzzled his nose with mine and said, "I'm not mad at you. I'm just … frustrated with … everything." He leaned to the sidewall and held me by my waist. I wrapped my arms around his lower back and waited for him to talk.

"I shouldn't have spoken to you like that. I'm sorry about that. It's just like… It's awful, you know? How I could dedicate seven years of my life to serving this country loyally and proudly, but still get treated like I'm less than them. Like no matter what I do, what accomplishments I achieve, I will still be a nigger to some people. Sometimes it pisses me off. Sometimes it just..."

Hurts. I knew that was what he wanted to say but didn't. I have had these talks with Afia too. With Afia, it's easier. I just hold her, reassure her that I see and value her, reaffirm her beauty and her worth in her skin color. I wasn't sure if that was what Jamel needed, so I asked.

"What can I do?" I held him tighter. "I can't change the world, but how can I make it better for you?"

He didn't say anything for a moment, but he pulled me against his body. For once, it was him leaning into my neck. I loved that we were nearly the same height, and he could lean on me like that, literally and figuratively.

Words of Affirmation was the last on his list, but I gave them to him anyway. I kissed his face and said in his ear, "I value who you are, even if others don't. I see who you are, Jamel Josiah Jones. A strong, beautiful black man. It's okay to let go with me. You promised that I would be safe with you always, and I make

♥♥♥ Chapter 10 ♥♥♥

that same promise to you. I promise to keep you safe when you are with me, Jamel. Always."

I let a moment pass, then said, "I will die before I let something happen to you." And I meant it.

He squeezed me tighter and said my name so quietly it could have been drowned out by the sound of the water, "Connor."

We held each other for a while. Then he backed me into the shower door. He kissed my lips, neck, and shoulders and ran his fingers through my wet hair. He traced his fingers down my back, held onto my bottom with both hands, and kissed me again. My dick sprang up immediately, surprising me that it had not been up this whole time. He turned off the shower and said, "Let's go."

I followed him out of the bathroom, and he went to grab a condom and lube. I moved toward the bed, but he pulled me close to him again, our naked bodies wet and needy. He backed me against a wall mirror as he kissed and grinded against me. Then he slowly turned me around, spread my cheeks, and lubed me up before guiding his sheathed dick inside of me. I had nowhere to hold onto, so I laid my palms flat on the glass as he bottomed out.

Jamel fucked me slowly against the mirror, kissing my neck, shoulders, and back. He stroked me from the front until I came all over the mirror that reflected our passionate faces. Then he moved me to the bed, laid me on my stomach, and fucked me slowly again, lying right on top of me, moving in and out of me. We were there so long that we heard the knocking from room service, but neither of us stopped. I'm sure they heard me moaning and decided to move on. Eventually Jamel silently came. He leaned up with his knees on either side of me, pressed his palms into my lower back to arch it further down, and pushed deep into me. I moaned as I felt him cum into the condom, longing to feel his sperm pool up inside of me.

One thing I hadn't yet realized is that while I use sex to not feel, my lover uses sex in the opposite way, to be emotional. Jamel communicates how deep he feels about me with his entire body, from his hands to his genitals. If I had been fully paying attention, I would have known that was his way of telling me he was in love with me.

The hotel staff left the food tray outside the door. The food was lukewarm, but we ate it anyway. We were in our underwear on the king-size bed, listening to music playing from the crappy clock radio on the nightstand. Robin Thicke's "Lost Without You" came on, and I started playfully lip-syncing the words. Jamel stood up and reached for my hand, and I took it. He pulled me close to him with one hand around my waist and held up my other hand. Suddenly, we were slow dancing in our boxer briefs in the middle of a hotel room, mouthing the words to each other. By the end of the song, our feelings became very real, and we just stared into each other's eyes and swayed. The song changed to "Always Be My Baby" by Mariah Carey, and we continued to slow dance.

"Are you ... thinking about going back? Reenlisting?" I asked him, almost afraid of the answer.

He smiled. "Did they tell you that?" I nodded.

Chapter 10

He let go of my hand and wrapped both arms around me. "When I got back in 2006, my plan was to stay. But then the housing market crashed in 2008 and started affecting the home inspection side of my business a lot. People still needed electricians but not so much home inspections if they weren't buying homes. So, last year, I had mentioned to them that if things didn't turn around in a year, I would just rejoin the Army."

"Things aren't turning around," I told him. I didn't really watch the news, but I knew the state of affairs, and we were definitely in a recession fueled by the housing market bubble burst. Who knew if or when it would bounce back?

"No, they aren't," he said, still looking at me. "So, if I decided to go back in a year or so, what would you do?"

I gave him a look. "I'm not going to cut and run, Jamel. We'll make it work. I'm not some *little*, pussy ass, *bitch*." I emphasized the words, and he laughed really loud.

"You've been talking to my cousin, I see," he said, and I chuckled.

He was quiet for a moment, then said, "I'm not going back. Don't worry about that. I'm going to stick it out here and make it work for myself. Plus, I have people that need me to stay. My dad. My brothers...."

Me. I needed him. We both thought it, but neither of us said it. Then he asked, "Connor, do you think you would ever come out fully? To your friends and family?"

"I don't know," I told him honestly as we held each other. "I never really had a reason to ... before now. But now... You should know, you being with me is giving me all the reasons to. So … maybe not tomorrow. But maybe … one day."

He nodded, then kissed my lips. I didn't know what came over me, but I heard myself say with a bit of fear in my voice, "Don't leave me, Jamel."

He looked at me incredulously, like I just said the stupidest thing in the world. He kissed the space between my neck and my shoulder and whispered in my ear, "I'm never going to leave you, Connor."

Yep. We were definitely falling in love with each other.

CHAPTER 11

WHAT THE FUCK AM I MISSING HERE?

We got back late on Monday, and I went to work on Tuesday. When I came home, Owen McIntyre shocked the shit out of me by making himself at home in my garage apartment. He had his feet up on my coffee table as he relaxed on my couch, watching baseball on my TV.

"What are you doing here?" I said sternly, forgetting for a moment that he scares me. I had to keep my anger in check to avoid him knocking my head off. But I was boiling over, mad that he came into my private space without my permission.

He said plainly, "This is my house, son. I go where the fuck I want." I didn't say anything. He must have found my garage key. *How could I have been so stupid?*

"Where have you been since last Wednesday?" he asked me. I didn't answer or move. Being with Jamel was slowly changing me not to accept less than my worth. At twenty-five years old, I didn't owe that motherfucker one explanation of where I had been.

He got up and started walking toward me, and I instinctively backed up. He stopped when he had me cornered against the wall near the kitchen sink.

I stammered out, "I… I… I … went out of town with Afia. Fuck!"

I raised my arm to protect myself and hated that he still had control over me, that I feared him the way I did. *Guess I haven't changed that much.*

He stood there and waited until I put my arm down and straightened myself up. I was kinda surprised he didn't say anything about my cursing or that he wasn't knocking me upside my head.

He got in my face and told me, "Don't get that nigger bitch pregnant. I will end your life and hers."

I didn't give him my standard, "Sir, yes sir," line. I just stayed quiet. He left after that. I was less rattled by his threats of killing me and the fact that he was in my house, in my space. I had to get the fuck out of there.

Jamel and I debated over text whether we should take a break from seeing each other. We decided we didn't need a break from each other, so he came over later that night. When I told Jamel what happened, obviously leaving out the racial epithets and threats of physical violence, he said automatically, "Just move in with me."

"No, you have a one-bedroom apartment in your family home. We won't have enough space for both of our stuff."

"Then let's get a place together," he said simply.

Chapter 11

"Are we there yet? Moving in together, spending all our waking moments together?"

"Don't we do that now? All the waking moments I can do are with you."

"You know as well as I do that it's different."

"How?"

"It's..." I wanted to say it was another level of commitment that I wasn't sure if I was ready for. I didn't even know what it felt like to live on my own yet. And if I did want to live with him, I definitely wasn't moving into the space he shared with his ex. But I didn't want to start a conversation about how and why moving in together would not be feasible for me. "It's just not the right time."

"Hmmm... Okay," he said. I was beginning to know and understand his tone, sounds, and moods, and I could tell he was frustrated.

I told him, "I'll look into some places close to you in North Providence. It's a little further out from my job in West Warwick, but it's okay. I'd rather be closer to you anyway."

He didn't say anything for a moment, but I heard him sigh. "Okay. Let me know if you need help."

♥

~~~June 2010~~~

Within a few weeks, I found a place in College Hill, a few minutes from Afia's family pharmacy. She could literally walk to my apartment building. It was also less than ten minutes from Jamel's house. I signed the lease, and my move-in date was June 1st. I was so excited about not living with my family that I was kicking myself that I hadn't done it earlier. I debated heavily on not saying anything to my family but leaving with a moving truck like a thief in the night. But Afia talked me out of it.

"He has to know he no longer has control over you anymore. And you have to know too. So face him, face them all, and tell them you are moving out and on with your life."

And of course she promised to go with me. June 1st was a Tuesday, so I waited until the Sunday right before to tell them, so no one could actually stop me.

Unfortunately for both of us, that was the Sunday Matty decided to come over with his frozen bitch of a wife, Stephanie, and their three kids, Madeline, called Maddy, a play on her dad's nickname, age ten, Deann, age seven, and Fredrick, called Freddie, age four. Matty and Steph were both eighteen and still in high school when she got pregnant. Which, if you asked me, he got her pregnant on purpose because I couldn't see Stephanie wanting kids ever, and certainly not at eighteen. But alas, Catholics don't have abortions, so she was keeping it. Matty married her right away and moved in with her family. Whether he loved her or not was irrelevant. She was his way out.

I actually really like my nieces and nephew and wished I saw them more, but their parents are assholes, so I didn't go anywhere near their house. I kinda feel bad for them having such awful parents who I'm pretty sure never hug or kiss their kids, so I try to

Chapter 11

every chance I get. I spent that Sunday playing video games, hosting tea parties, and rolling around on the floor, tickling them until dinner.

We spent most of the dinner listening to Matty drone on and on about his work as a general manager at a GMC car plant and warehouse. Finally, the conversation died down. I don't typically talk at the table so if I do, they usually listen.

I cleared my throat and said, "I have an announcement."

As expected, everyone looked up. Afia squeezed my thigh as encouragement. "So. I... I found a place. In... Providence. Closer. Closer to my job." Everyone was waiting for the punchline as I avoided my father's eyes. "So. I'm moving. Out. This... this week. To my apartment. In. In College Hill."

My father didn't say anything, so my mom said, "Why such short notice? Why didn't you—" But she was silenced by my father's index finger rising in the air. We all knew that was his sign for "I'm talking, and everyone should shut the fuck up."

He started, "When did you make the decision to move out? After I told you I didn't want you having unmarried sex under my roof?"

I could feel the heat of embarrassment off Afia even though she knew she wasn't the one, but everyone else thought she was. Stephanie tsked loudly and I resisted the urge to glare at that hypocritical bitch. I took Afia's hand under the table, squeezed it, then answered my dad.

"I have been thinking about it... for a while. Because I'll be 26-years-old in July, and if I'm ever going to be a man, I need to stand on my own two feet, pay my own bills, and make my own way in this world, sir." I had that line practiced.

He didn't say anything for a moment but then ordered, "You will still attend Mass and be here for Sunday dinner."

I had this line practiced too. "Actually, sir, my parish will change to St. Joseph's Church. According to canon, St. Cecilia's won't be my home church anymore. I'll still be here for dinner on Sundays as long as I'm not working. But... but I'll be over in Providence now. Sir." I knew he would try this bullshit, and I wasn't going to get stuck there every fucking Sunday.

I could see it in his eyes that he wanted to yank me out my seat, slap me around, and tell me I wasn't going any-fucking-where, but with everyone at the table, he wasn't going to do it. Yet.

Instead, he said, "I don't think you should go. I don't think you're ready to move out on your own."

I took a deep breath and looked him in the eye. "I have a full-time job with benefits. I have money saved. I pay my own bills on time, including the rent and utilities I pay to you, my car note and insurance, my credit card, and my phone bill. I've lived without the supervision of my parents for almost five years before I came back home. I went to war, became a Corporal, and led a Fire Team as a Squad Leader. I have proven myself responsible in numerous ways, so I know I can take care of myself. I'm ready. I move out on Tuesday. Sir."

His face was stone, and he was angry with me. But what could he say after that? I made a case for leaving, and I was doing it.

♥♥♥ Chapter 11 ♥♥♥

Angie spoke up first. "Connor, I think it's great. And I can't wait to visit you and see your space." She smiled at me, and I gave her virtual hugs for her support.

My mom followed, "Well, I do wish you would have told us sooner to prepare for it."

"It's just thirty-five minutes away, Mom. I'll be around just like Matty comes around," I lied. I was making my great escape, and I was never coming back if I could help it.

"Well, good because I will miss you too much, Connor. I love having you around the house," she said sweetly. I couldn't tell if she said it because she meant it or because company was there. My mother could be very sincere and also sincerely fake. It was her coping mechanism for having an abusive husband. I gave her a smile.

And here comes Matty's bitch ass. "College Park? Afia, isn't your pharmacy in College Park?"

I squeezed her hand; she hated when he spoke directly to her. "Yes," she said simply.

"Huh. So does that mean you're going to be moving in too?"

We both said simultaneously, "No."

I kept going, "Afia is not moving in with me. Me moving into my own space has nothing to do with her."

He smirked and said, "Oh, I'm pretty sure it has a lot to do with Afia. I'm sure she's going to be over there every day and possibly every night." I wanted to reach across the table and stab him with my fork.

She said calmly, "No, Matthew, I won't be. I'll still be at my folks right here in Rockville." If she had to acknowledge him, she refused to call him Matty. It was her way of saying, "We're not fucking friends, asshole." I love her for it.

"Uh-huh. I just find that hard to believe, you know? Considering how close you two are."

Why won't he just shut the fuck up? He's trying to start something, the bastard. I said again, "She's not moving in with me. If she was, I would say it, but she's not. Drop it."

"Sure, sure," Matty said unconvincingly. "Maybe not right away, but it's only a matter of time. Seeing as how you two are, you know ... doing it. I mean, do you even use condoms?" He sat back smugly.

My mother tried to shut it down. "No, none of this talk at the table."

"I'm sorry, Mom, I didn't mean to upset you. It's just that when I see two lost souls, it's my job to bring them back to Jesus. And I've never seen two more lost souls than these two," Matty said innocently. I gave him a death glare.

Angie rolled her eyes from across the table but didn't say anything. No one said much of anything else for the rest of dinner. But at the end of it, my father began.

"Fornication grieves the Holy Spirit. It is a sin against your own body and God Himself. Fornicators will not inherit the kingdom of God. The Bible says in 1 Corinthians 6..."

And the whole family, Afia included, had to sit there for the next twenty minutes as Owen McIntyre, preacher wanna-be, gave his sermon about fornication, sexual immorality, and sin against the body. My brother and his wife nodded their heads and amened right

♥♥♥ CHAPTER 11 ♥♥♥

with him. Afia was annoyed but kept her face unreadable. We held hands under the table and squeezed each other now and again to make sure we were okay.

If it had been a normal Sunday, I would have already shrunk with embarrassment. But that day, I was happy to hear one of the last sermons I would ever hear from that abusive fuck. I wondered what Jamel was doing at his Sunday dinner. Probably arguing over The Affordable Care Act and whether it would really help Americans in the long run. Fuck, I missed him and his entire family so much at that moment.

Owen McIntyre ended his sermon with, "I hope all the unmarried men and women at this table understand the seriousness of the sin of sexual immorality. We have some sinners among us at this table. End it now, before your soul burns in hell forever."

He stood up and held out his hands. My mother grabbed one hand and Mary Kate on his other side took the other. We all stood together and held hands as he prayed for the next ten minutes for the souls at the table, throwing in a few jabs about how people should be equally yoked in mind, body, and spirit before they even considered marriage, let alone being fruitful. I knew that was all about her being black and me being white. *Fuck him for that.* When he was done, my father left the table first, glaring at me. It sent a chill through my body.

I held Afia's hand and walked her to the car afterward. "I'm sorry," I told her. "I know that was uncomfortable for you, especially since you're not the person I'm sleeping with."

She laughed. "I'm heading over there tonight. Do you want a ride?"

"No, there is something I need to do tonight. But could you spend the night here with me tomorrow night? Just keep me company on my last night here."

"Okay, yeah sure. You okay, Connor? You're looking a little lost right now." Concern was all in her eyes, and I had to get her off my scent.

"Am I? Maybe I'm just stunned that I told them, and I'm really going to do it. Move out."

"No, it's something else." She looked at me intently. "Do you want me to stay tonight?"

I really, really fucking did because I knew what was coming. But I needed her to go so I could just get it over with.

"No, go be with Ty. After that whole ordeal, I think you need to be up under him. Try not to think about burning in hell while you're riding his dick, though." She punched my arm, then hugged me.

"Call me later. Love you." She kissed my cheek instead of my lips. She had been doing that more and more now, and it was better that way.

"Love you, Lovie. Text me when you get home." After watching her drive off, I went into my garage apartment.

I hadn't started packing just in case I got another unwanted visitor and tipped anyone off. But I pulled out the folded boxes from under my bed, taped them together, and started packing. I took off Monday to Wednesday for the move. The only person I asked to help me was Jamel, who kept his Tuesday open so he could help. I packed and tried not to tremble

Chapter 11

as I waited for him. I didn't think he would bother knocking since I know he has a key. How long he'd had it I didn't know. But it didn't matter because I was out. *I'm almost out.*

♥

I was right. Around 11pm, as I was packing up the kitchen, I heard my front door open. I heard him come upstairs and try the knob of my main door, which I locked on purpose. Then he knocked.

"Connor," my father called. "Open the door, Connor."

He had the key to open it himself, but that was part of this whole schema. I had to let him in.

Against the better judgment of every nerve in my body, I opened the door. My father walked in and looked at all the boxes, my clothes on the bed, and my unplugged electronics. He looked surprised, as if I didn't just have the conversation with them four hours ago.

He started, "So you're moving out."

I nodded slowly. "Yes, sir. I think we both know it's time."

"Time for what?" he snapped at me.

I swallowed. "Time that I move on and start my life," I said calmly. "Sir."

"Do you think there is something better for you out there? Something that my home doesn't provide?" He was becoming dangerous. I could feel it, but I kept my voice calm.

"No, not at all, sir. I am grateful to you providing for me all these years. I just believe that right now—"

But I was cut off by him grabbing me by the neck of my shirt, lifting me off my feet, and shutting off my air supply.

"Where the fuck are you really going? Answer me!" he spat.

I could barely breathe. I grabbed his wrists to tell him that. He let me go, and I dropped to the floor like a rag doll. "I told you." I started heaving and talking. "I found ... An apartment ... in College Park. It's ... a real place." I started coughing. He towered over me and said, "You'll give your mother a key to your place, so she'll have access to you." *So, he'll have access to me, he meant. Fuck that.*

I looked up at him and started to say, "I can't give her a key. I am only allowed one per unit, and then I have to pa—"

But then I was met with a punch to the face, and I knew I was going to have a fucking black eye. *Now I'm going to have to explain this shit to Mel. Great.*

He must have been furious because he typically didn't hit me where bruises could be visible. I moved to dodge his next blow and crawled away to create distance between us. But he was right there, kneeling behind me, putting me in a chokehold, and telling me how he should kill me for being an insubordinate, worthless piece of shit. As I began to lose oxygen, the same thought that always came during such times passed through my mind: *I am a fucking Marine and a trained killer. I could kill this motherfucker with my bare hands if I wanted to.* Yet there I was, once again, letting him beat the shit out of me and assert his control over me.

♥♥♥ Chapter 11 ♥♥♥

It was probably the fourth time he had done that since I had been back home. The first time was when I brought Afia home for dinner a month after I came home for good and let everyone think she was my girlfriend. He came into my bedroom and beat the shit out of me with his bare hands. That was for "bringing home a nigger bitch." He threatened to kill me if I ever knocked her up or married her. He was letting me know he could still kick my ass if he wanted to, Marine or not. I moved into the garage after that.

The second time was at the Sunday gathering after Mass when I opted to sit with Jack and talked about him falling in love with Ethan. Ethan had just moved to town that year with his two-year-old son, EJ, and bought the old Inn to manage. I didn't even know he was gay until he and Jack started dating. Jack implored me to come back to their family farmhouse for their Sunday dinner instead of my family dinner, and I happily agreed. I had only met Ethan a handful of times before then, but I got to know him better that day. And with Mina there, we had so much fun. The next day, Owen led me into his den and kicked the shit out of me for consorting with "faggots" and "sexually immoral cretins" who should be shot and killed. He broke two ribs that day, and I never went over to Jack's for Sunday dinner again.

Then last summer, I tried to get away with not going to Mass at all. My Catholic faith is actually really important to me, but it was more important to rebel against this fascist regime. Every Sunday in July, I had an excuse. At 5am on the fifth Sunday, my father woke me up with a softball bat. He gave me a minor concussion and dislocated my shoulder, but other than that, I just had a few bruises and welts. He told me he would wake me up that way every Sunday if I didn't bring my ass back to church, so I did. But that was also why I changed the locks and put a deadbolt on the inside of my door. No more beat-down surprises.

He used to beat the shit out of me at least once a week as a kid before I left. That's the real reason I joined the military: to get the fuck away from him and learn how to kill him one day. I just never got the balls to kill him. *Today isn't the day either because I'm almost out of here.* So I let him continue because this would be the last time he would ever put his hands on me.

He finally let my neck go, and I was heaving and spitting up. Then he told me how I make him so angry with my stupidity and how I can't leave because it's his job to keep me in line, and he won't be able to do that from so far away.

I stood up and told him, "I'm sorry, sir. I'm leaving on Tuesday."

I waited for the blow, which came seconds later to the same eye. He grabbed my neck again and delivered three punches to my gut. Then he bent my right arm back, and I swore he was going to break it as he reminded me how I couldn't cut it in the Marines, and that's why I came home. And I wouldn't be able to cut it out there, so I would be back. He gave me a couple more knockdown blows for the way I disrespected him at dinner, a few kicks to the groin area as a reminder that if I got Afia pregnant, he would kill both of us, and it was all over before midnight. And I was free.

♥♥♥ Chapter 11 ♥♥♥

♥

"What the fuck happened to your eye!?" Jamel exclaimed when he saw me Monday evening.

I didn't expect to see him until Tuesday morning. Afia brought him over with her to surprise me. *Great.*

Afia looked at me with sad eyes. She knew. "Fuck, Connor, I knew I should have stayed. Why did you tell me to go to Ty? Why didn't you say something?"

"Because I didn't want you to stay. I just needed to let it happen," I said as she touched my face.

"Yo! What the fuck am I missing here!?" Jamel yelled angrily.

That was probably the loudest he had ever gotten in anger and frustration with me or with anyone, as far as I could remember. Afia, the keeper of my secrets, said nothing, but she gave me a you-better-tell-him look, complete with eyebrows raised.

I sighed and said, "My father. It's fine. It is what it is. I'm leaving, so don't make a big deal out of it." The look on Jamel's face was murderous, but he did not respond.

Afia went into my bathroom medicine cabinet. "What did you put on it? Cold compress or hot?" she called out.

"Cold. The swelling went down, and Advil helped with the pain."

"Did he break another rib?" she asked.

"No, just sprained my arm, but—"

She came out of the bathroom with my Tylenol with Codeine. "Take this instead."

"No, if I take it, I can't drink tonight, and I plan on getting fucked up."

"Don't be a dumb ass. Get fucked up tomorrow night in your new apartment. But tonight, ease your joints and get some rest, okay?"

"Okay, Lovie." She went into the kitchen to get me water. I looked over at Jamel standing in the same spot near the door, looking at me angrily.

I snapped at him, "*What?* I'm sorry, but you don't have to be upset with me for not telling you."

He shook his head and walked over to me, then asked quietly, "How often does he do this to you? Because I've been with you for months, and I haven't seen any bruises on your body until today."

He reached over and touched my pink neck, which looked a hell of a lot better than it did when I woke up that morning. I couldn't lean to the left without pain, but really, I was fine.

I backed away from his touch. "That's because he hasn't done it in months. He saves the ass whippings for special occasions, times when I've really pissed him off. My leaving is pissing him off. I knew he needed to let off steam, and I let him because I knew it would be the last time. It's not a big deal," I told Jamel as I took the cup and two Tylenol 3's from Lovie and swallowed.

Jamel walked closer to me, saying, "And you two are acting like this is normal. It's not normal."

I backed up again. "Stop," I ordered.

He stopped for a moment, narrowed his eyes, then came toward me again. I kept stepping back until I was up against the bed. Suddenly, I didn't like that he was bigger and stronger than me. He was clearly angry.

♥♥♥ CHAPTER 11 ♥♥♥

But then he reached under my t-shirt and gently put his hands on my waist. He said into my neck softly, "It is a big deal, Connor. He hurts you. And that's a big deal to me."

He backed up and lifted my t-shirt over my head while looking into my eyes. He dropped the shirt on the floor, and his eyes traveled downward.

Even Afia gasped when she saw the bruise on my side and my red-streaked chest. "Connor!" she exclaimed between her hands over her mouth.

She came toward me to hug me, but Jamel held his palm out to her, saying sternly and loudly, "NO!"

He stopped her in her tracks, shocking her and me. She looked at him wide-eyed, then looked at me with the same expression, and I knew my face mimicked hers. It was the second time I had ever heard him raise his voice, and both times occurred in the last five minutes.

He took a deep breath through his nose to calm himself down, exhaled, stepped back, and looked at my body. He ran his fingertips gently along the black and purple bruised rib and red splotches across my chest, all the way up to the ring of pink around my neck, shaking his head the whole time, and saying quietly, "This is not okay. None of this is okay."

I shrugged. "It is what it is."

He opened his mouth to speak, then closed it. He watched me for a moment, then turned to my Lovie. "Afia, sweetheart, can you give us a moment? Maybe pick us up some dinner. Be back in an hour or so?" He reached into his wallet and handed her his credit card.

She looked like she wanted to tell him no, and I kinda didn't want her to leave either. But then she looked at me, and I knew she had changed her mind.

She took it and said, "Two hours. I'll be back around 8:30."

She left me alone with Jamel, who I was trying to read but couldn't. I couldn't tell if he was angry at me or the situation.

He came back over to me and said, "Let me see your legs."

I sighed again, and I let him pull down my pants. He saw more red splotches and black and blue bruises on my thighs and groin area, but there was nothing to be concerned about.

I said again, "It is what it is. I told you, he is an abusive fuck."

"Yeah, Connor, verbally abusive, but not physically. Not this. This is … criminal." He reached up, touched my face, and looked me in the eye. "He is never going to put his hands on you ever again."

"I know. I'm leaving, remember?"

He shook his head again and said slowly and quietly, "I don't think you understand what I'm saying to you. I will put your father in the fucking ground if he ever, ever lays a hand on you again." He had both hands on my face, caressing my cheek with his thumbs. "You get me, Connor? I mean, do you really understand what I'm saying? I am not a violent man. But I will kill him. Just say the word."

He stared at me intently, and I stared back, seeing and hearing the seriousness, unsure of what to say. I

Chapter 11

eventually shook my head and pulled away from his hands on my face.

"No. I'm fine. I'm getting out. I am out. As of tomorrow, I'm out. It won't happen again."

He looked thoughtful. "Is that why you asked Afia to spend the night here with you?"

I nodded. "If he sees her car, he won't come up here, especially at night."

"But you told her to go to Ty last night. Why?"

"Because he was going to catch me at some point in the next 48 hours. So, it was best if it happened on Sunday so that I'll be fine for moving on Tuesday."

"And what if he killed you last night?" he asked me.

I let my mouth hang open but didn't respond. Jamel nodded, "I wasn't going to stay the night. But I am now. I'm going to stay here with you all night. And no one is ever going to hurt you again."

Jamel hadn't spent the night since that first night we slept together, but I was not going to argue his direct order.

He reached back to my waist and connected his soft fingers around my body. He moved his fingers slowly up my back until he reached my shoulder blades and pulled me against him. My hands instinctively went up and around his neck. *We're so close we could be one person.*

"You can't kill my father," I said to his lips.

"I can. And I will. Just say the word." He breathed his response on my lips.

"I won't tell you to do it," I breathed back to him.

"Okay. But then he better not ever put his hands on you again."

He leaned back to look me in my eyes, and again I could tell he was deadly serious. My man would kill for me if I asked him to. It was so fucking sexy that I attacked him with my lips, and he kissed me just as passionately. I pulled off his shirt, kissed his hairy chest, and sucked on his erect nipples. I unbuckled his jeans and began to get on my knees, but he stopped me.

"No. Let me make you feel good. I'll be gentle."

I was already naked, and the only thing left to take off was my briefs. Jamel got on his knees, pulled down my underwear, then proceeded to blow me and let me face-fuck him hard until I came down his throat and my knees got weak. The codeine in the medicine was starting to get to me, and I felt very relaxed with less pain in my body. I moved backward on the bed and watched him take off his pants.

He opened the drawer of my anal toys and sex items and looked at me because it was empty. I pointed to the small cardboard box on the couch. "It's in the box over there."

He went over, pulled out a condom and the lube, and prepared me, then himself. He then pulled me to the edge of the bed and leaned over while guiding himself inside me. As usual, I gasped, winced, and moaned as he filled me up. When he was all the way in, he kissed my neck and ears.

He whispered, "I'm so sorry, baby. I'm so, so sorry."

And at first I didn't know what he was sorry for because he wasn't hurting me any more than usual. But then he said, "I'm so stupid for not seeing it. Someone was hurting my baby right underneath me, and I didn't

Chapter 11

protect you. I'm so sorry. I promised to protect you, and I failed. And I'm so sorry for that."

I touched his head and said, "Mel, I've lived with this for almost twenty-six years. There was nothing you could have done, especially since you didn't even know what was happening. And I'm fine."

He looked up at me. "I swear to God, on my life, I will never let another person on this earth harm you for as long as I live. I will die first. What he's done is not okay. You're not fine. But you will be from this moment on. I promise you that."

I could see his eyes were watery, and his holding back tears made me want to cry. I pulled his face down to kiss me again, and he began to move inside me. I closed my eyes and let my tears fall, not from pain but from how emotional it all felt. I wrapped my legs and arms around him and let him love me with his deep strokes until we came together.

I was immediately sleepy after I came. He got a warm rag to wipe me down. I could barely keep my eyes open as he dressed me in underwear and a t-shirt, laid me in the bed and held me until I fell asleep seconds later. I didn't hear Afia come back in, but at some point, I knew she was in bed talking to him about me, but I couldn't remember what they were saying.

I woke up in the middle of the night and felt sandwiched in and couldn't move. I realized Jamel was behind me, holding me to his chest while Afia was in front of me, leaning into mine. And I have never felt more loved or more safe in all of my life.

CHAPTER 12

IT WAS THE PERFECT DAY.

~~~July 2010~~~

I woke up that Saturday like I always do, right up against my lover. It was already warm outside, but a nice breeze flowed through my third-floor window. I didn't want to move just yet. My back was against Jamel, and he was holding me and snoring lightly. I could feel the small rumble in his chest as he slept peacefully. He had to work later, but he took the morning off so we could wake up together on my birthday. I didn't need him to do that. It was just another day for me since I also had to work later. But when I woke up next to him, I was grateful for his warmth and thoughtfulness.

I didn't have any furniture in my apartment. I brought my bed from the garage apartment, and I recently bought a full bedroom set, but that was it. Sometimes I feel like I have too much space, living in a 500 square foot, one-bedroom apartment. Jamel and I still spend

Chapter 12

all of the waking moments we could spend together, mostly at my place now. It felt lonely during the rare moments when he worked and I was home. Maybe living together wouldn't be a bad thing. He asked me about it a few days before, and I avoided the question. Even if we did, I would still be just as lonely waiting for him to come home. That reasoning solidified my confidence that I had made the right decision. I did not want to depend on Jamel too much. I was glad about my decision to move out and away from my family and be on my own. Living with Mel would have been easy but not as satisfying. Living alone was definitely something I needed to do, and I felt so good doing it.

We didn't have sex the previous night. We drank wine in bed and discussed plans. I talked about the places I would love to take Vinnie's Vet Buddies. Jamel shared that he wants to expand his territory outside Rhode Island to Massachusetts and possibly Connecticut. That way, when he takes over Jones Maintenance and Construction from his father, he could expand there as well. We talked and talked, and I think I fell asleep first, laying against him. It was one of the best nights of my life.

My heart was so full that it just came out. I whispered into the bed, "I love you, Jamel."

He didn't stir, and I didn't think he would. I was sure he did the same, telling me he loves me when I'm sleeping. I don't know why we didn't say it to each other. I didn't say it to him because, basically I'm a punk. I never said it to Jack, and the one time I said it to Vinnie was when he was dying in my arms. Afia was the only person I said it to consistently because she has told me she has loved me since she was fourteen.

But I was in love with Jamel Jones. And the best part was, I knew he was in love with me too. *Who needs Words of Affirmation when he tells me he loves me with his touch, his sex, his actions, his eyes?*

My phone buzzed on the dresser, and I knew it was Lovie wishing me a happy birthday. I didn't reach for it, but the ringing woke Jamel; his breathing changed behind me. He squeezed my arm a little tighter and sniffed.

"Morning," I said softly.

"Morning," he croaked out in his baritone voice. He put his nose in my hair and sniffed. "Happy birthday."

"Thank you."

"We have dinner plans tonight with the family."

"Okay. What time do you need to be at work?" I asked.

"When I get there," he answered smugly, making me giggle. "The Major knows I'm spending my morning with you."

I turned all the way around to face him. He blinked at me a few times, and I leaned in to kiss his full lips softly. "Spending it in bed?"

"If that's what you want. I'm not complaining," he replied with a twinkle in his eye.

I kissed him again, with more fever. Both our mouths were dry because of the sauvignon blanc we finished last night, but our bodies quickly heated up.

"Turn around," I told him between kisses. He did.

I reached back and grabbed the lube off the nightstand. That's the other thing I liked about living on my own. I don't hide shit. Lube and condoms lay openly on my end tables. I quickly prepared him and myself

Chapter 12

and slid inside him until our sides fully connected. I wrapped my arm around him and held onto his arm the way he was just holding onto me, and I began to move inside of him. He moved with me. We were so close, we could be one person.

It didn't take me long at all. I bit the space between his neck and shoulder and came. I knew he hadn't cum yet, so I slid out of him and turned him onto his back. Before he could speak, I was crashing my lips on him and pushing my tongue into his mouth. He grabbed my face and kissed me with the same amount of aggression. I moved downward, kissing his nipples, licking his hairy abs, and making my way down to his hairy groin. I dragged my teeth in through it, getting his pubic hair caught between before I licked up his cock and put it in my mouth.

Jamel groaned loudly. He put his hands behind his head and watched me slide up and down, filling my mouth with his cock. I took my time, moving slowly at first, making him squirm by bringing him to the brink but not taking him over the edge. It was probably the slowest and longest blow job I had given him. I think his orgasm snuck up on him because of the way he called out, "Ugh!" His warm, thick cum began to fill my mouth while I licked the underside of his cock to encourage more ejaculation. He didn't stop moaning, and his body trembled underneath me until he stopped cumming and sighed loudly. I swallowed and let his cock fall from my mouth. I put my head on his thigh and looked up at him.

When his eyes uncrossed, and he came down from his climax, he looked down at me. "Shit. I'm supposed to be the one satisfying you."

"Trust me, I'm satisfied. Everything about that was perfect. Waking up with you is perfect."

He gave me a small smile. "Yeah. Same," he said softly.

He reached down and ran his hands through my hair. I closed my eyes and let him tell me that he loves me with his touch. Then we got up, took showers together, and made breakfast.

♥

"Happy birthday, my sweet Connor!" my mother sang out when I answered the phone.

I was sitting at my cubicle in the office doing the notes for my installation when my phone rang. "Thanks, Mom."

"Will I see you today?" she asked.

"No, I have to work, sorry. And I have dinner plans."

She sighed. "Well, of course you do. I can't expect my 26-year-old son to want to spend his birthday with his mother."

I rolled my eyes. "Not the guilt trip, Mom."

"Well, come to St. Cecilia's for church tomorrow and spend the day with us. That will make me feel better. And I miss having you around the house."

Ah. That's what she wanted. I'm on to this woman. "That depends," I said cautiously. "Will Matty be there?"

"Oh, Connor, that's your brother, you know. He has a bit of a mean streak, but he's always looked out for you."

"Yeah, well, it's my birthday weekend, and I want to spend it with people that actually like me. So,

Chapter 12

guarantee that Matty won't be there, and I'll be there with bells on."

"Oh, Connor," she said again and sighed. "Fine. Will it be just you, or will Afia join us for dinner?"

"Um… I think it will just be me. She may have plans."

"Oh!" I could hear her voice go up an octave in surprise. Almost … joy? I ignored it.

"But we're hanging out tonight and going to dinner with a few friends."

"Oh, that's so nice," she said sweetly. "Well, enjoy your day. And don't forget about tomorrow, no matter how late you stay out."

"Sure, Mom. I'll be there."

I hung up and thought about my mom. Ever since I moved out, which had only been around six weeks at that point, she had been trying to get me to come over weekly, outside of Sunday dinners. The problem was I didn't know if the pleading for me to be around more was actually coming from my mother or him. My mother has never been the reason I stayed away. I truly loved her, and I get why she is the way she is. If my father suddenly died of a heart attack, I would be over there all the time. But as long as he was alive, he called the shots, no matter how independent Katherine appeared to the outside world. So, even though I don't live there anymore, I still have to tread carefully. The last thing I wanted was for him to take out his anger on her because I wasn't falling in line.

I sent her a quick text:
[Connor: I'll see you tomorrow. Love you, Mom.]

She texted me back right away:

[Katherine: Love you too my sweet Connor.]

Bryson tapped my shoulder. "Hey, come talk to me for a moment."

I followed my boss back to his office. He closed the door and motioned for me to sit. "Dawn is retiring in three months, and I want you to apprentice under her so that when she moves on, you move into that position."

I was surprised. "Seriously?"

"Yes, seriously. You've been here for three years, and the others already look up to you. Dawn also thinks you would be the best person to take over Field Operations for South Providence."

"Wow. Um... okay, yeah."

"Here's the thing: the brass is going to want me to put the job out there first, and they will be a part of the hiring process. I have a say, so I want to put my best candidate forward. So, I'm starting early by letting you know now. When the application opens in October, I want you to be ready to apply and have the skills needed for the position. Dawn can help you do that."

"This is such an honor, sir. Thank you for thinking of me."

He shook his head. "It's been an honor having you a part of the team, Connor. You're smart, quick thinking, and a natural-born leader. Maybe when I'm ready to retire, you'll be taking over my job."

I thought about it. Comcast was definitely not my long-term gig, but it was a good, steady-paying job, and I love what I do. I smiled. "Maybe, Bryson. Watch out. I may be coming for your job earlier than that."

♥♥♥ CHAPTER 12 ♥♥♥

He laughed. "Get the fuck out of my office." I laughed as I stood up. He stood up as well, and we shook hands. "Great work here, Connor. I mean that."

"Thank you, sir."

♥

Jamel greeted me with a kiss on my lips and a glass of Pinot. "How was work?" he asked as I followed him to the kitchen in the upstairs part of the family home. I watched him pull out the mac and cheese and mix the collard greens with turkey necks in it, his mother's recipe.

"Fine." *I'll tell him about the possible promotion later*, I thought as I sat on the stool in the kitchen. "You?"

"Technically, we're done. But are you okay to stay here tonight? Only because I have to get up early and head to Mt. Hope to let the realtor in to take pictures of the house we just finished renovating."

"Yeah, that's fine. I—"

But I was cut off by soft, brown hands wrapping around my neck. I patted her hands. "You didn't call me back," my Lovie scolded.

"Sorry, I was … busy this morning." I smiled at Jamel, who chuckled.

"Ew," she said playfully. She came around and checked her famous rhubarb pie on the kitchen counter.

I looked around and said, "Why is there so much food? I thought we were having a simple dinner."

"We are having a simple dinner. A dinner to honor your life and presence in all our lives," Afia said.

I grimaced. "What?"

Honestly, I didn't even remember the last time I wasn't shitty drunk on my birthday, waking up with one or two strangers. To go from that to this family thing was a little much. "You all are doing way too much."

"I told you he was going to freak out," Jamel murmured.

"And I told you, I don't give a shit," Afia said to him. "We all love him, and we're going to celebrate him whether he likes it or not." She turned back to me and gave me a stern look.

I rolled my eyes and said nothing else. She took that as a sign to grab plates and set the dining room table.

Donell came into the kitchen, winked at me, walked right up to the mac and cheese, and tried to put two fingers in there for a pinch. But Jamel saw out of the corner of his eye and quickly grabbed his wrist, twisted it, and pushed him against the counter.

"The fuck, Captain America!?" he howled.

"Keep your grubby hands out of Afia's mac and cheese, son," Jamel growled playfully. Donny pushed him off him and pretended to swing on him.

"Captain America's not black," Ty said, coming behind him. "You were better off calling him Blade." He made a fist and reached out for a dap, and I held my fist out and gave him one. He went out the other side of the kitchen to help Afia.

Lavell overhead from the living room and called out, "He'll be black one day. According to the trajectory of—"

"Shut up, Lavell," Donny and Ty chorused. I chuckled.

Chapter 12

"Don't tell your brother to shut up!" Mama Denita yelled from somewhere in the house. "He's gonna rule over you one day!"

"Fuck outta here," Donny murmured.

Jamel and I chuckled again. Afia came back into the kitchen. I watched them rally around, grab the oven-fried chicken out of the oven, and move food to the dining room. I sat next to Jamel and across from Afia and Ty. It was my assigned seat when I was there. Lavell sat next to me, and Donny sat across from him. There was small talk until the Major entered with Mama Denita. We all stood up until the Major got to his seat.

He stood on his end and waited until Mama Denita made it to hers. She sat first, and the rest of us sat after her. No one spoke as everyone waited for the Major to say grace. But before he bowed his head, he said to no one in particular, "This food was labored with love."

Afia smiled at me. Ty rolled his eyes. Donny winked. Jamel, as expected, did not react, and neither did I. I just closed my eyes and bowed my head in prayer. "Merciful and gracious God," the Major began, "We thank You for the food and the hands that have made it. We thank You for all family members at this table, and we continue to be grateful for Your blessings upon their lives. We thank You for those that have joined our family in the last year, Afia and Connor, and we especially thank You for Connor's life and service as he celebrates another year on this earth. May You continue to hold him in the palm of Your hand. In Your name, we pray."

We chorused, "Amen."

Everyone began to dig in, grabbing spoonfuls of food or fighting over who got the biggest chicken breast, although there were enough chicken pieces to feed a small village. I found myself watching them: Lavell humbly grabbed a few chicken legs and let Donny and Ty argue across the table. Mama Denita threatened to get the switch if they didn't stop being rude. Afia silently added food to Ty's plate, and when he noticed, he gave her a sincere thank you with a kiss on her cheek. Mama Denita complimented Jamel on his collard greens. My new family.

My eyes landed on the Major whose eyes were already on me. His expression was unreadable, just quietly watching me. Then he gave me a look of concern. He cocked his head and mouthed, "You okay?"

How could I explain how perfectly fine everything was? How could I explain that a simple family dinner with people who weren't even my family was more intimate and loving than anything I had ever experienced? That the last time I had a birthday party was when I was seventeen, and the party ended with my father pulling a gun on me for inviting Jack, my gay best friend? That it was so perfect being a part of this family that I was afraid any moment someone at the table would turn to me and see me as a fraud, an outsider, someone who didn't belong there?

I couldn't explain. So instead, I nodded respectfully, turned my head to the table, and started adding on food.

♥

❤❤❤ CHAPTER 12 ❤❤❤

Donny tapped me on the shoulder and said into my ear, "Come outside for your real present."

Jamel, sitting next to me on the couch drinking his cognac, rolled his eyes. I winked at him and followed Donny to the front porch, and the automatic light came on. He pulled out his bag, sat on the steps, and we rolled joints together.

"How's Vanessa?" I asked him. Vanessa was his on-again, off-again girlfriend.

He shrugged. "I think she's seeing someone else now."

"And you're okay with that?"

"As long as it ain't one of my frat brothers, I'm good." He lit his joint and pulled, then handed it to me, letting out the smoke as he talked. "Good kush from Atlanta. Homegrown, nothing mixed."

I took a puff, held it in, then released slowly. I felt the effects immediately. It was strong. We passed the joint back and forth for a while, then Donny asked, "You and my brother, y'all, gonna stay together?"

I took a long drag, closed my eyes, and breathed out, "Yep."

When I opened my eyes again, he was looking at me. "Cool." Then he started giggling, making me giggle too.

The front door opened. "That shit will rot your brain cells," Lavell said and hopped on the ledge.

"Or it may help you focus, like it did for Barry in college, Blerd," Donny teased him.

Lavell scoffed. "I doubt it."

Donny held the joint out to him. "You never know unless you try. You about to be a college man in a few weeks so—"

I slapped his hand down. "Don't do that."

He looked at me, surprised. "Do what?"

"He doesn't want to smoke. Leave him alone," I told him sternly.

"Well, maybe I do want to try it," Lavell said hesitantly.

I looked up at him and shook my head. Lavell was headed to M.I.T. in the fall. The last thing I wanted was a genius kid like Lavell using drugs of any kind.

Donny reached his hand up, and I slapped it down again. He started laughing. "Damn, you and Jamel belong together. Y'all both a little uptight."

The door opened again, and Ty walked out with Afia. "Why are you out here, Lavell? Go inside the house," Ty ordered their youngest brother.

Lavell quickly did as his brother told him to. Ty snatched the joint out of Donny's hand and took a puff. "Y'all should be ashamed of yourselves. Peer-pressuring-ass motherfuckers."

Donny started laughing as Ty passed it to me, and I spoke. "For the record, I told him not to."

"Well, then there's hope for you yet," Ty said sarcastically. I rolled my eyes and passed it to Donny.

Donny took a pull and tried to pass it to Afia, but Ty and I said at the same time, "Afia doesn't smoke." Then we looked at each other.

"Shit, do you two defenders of Nation Afia want to let the lady speak for herself?" Donny asked with a smile.

Chapter 12

Ty responded by pulling Afia closer and kissing her on the lips. "Only one occupant of Nation Afia around here."

She smiled at him, and I resisted the urge to roll my eyes again. I don't know if Ty and I will ever actually be friends, but since he was literally and figuratively occupying Nation Afia, I would continue to keep it civil between us.

She kissed her boyfriend's lips and turned to Donny. "You know I don't smoke, jackass."

He started laughing again. He passed it to me, and I pulled from it as the front door opened again.

"God damn, could y'all stop coming outside before Pop yells at me for the smoke smell in the house?" Donny yelled.

Jamel said, "Shut the fuck up," as he walked over to me and bent down to take the joint out of my hands. He took a long pull, then looked at it and said, "This is strong."

"Only the best for Connor's birthday!" Donny said and laughed again. I started laughing too and looked up at Jamel.

We stared at each other as he took another pull, held it for a moment, then released slowly. "You high?" he asked. I nodded slowly. "Good. Come inside."

He handed the joint to Ty and reached for my hand. I gave it to him, and he pulled me to stand. He laced his fingers with mine and took me into the house without another word to his brothers. I heard Donny snickering behind me, but I didn't care. I was about to get fucked in the best way.

Jamel held my hand into his apartment, locked the door, and kept going. When we got to his room, I started to say something, but he pushed me against the door and kissed me. He kissed me gently and sweetly, licked my lip, pulled my top lip, slid his tongue inside to lick my tongue, and kissed my lips fully again. I still loved his kisses. He moved down to my neck and left a wet kiss there and another wet kiss behind my ear. I didn't touch him. I kept my hands at my side, my eyes lidded and bloodshot, and I let him work me. He stepped back and lifted off my t-shirt, leaving my tank top on. He moved against me and kissed me again. He pulled at my bottom lip, kissed my chin and down my neck again. I reached down and began to unbuckle my belt. I unzipped my zipper as he continued to show me he loved me with his kisses. When I reached down and pulled it out, he grabbed my wrist and moved my hand away. He looked me in the eyes, and slowly got on his knees. We held eye contact for a long moment. Then I gently put my hand behind his head. He took my cock in his hands and mouth, and I stifled a moan. I guided him up and down, watching his lips purse together on the way down and spread wide on the way up. I always said that the sight of a man's dick in my mouth was the most beautiful thing ever. But Jamel, in all of his alpha maleness, was more than just beautiful when he serviced me like this. It was devotional. Jamel continued to devote himself to me. A fleeting thought that I had was if I was just as devotional to him. *I think I am.* Like the way I made love to him earlier in the day. I hope I showed him that I love him with my touch, my sex, my actions, my eyes too.

♥♥♥ CHAPTER 12 ♥♥♥

I moved my waist backward and slid out of his mouth. He looked up at me. I smiled at him, stepped to the side, and went around him to sit at the edge of the bed. He stood up and came over to me as I took off my sneakers and pulled down my pants and underwear together. I left on the Army green tank top I was wearing, his tank top. He took off all his clothes, completely in the nude. When done, he nuzzled his nose with mine, and kissed me again, falling between my legs and laying my back on the bed. His bare cock rubbed against mine, and I thought he would just put it in at that point, but he rolled off me to grab a condom. With his back turned, I smiled at the ceiling first and then turned to my stomach. Why were we still using condoms eight months later, I did not know, but I was not going to ask to change it. I knew him well enough to know that when he was comfortable, he would just do it.

I laid there with my arms crossed on my chest and stared at his wooden headboard as I felt him scissor me with his fingers and lube, opening me up. I felt him lean over me and press against my backside. I winced and moaned in my throat but let him in fully until his pubic hair brushed against my cheeks and his heavy balls nestled between my thighs. He gave me a moment, then began to move.

All thought processes went out of my head. All problems faded. All worries were gone. All that was left was he and I, and how good he made me feel when he was inside me, his body pressed against me, his lips on the back of my neck, his hands through my blond hair. I closed my eyes and let him make love to me, with the marijuana and wine at dinner enhanced my emotions and nerves. He pressed against my prostate one too many times, and I climaxed hard, crying out loudly and cumming, hands-free, on his dark blue sheets.

"Shit," he said quietly and slowed down.

"Mmmm...." I responded, still coming down from my sexual high, the chemical high enhancing it tenfold.

He hadn't cum yet. He came off me and laid on his back. I opened my eyes and looked at him. He smiled, and I smiled back. I knew what he wanted, and he knew I wanted to give it to him. I moved on top of him, kneeling first. He held himself steady, and I impaled myself with his ten inches. I gave myself a moment, put one hand on his chest and the other on the back of my neck, then began to bounce up and down on him. He put his hands on my waist, closed his eyes, and let me bring him over the edge for the second time that day. But right before he did, he grabbed my cock and began to jerk me hard and fast. I bucked faster without realizing it as he fell off his climatic cliff and took me with him. I felt his cock twitch in me as mine twitched in his hand, and we came at the same time.

I slid off and fell on the pillow next to him, completely spent. But before he could do it to me, I rolled over and threw my arm over his chest. He rolled the condom down carefully and tied the end before dropping it in the garbage pail by the bed. Then he rolled over to his side and put his hand on my waist. He didn't say anything, but he didn't need to. He told me he loved me with his eyes. I moved closer to put my head on the same pillow he occupied and gave him a

♥♥♥ Chapter 12 ♥♥♥

simple kiss. He wrapped his arms around me, I did the same, and we quickly fell asleep.

♥

"Think we'll ever be happy, Connor?" Vinnie asked him.

"What do you mean? I'm happy right now."

"You know what I mean."

Connor sighed. "I don't know, man. But I meant what I said. I'm happy right now."

Vinnie sighed too. "I'm going to die with this secret. No one will ever know."

"That's impossible. I know your secret," Connor said slyly

Vinnie smiled. But then he said, "I'm going to tell Bethany. After this tour."

Connor scoffed. "Why?"

"Because I don't want to die with this secret."

Connor rolled his eyes, "You're not gonna die, Barrone. I won't let you."

"Connor, I'm serious."

"I know. Lighten the fuck up. We head out tomorrow. We'll get serious then."

"I don't think you think about this hard enough—"

"And I think you think about this too much. Let it be what it is. Don't tell Bethany or anyone. It won't change anything, and it will just make her hate you."

Vinnie was silent for a long time. "Connor, do you think we'll ever be happy?" he asked softly again.

"I don't know, Vinnie. I just don't know," Connor replied softly back.

Vinnie turned to him and looked him in the eyes. "You're happy now, though."

Connor turned to him in complete surprise. "What?"

"You're happy, Connor."

Connor was confused. "That's... that's not what you're supposed to say. That's not what you said that night. You said... You said 'I love you, Connor. And that makes me happy. Maybe that's enough.'"

Vinnie said again. "You're happy, Connor."

Connor sat up. "Stop. What's happening?"

"It's okay to be happy. It's okay if he makes you happy. Go be happy. I'll always be here. Go be happy."

"Vinnie—"

Vinnie smiled at him and closed his eyes. "Vinnie!" Connor called his name again.

♥

My eyes flew open and my heart was racing. It took a moment to adjust to the darkness around me and remind myself I was in Jamel's bedroom. I hadn't dreamed of Vinnie in years. Not since before Jamel came into my life. It started as a memory. It was the night before we were to deploy to Fallujah. I was on my third ten-month tour; Vinnie was on his second. It was our last tour together. We had just finished making love and were lying on the floor of my room, trading cigarettes and talking. But that ending part, when he told me to go be happy, that wasn't a part of my memory. That didn't happen. Vinnie was sending me a message from the grave. I knew it.

Jamel was lying on his side, his arm still laid across me. I gently moved his arm so I could get up, put on his sweatpants, and head to the bathroom. I came out

Chapter 12

but I didn't go back to the bedroom. Instead, I opened his door and went outside to the front, and the porch light came on. It was warm, but a nice breeze hit my skin. The Joneses lived on a quiet block, so all I heard around me were crickets scurrying in the front yard. I sat on the porch steps and thought about my life so far.

I've never really been happy in all areas of my life at the same time. I spent so many years unsure of who I was. My abusive childhood was a big part of that, but I also didn't help myself by sleeping around so much, first with girls in my youth, and then with men. A part of me thinks I've always been gay, but sleeping with females was what was expected of me as an attractive male jock, so I did what was expected. But outside of Afia, I've always been emotionally drawn to males: first Jack, then Vinnie and now Jamel. And all three saw the real me: My insecurities, my fears, and my uncertainty of who I am. The military changed me, not just because of Vinnie, but it made me discover my strengths as a leader and mentor. I'm still insecure in a lot of ways, I still am afraid of people I love leaving me behind. I still don't know where I fit in this world or what I want to do with my life. But I know a few things now. I know that I am strong. I know that people look up to me. I know that I am loved. And I know that no matter what happens, Jamel will never leave me. And Vinne was right. I am happy. Jamel makes me happy.

The front door opened, and I looked up. Afia stepped out, and I smiled at her. Her hair was out and frizzy, and she had on Tyrell's t-shirt and boxers with her pink socks. She wordlessly sat next to me and put her head on my shoulder.

"How did you know I was out here?" I asked.

"I guessed. I saw the porch light go on from Ty's window, and I knew it had to be you."

"He's asleep?"

"Yeah. Jamel?"

"Yep." We sat quietly for a long time. Then I said to her, "Now that I have it, I might be afraid of losing it."

She knew exactly what I meant. "Don't be. Jamel's family thinks of you as family now. We have both been indoctrinated into this family. Unless you want that to change, it won't."

"But Lovie, you already have a stable family that loves you. If I lose Jamel, I lose this family. And I'll have ... nothing."

She lifted her head from my shoulder. "You have me, Connor. You will always have me, no matter what."

I touched her face and pulled her close so I could kiss her forehead. "I love you, Afia."

Why was it so easy for me to tell her verbally but not Jamel? I don't know. But it was just easy with her. My love for her was deep and timeless.

"I love you too, Connor," she replied. She put her head back on my shoulder, and I put my arm around her. "Are you in love with Jamel?" she asked.

I scoffed. She giggled. "Are you in love with Ty?" I asked her.

"Yes," she said automatically. "I love him so so much. I feel like my heart is going to burst."

I nodded. "Good. He loves you that much too. He's your perfect match."

"And Jamel is yours."

"I know. Trust me, I know."

♥♥♥ CHAPTER 12 ♥♥♥

We sat in silence for a while longer until she said, "I'm going to go back inside to him."

"Okay." I let her go. She kissed my cheek and went inside.

I sat there and thought about my Lovie. She will always be a big part of my story. But Jamel was my rock and everything now. She gave me over to him completely that day when Jamel found out about my father's abuse. I saw it in her eyes right before she left us alone. It should have frightened me, but again, I went back to the things I knew, things that she discovered too that day: that Jamel loved me and will never leave me. He'll always be there for me. And that was more than enough of a reason for her to let me go.

I went back into the room. Jamel was still asleep, but he had rolled over to stomach. I laid down next to him gently to not wake him. I rested on my stomach to watch him sleep and listen to the sound of his steady breathing. I whispered to him like I whispered that morning, "I love you, Jamel, so, so much."

I heard his breath go up and pause, and I froze. *Holy shit, did he hear me that time!?*

He didn't move a muscle, and neither did I. I heard him exhale, and his breathing returned to normal. Maybe it was a fluke, or maybe he did hear me. Either way, I found myself smiling. I leaned over and kissed the scorpion tattoo on his shoulder and closed my eyes. His steady breathing lured me into a restful sleep beside him. It was the perfect day.

♥ ♥ ♥ AUTHOR BIO ♥ ♥ ♥

Wife, mother, partner, daughter, sister, friend, social worker, life skills coach and part-time erotic romance novelist, Eskay Kabba finds the complexity of human nature with characters that reflect the notion that no one is all good or all bad, but we are all just trying find love in hard places. Eskay pens erotic romance novels that celebrates the LGBTQ community, people of color, and interracial relationships.

BOOK CLUB QUESTIONS

1. Connor is a closeted gay man who is sexually promiscuous and had no desire for a relationship with anyone. What was it about Jamel that made Connor want to give the relationship a chance as opposed to trying to build a relationship with Xavier "Lex" Lemos?

2. Are Jamel and Connor a "perfect match"? Why or why not?

3. What social, emotional and mental health themes of each character stood out to you?

4. Afia and Connor have a very close relationship with a sexual history. How does their emotional connection impact the storyline for Connor? For Jamel? For Tyrell?

5. What line literally made you laugh out loud?

6. What part made you angry?

7. What part made you sad?

8. Connor and Jamel's family have some similarities as well as obvious differences. What do you think the author was trying to show in comparing their family structure and dynamics?

9. What scene would you point out as the pivotal moment in the narrative? Explain why?

10. What was your favorite chapter and why?

11. What do you think the author's goal was in writing this book?

12. What did you like most about the book? What did you like the least?